Praise f

A TOUGH NU

"Warm, witty, and full of Texas charm an… Clear a space on your keeper shelf for the Nut House se…
—Duffy Brown, national bestselling author of the Consignment Shop Mysteries

"A family nut tree with some branches missing, sly old ladies, and a tall, dark stranger come to town. Or is he? Chomp into this engaging new mystery series, and it just might Bite-U-Back!" —Mardi Link, author of *Isadore's Secret*

"Elizabeth Lee delivers a delectable mystery that's pure Southern comfort. Readers will go nuts over *A Tough Nut to Kill*."
—Riley Adams, author of the Memphis BBQ Mysteries

"What a wacky group they are in Riverville, Texas. From the Blanchard family to all the townspeople, they had me laughing and shaking my head . . . A solid start to the series." —Socrates' Book Reviews

"[Lee] has given us the most important ingredient of a cozy mystery—quirky characters! She has created some real treasures . . . A well thought out whodunit. Plenty of suspects and red herrings to keep the readers guessing. There is also a great deal of humor and Southern charm spread throughout the entire story." —Escape with Dollycas into a Good Book

continued . . .

"Church ladies, wild hogs, competition over who bakes the best pecan pie—you know you're somewhere else, and you're darned glad to be there, chasing down the clues with Lindy and her meemaw . . . Great fun!" —Books in Northport

"Lee shows her talent and humor with every turn of the page. With some interesting characters like Miss Amelia and the Chauncey twins, Lee is sure to keep readers wanting to come back to Riverville, Texas, on a normal basis. A great first book in a new series!" —Debbie's Book Bag

"An exciting new mystery series filled with Southern charm."
—Melissa's Mochas, Mysteries & Meows

Berkley Prime Crime titles by Elizabeth Lee

A TOUGH NUT TO KILL

SNOOP TO NUTS

NUTS AND BURIED

Nuts and Buried

ELIZABETH LEE

BERKLEY PRIME CRIME, NEW YORK

An imprint of Penguin Random House LLC
375 Hudson Street, New York, New York 10014

NUTS AND BURIED

A Berkley Prime Crime Book / published by arrangement with the author

ISBN: 978-0-425-26148-4

PUBLISHING HISTORY
Berkley Prime Crime mass-market edition / November 2015

PRINTED IN THE UNITED STATES OF AMERICA

10 9 8 7 6 5 4 3 2 1

Cover illustration by Robert Crawford.
Cover design by Diana Kolsky.
Interior text design by Kristin del Rosario.

For Tony, who keeps me going.

Acknowledgments

With thanks to:

Patty Sumter for her recipes and the laughs at Diana Rodabough's country store on Starvation Lake Road. What a great place to come up with recipes with a lot of bourbon in them.

Andy Sherrod, manager of the Royalty Pecan Farms outside Caldwell, Texas (Info@Royalty Pecans.com), for his pecan knowledge and love of his job. The time we spent at Royalty Pecan Farms was magic. Any errors about anything "pecan" are all mine. I was so busy looking at the groves and listening to Andy, I forgot to take notes.

Mary Ann Warner for sharing good friends with me.

Kathy Botard of Sheridan, Texas, along with Sara, who is sorely missed.

Mary Sherwood for the cake that weighs a ton.

Kathy Gibbons for the great tour of Texas. How I learned to love the small towns, and the Colorado River, and San Antonio and LBJ's Texas White House and all the tourist things we did and all the off-the-beaten-track things we did. And the cowboys we met. And the saloons she kept me out of.

Shawn Mullin for his knowledge of sniper rifles and scopes and bipods and distance and ammo. I held that gun, but I still can't shoot it.

Jake Anderson for making me understand different firearms. Seems a lot more complicated than it should be to just pick one up and take a shot.

John Mullin, master of the web, and Josh Mullin, master of the crows.

Chapter One

That night I dragged myself, in noose and shroud, out of my dusty white pickup in front of the Wheatley mansion. I put the keys into the hands of a disgusted-looking man who waited to park it, or hide it, behind all the shiny brand-new pickups covered with chrome and expensive gun racks, and all the big Cadillac Escalades parked on a fitful lawn, back toward a wall of low, honey mesquite trees.

It wasn't because I expected a murder at the party that I looked the way I did. My costume was a protest because I didn't want to go to Elizabeth and Eugene Wheatley's gala to begin with. They were throwing it to introduce Eugene's new wife, Jeannie, to the "elite" of Riverville, Texas—or at least to a good number of the best and oldest citizens. I didn't want to be one of those citizens. My friend Deputy Hunter Austen of the Riverville Police Department, a man who protected all those rich people, wasn't invited, and if he wasn't good enough to be asked to their costume party, then I wasn't either.

I was mad at the Wheatleys and all my family, the Blanchards, and just about anybody who might get in my way that night.

"COME AS A FAMOUS TEXAN," the invitation shouted, and I knew it was all Elizabeth Wheatley's idea, owing to her expertise in Texas history, as she was eager to tell anybody and everybody since I first knew her back when I was in high school and she was already in college. She was Eugene's sister, so I put up with her bragging and strutting and putting on airs because, after all, they were Wheatleys of the oil Wheatleys of Dallas, but living in Riverville for no good reason I ever got out of Eugene.

It was no skin off my nose if she wanted to play lady of the manor. Yet . . .

"I'm not going," was what I first told Mama and Miss Amelia, my grandmother, the day before the party.

"The hell you're not going," Mama said and finished off her breakfast of scrambled eggs and Texas toast, picked up her coffee cup, and gave me one of those long stares that told me I was going to lose this battle.

My meemaw was saying, "Watch your mouth, Emma," to Mama, which made Mama get red in the face and steam the way I was steaming. My younger sister, Bethany, saw what was coming and got up, dumped her dishes in the sink, and headed out to the event tent, where she saw to weddings and showers and graduation parties under our tall, old pecan trees. Justin, my older brother, who took care of Rancho en el Colorado, the pecan farm we lived on, grunted something about meeting up with his men for spraying and was out of there.

I liked Mama's steaming because she was wrong, and it felt good puffing up like a pigeon because I was right. "I'm a grown woman and I can decide for myself whether I want to go to some awful costume party. You know Hunter's my best friend. They could've asked him."

"There's always somebody has to be left out, Lindy. A house can only hold so many people."

"Then let it be me. Anyway I feel cramps coming on. And I don't have a costume. And some man from some European lab is coming to look at my trees. And . . . I just don't want to go if they snub Hunter."

Mama leaned back from the breakfast table, stretched her arms over her head, and then ran fingers through her cropped blond hair. "Me and your grandmother are Hastings—and proud of it. But here in Riverville we are also Blanchards—all of us. We're invited to a party given by old friends where we have to dress up as a famous Texan. You a Texan or not?" she demanded, her hair now standing on end, making her look kind of wild. Who can take a woman seriously when she looks crazy and she's your mother, but you are grown and should be able to do what you want to do in life?

My meemaw cleared her throat and knocked her clasped hands together on the tabletop. She had something to say, and when Miss Amelia made a pronouncement, it was somewhere up there near treason to go against her. Miss Amelia's seventy-six, tall, stately (like our pecan trees), and sweet as an angel to customers in the Nut House, our store in town, where she sells everything pecan, and sweet to everybody in the family unless she comes at you with a "Bless yer heart" and "Why, you dear thing you—" That's when the knife comes out and you better watch your back.

"Why, my sweet girl," she said and the hair on my neck stood up. Right then I knew I'd lost, but I wasn't going to make it easy on anybody. I knew who I'd go as and figured it would be the one costume at the party that would shock the devil out of all of them.

Chipita Rodriguez. That's who I picked. Born in 1799, in Mexico. The only woman ever hanged in Texas; accused of killing John Savage with an ax, then hanged from a mesquite tree with her last words being "*No soy culpable!*"

("I am not guilty!") After I got my shroud together—old gray burlap wrapped around me and sewn, in places, to my jeans and T-shirt underneath—I tied my noose from a nice hefty rope and put it around my neck. I floured my face and wild hair then drew red grease pencil under my eyelids. I planned to walk around their big old ballroom intoning *"No soy culpable,"* but I knew I'd lose my nerve after Mama got a look at me.

I almost fell over the noose as I crossed the gravel drive circling in front of the huge old mansion. I hefted the noose higher, wishing I'd gone for a shorter, lighter rope.

Brave woman that I am, I was already feeling dumb and wishing I'd come as Barbara Bush with a string of pearls around my neck instead of a noose. I walked slower and slower toward the heavy front door standing wide open. I could hear music from the back of the house.

My bravado was kind of failing me. Nobody would know my costume was a protest against anything—like Texas hanging a woman, I told myself. They'd think it was just me, Lindy Blanchard, making a stubborn fool of myself though I was twenty-eight, had two degrees from Texas A&M, and was deep into biotechnology—genome selection—so the pecan trees on our ranch would grow and bloom and produce even in drought years. *"A selfless deed,"* I always told myself though I loved doing the work just for the doing. But wasn't I helping my family and all our neighbors? And I was keeping a promise to my Daddy, who'd been proud of me back then, before he got killed out on his tractor, mowing under those big old trees.

Naw, when they got a look at me, they'd all say I should've known better.

The argument with myself was short. Too late. I took the rope and wrapped it around my upper arm a couple of times.

I tried to smooth down my hair and brush a lot of the white flour off my face. Couldn't do a thing about the shroud.

I walked across the portico with tall Ionic columns and through the open double doors, which looked like every doorway to disaster from every scary movie I'd ever seen. In the grand front hall I was met by a butler holding a silver plate, waiting for my invitation. I knew the butler as Roy Friendly, an old cowboy who hung out at the Barking Coyote Saloon. Roy looked embarrassed when I raised my eyebrows at his tux. He was smiling, though his rough and grizzled cheeks barely moved as he asked for my invitation. I said I didn't have one because Mama came ahead of me and she had it.

All Roy did was shrug and pull uncomfortably at the collar of his white shirt.

"I gotta ask, Lindy," he said while giving me the once-over. "What in hell's name you come as? Is that Davy Crockett after the Alamo?"

He snickered and picked at his tongue as if he felt tobacco there. I ignored him and headed back toward the music. I wanted to see my family, make sure they knew I'd been there, say "Hi" to a few folks, and then get the heck on home while I had at least a little dignity left.

Chapter Two

First to spot me when I entered the high-ceilinged ballroom lined with huge, gold-framed portraits of every last Wheatley, and—I swear—golden chandeliers shedding golden light on the illuminati of Riverville, was my younger sister, Bethany, in her wide red hoopskirt with very tight embroidered bodice. She looked like Scarlett O'Hara to me, but since Scarlett didn't live in Texas, I figured she was some other femme fatale or just all Texas femme fatales because she found the outfit before she thought out who she'd be.

Bethany threw her hands to her cheeks. Her mouth made a bright red oval. The fat blond curls on her head were puffed up larger than normal. She left the much older—bordering on ancient—man she was dancing with to come stand in front of me, wide-eyed, astonished, and unhappy.

"Who the devil you supposed to be, Lindy Blanchard?" she demanded in her best irate voice.

"Bunch of famous dead people," I hissed back at her.

After all, I was older than she was, a lot smarter, and didn't like feeling dumb right there where other people could see.

"Are you out of your mind? You come to a wonderful party, with wonderful people, to celebrate their wedding—like that?"

"Second wedding. Sally was shot, remember? Remember Sally? I liked Sally."

"I remember Sally. Loved her clothes. Sad—just a hunting trip over near Austen and then Sally gets a bullet to her head. But that's history now. 'Course Eugene's married again."

I was finished with Bethany. I didn't need my sister's sibling stuff right then. "Hey, maybe you should go back to that dashing man you've got waiting impatiently there on the dance floor." I nodded to where the old gentleman stood looking confused, as if Bethany had disappeared on him.

Bethany stuck her tongue out at me, put on a big smile, and clapped to the music as she hurried toward her very old and very oil-rich partner with many friends who might give parties in Bethany's event tent, or could have political cronies needing a space to hold rallies and such. You had to give it to Bethany, since taking over our entertainment business she was never off duty.

Next it was Meemaw who blindsided me. Lady Bird Johnson, I guessed. Dressed in a very neat denim outfit with a cowgirl hat tied under her chin. Personally I thought Meemaw did Mrs. Johnson proud.

"Chipita Rodriguez, right?" Meemaw, as usual, was way ahead of me. Nothing gets by this woman who can look at a man in ragged jeans and an old cowboy hat and figure he's a billionaire. Or look at a fancy cowboy in a ten-gallon hat, best boots ever, and whisper, "All hat. No cattle." Or look into somebody's eyes and know right away if they were capable of murder.

"Thought that was who you'd be. Maybe not going to

impress any of the men here—as your mama hoped. Not with you looking like something pulled out of a moldy grave. But good for you, taking on somebody like Chipita."

"Took the Texas legislature over a hundred years to claim she didn't get a fair trial," I groused as loud as I dared, wanting people around us, staring at me, to get it. "That's famous enough for me."

"Yeah, well, lot of men hung didn't get that much attention. But I'll tell you, Lindy, I had a friend back in Dallas who swore she saw Chipita's ghost riding the river bottoms over to San Patricio County. Hope you don't stir her ghost up around here."

Meemaw looked well satisfied, passing on that small fact, and fixing me in her own way.

"Are you mad at me?" I leaned in close to ask because of all the people in the world I never wanted mad at me, Meemaw was at the top of my list. Along with Mama, I suppose, but there's always been something very special between my grandmother and me, like we could look at each other and know what we were thinking.

"Mad at you?" Her faded blue eyes went wide. She rocked back on the heels of her sensible shoes. "How could I be mad at you, Lindy? You got all that feistiness straight from me. Wish I still had some of it. But I've got you. I'm awful grateful for that."

I hid my embarrassment at pushing Meemaw to that extreme edge of grandmotherly love by turning to the tall, dark man standing behind me, a tray of barbecued shrimp with lemons heaped into a bowl of ice on his tray. He lowered the tray to within my reach as his dark eyes went over my costume and his nose wrinkled with distaste. Funny that I didn't know the man. Weren't many strangers in Riverville. From the look of him—with his dark curly hair and judgmental eyes, I imagine he'd been brought from Dallas with the Wheatleys. I'd say some old family retainer except he didn't look old and that insolent stare . . .

Whew. I grabbed a shrimp on a toothpick and turned my back to him.

I was looking around for a place to stash my toothpick when Mama came up fast and mad in her Laura Bush chinos and flowered blouse, short blond hair brushed up pretty and neat. She had one of her big, phony smiles meant for the people around us as she put her hands out and grabbed me by the shoulders, pulling me into a big hug, then whispering in my ear, "Just what are you supposed to be?"

"Why, Mama! I'm the only woman ever hanged in Texas."

She leaned back—phony smile stuck in place. She tipped her head to the side and said, around all those white teeth, "Really? Unless you want to be the second one hanged, you'd better ditch that noose pretty fast and get over there and talk to your hosts. If they ask, tell 'em you're the ghost of a dead pecan tree. Don't care what you say—just get over there."

She smiled again and hugged me and blew on past, leaving me like a battleship on a lake—with no place to hide.

I looked over to where Eugene Wheatley, a man I'd known since high school days, and his new wife, Jeannie, stood. He must've come as some old politician, in his straight black suit and high white collar. Jeannie, well, I didn't know for sure why, but she was wearing a lot of yellow.

The Chauncey twins stood with the Wheatleys. "The girls," as everybody called Melody and Miranda, were over eighty and tough as nails. They ran their old family pecan ranch by themselves, shot a mess of rattlers just about every day, and were the first people there if a farmhouse burned down or somebody died or a child got sick. Good people, "the girls."

Miranda, with her arthritic hands, could shoot the eyes

out of a snake at a hundred feet, pick him up, strip him of his rattles, open a screw jar, drop in the rattles, then pull that jar out whenever you saw her, proving how many snakes she got that year, and insisting you take a look at how small the rattles were. "Something up, I'll tell ya," she'd say. "Bad year for the snakes."

Every January, Miranda started out new with a little ceremony in the garden behind the Rushing to Calvary Independent Church, where the pastor would bless the jar and both women, then wish them good luck in the coming year.

Melody was into what she called "gentility." She'd taken, as the girls aged, to upbraiding Miranda for her crude ways with people; the way the ranch house looked when folks came to visit; and for pulling that jar of rattles out of her pocket whenever she had a captive audience.

The girls had come as themselves, far as I could see. Boots that looked a hundred years old. Pants with patches low on the butt, washed-out cotton plaid shirts hanging oddly over their spindly shanks. Their ancient Stetson hats sat far down on their backs. Same outfits they wore every day of their lives except they'd evidently marked this occasion by a trip to Lena's Salon in town. They were a lot curlier, and a lot grayer, than usual, with their hair teased up like two elderly angels. Melody had spots of rouge smeared on her cheeks for the occasion. Miranda, old eyes squinting and looking around from under her bushy white eyebrows, seemed about as ready to bolt as I was.

I knew this pair was going to laugh when they saw me, and tell me I looked like ten miles of bad road or something they found equally funny.

Miranda was going on and on about cottontails and how she was shooting them at a great clip when Eugene looked up and waved, almost begging me to save him from another rabbit story.

Ethelred Tomroy, a cranky old friend of Meemaw's, who

spent most of every day over to the Nut House, was standing beside Melody. I was in no mood for her sniffing and screwing up her mouth and guessing I was dressed as old Texas dirt or something else she hoped was offensive enough.

Trouble was, I didn't have a choice. I joined the circle and nodded to everyone. I hugged Miranda and Melody and gave Ethelred one of Mama's phony smiles. The woman looked like she'd come as the original flour sack, in a down-to-the-floor sprigged dress with a scalloped hem. Had to be homemade. No self-respecting dressmaker would have turned out an outfit like that one.

When Eugene introduced me to his new wife, Jeannie, dressed in a very fluffy, very yellow ball gown, I walked up and hugged her hard, welcoming her to Riverville and saying how happy I was to meet her.

"I was just asking who Miz Wheatley was dressed as, in all that yellow." Ethelred gave me a hard look and sniffed as she rocked back on her black oxfords.

Jeannie looked down at her yellow gown, did a half turn and back, then shrugged. "Just like yellow, I s'pose." She smiled wide and looked happy.

I knew right away what Ethelred was going after: A new bride in something that yellow and obvious. Yellow roses wound through her yellow hair. Yellow gloves and yellow shoes.

Had to be the Yellow Rose of Texas, though why this new society wife would choose that particular famous Texan was beyond me. The Yellow Rose of Texas, Emily West, was a hero in the Texas War of Independence all right, but the problem was that she kept General Santa Anna busy in bed while Sam Houston attacked San Jacinto. Houston won the battle in eighteen minutes—which I guess said something about Santa Anna in bed and how the man could keep his focus when he was occupied.

Famous Texan, all right, but for a new bride?

Still, who was I (or Ethelred) to judge? Hey, she wasn't dressed in white, pretending to be something she wasn't. I kind of liked this Jeannie Wheatley more, thinking she had a great sense of humor, coming as her own kind of famous Texan.

Eugene looked relieved to get away from rabbits and dry arroyos. "Well, Lindy. Don't remember seeing you since you beat the devil out me that time in high school."

"Gave you one black eye. You deserved it."

"All I said was you were pretty." He leaned back and laughed. "With most girls, that line got me a little better than beat up."

Jeannie was frowning, then asking me which famous Texan I was supposed to be.

"Looks like somebody got run over out in the road, you ask me." Miranda leaned back, narrowed her eyes and wiggled her eyebrows.

"Watch yer mouth, Miranda," Melody chimed in. "I think Lindy looks like some poor soul from the old days. I'm guessing Sully Browne. Seen her headstone out in the cemetery. That right, Lindy?"

I didn't get to answer before the two women set to arguing, in low voices, over who I was. I heard the words "death warmed over" and turned back to Eugene, asking him how he'd been doing since he moved away from Riverville. I felt like asking why he'd come back now but didn't, thinking it wouldn't come out sounding friendly.

"I'm glad you came to the party. Want everybody here in Riverville to get to know my bride," Eugene said and hugged the yellow lady to him. "We're thinking of settling right here, in this house. 'Course, I need to work out everything in Dallas. Still got my office and business. But Jeannie likes it here and she doesn't like Dallas much. Too big." He smiled down at his bride. He'd grown from the gawky, gangling kid I knew in high school into a tall, skinny man. I'd lost tract of Eugene after his father sent him off to a private school in Houston. He wasn't a bad guy. A little too much daddy-money, but how could he help it, with all those wells flowing all over Texas?

I turned to Jeannie. "Are you really the Yellow Rose of Texas?" I asked by way of making conversation. Behind me came a gasp from Ethelred, who was more into dropping hints and slurs than taking anything on directly.

"You like it?" She twirled again. "Elizabeth thought . . ."

I caught on fast that this wasn't a joke. Probably ignorance. My estimation of Jeannie Wheatley dropped a couple of notches. Or maybe it was just Elizabeth's meanness that got me.

"You're the one working on all those new trees?" Jeannie started right in with the information, whoever prepped her for the party, had put in her head. "What a great thing to be doing. Hope I can come over someday and see your greenhouse. I'd love to hear how you do all that experimenting." She kept smiling. Her round blue eyes smiled, too. I began to warm to our new resident.

Eugene excused himself from the circle of women pretty quick. "Promised the men I'd put out some of my gun collection. Gotta set things up in the gun room." He smiled over at Jeannie in that way men smile at new wives. A way that made me uncomfortable and not wanting to be in the middle of something between them that should be kept secret.

Jeannie showed a lot of white teeth, and a lot of love in her big blue eyes.

"Bet you'd be interested, Lindy." Eugene turned back to me. "Got a Browning machine gun, 1919A4 semiautomatic. Really rare. Got a couple of great Colts—1911s. A few of Wesson's own guns. Maybe three hundred guns altogether. Can't put 'em all out. Most stored in my gun safe. If you're interested in guns, come along in a while?"

He looked around at all of us. "I'll be holed up for half

an hour or so. Enjoy the buffet. Looks like they're going to open it soon."

"When are you gonna eat, honey?" Jeannie caught at his arm.

"Don't worry. There's a tray being sent out."

With a pat to my back and a buzz to Jeannie's cheek, Eugene made his way around the groups of talkers and cut across the dance floor between couples slow dancing to "You Two-timed Me One Time Too Often." He went out into the hall and, I supposed, to his gun room.

That left me and Jeannie, Ethelred, and the girls. I'd done my duty. Time to go.

I looked around for Meemaw, to tell her I was leaving, when I spotted Elizabeth Wheatley, Eugene's older sister, looking over at me. Elizabeth is not my kind of people. She's a pretty woman. Maybe thirty-eight. But she does a lot of sticking her nose in the air and letting you know you will never come up to her expectations—at least that's what she does to me. And smiles with tight lips. And blinks her eyes a lot while she's talking. And looks over my shoulder, hunting for somebody better to talk to . . . all those things.

Elizabeth had fire in those big, and very round, eyes of hers. She headed straight toward me. It didn't take much to smell the fight coming, though what she was so mad about was anybody's guess. I should've turned and run. I should've done anything but stand there with a rope hanging around my neck, in a gray burlap shroud, with white flour all over my face and hair. I shouldn't have stuck out my hand and smiled as the woman came at me like a blooming missile.

Chapter Three

Elizabeth, in some kind of nineteenth-century getup, had her hands to her cheeks and her eyes blinking at a great rate. She stopped dead in front of me, lifted one long finger, and pointed up and down, then up and down the length of me again.

"Lindy Blanchard. Why on earth'd you come to my party dressed like that?" Her voice was loud and full of outrage. "I mean . . . my dear woman . . . well . . . I hope I'm wrong. But you didn't come as poor Sally Wheatley, did you?"

My turn to be shocked. "Why, Elizabeth. How could—"

"You look dead as a doornail to me. I'd say that wasn't exactly the right thing to wear when all we asked is for everyone to come dressed as some stalwart, famous Texan."

I turned around, hoping Meemaw or Mama would step up and save me from this awful woman.

I said the first thing that came to me. "Sally Wheatley didn't hang, Elizabeth. She was shot, remember?"

"That's even worse, drawing attention to a violent death

the way you're doing. What on earth was in your head? Thought you were supposed to be a smart college graduate. Two degrees, is what I heard. Looks like they didn't take."

She was getting louder; drawing attention to us. The music stopped and the band chose that minute to take a break. Dancers turned our way, listening. My face had to be burning bad through what was left of the flour. And I was sorrier than I'd ever been for trying to make some point with Chipita, though I couldn't remember now what exactly that point had been.

"Just imagine what you're doing to poor little Jeannie here." Elizabeth moved over to put her arm around Jeannie Wheatley, who looked more puzzled than devastated. "Our poor, poor Jeannie. Just awful, you ask me. You okay, dear?" She leaned close to Jeannie, who only looked startled as she nodded and said, yes, sure she was okay.

"How could you come here and hurt my new sister-in-law this way?" Now Elizabeth's voice was deeply hurt, her face a mass of sorrow. She wasn't going to drop it. "Why, Lindy Blanchard, I'm truly surprised at you."

And then Mama was there and she was mad, demanding, "Elizabeth Wheatley. What on earth are you insinuating about my daughter?"

"Look at her! Came as a dead woman. Why, she even resembles Sally with that pale skin and those big eyes. Terrible. Don't know why Eugene didn't see it and get her out of here." The woman's face went back to shock and then she went for sympathy, working up a phantom tear she brushed off her cheek.

"We loved Sally a whole lot—the whole Wheatley family. This is such a . . . an attack, you ask me." She wasn't going to stop.

"Don't have to worry about that." Meemaw was next to me in full Lady Bird Johnson mode: hands on her hips, chest puffed out. "We'll be outta here faster than you can snap your mouth shut, Elizabeth."

My brother, Justin, came running over, dressed in his best Sam Houston suit. "What's going on?" he demanded.

"Elizabeth Wheatley's lost her mind." Mama stepped in. "And we're getting outta here."

Justin knew the family drill. He didn't ask questions, only nodded, ready to give whatever the family needed though he did whine once about wanting to see Eugene's guns, that being the only reason he'd come in the first place.

Then Bethany ran over, face redder than her dress. She didn't ask a single question, just balled her fists at her sides.

Elizabeth was going on. "I have not lost my mind, Emma Blanchard. You allowed your daughter to come here to insult us. I don't know what I, or Eugene, ever did to you, Lindy. But this is an outrage . . ." With no music, and the guests standing around quietly listening to what would be their bit of gossip at The Squirrel restaurant in the morning, the sound of a gun going off was louder than it might have been. It came from somewhere outside the ballroom. Somewhere beyond the open double doors to the hall.

At first everybody held still in place. Then came a startled intake of breath as the crowd went from watching the Blanchards and the Wheatleys going at it, to rigid stillness.

We listened for a second shot.

Nothing happened. The floor creaked. I could hear muted voices coming from out in the kitchen. There was a long moment when everybody looked at one another with startled eyes.

In a few seconds or minutes or however long it took all of us to stop listening for the next shot, there was another huge intake of breath and then a clink of metal as men in the room, just like in an old Western, pulled guns from costume pockets and cocked them.

We were a tableau of frozen people until somebody screamed and Miranda Chauncey, .22 in hand, yelled, "Hit the floor!" from the far side of the buffet table.

"Gunshot!" somebody yelled belatedly and people inched, then pushed in panic toward the hall, while others tried to fade into the walls behind them.

Meemaw put her hands on my back. Mama was beside her, holding on to Bethany. Justin was on the other side of Mama. One thing we Blanchards knew was how to circle the wagons fast.

It crossed my mind that it was some kind of entertainment—fireworks maybe. A few of the women around me still had their party smiles on. Some looked embarrassed, like being caught crouching after hearing a gunshot could be a silly thing.

It didn't take long for everything to change. Me and Meemaw followed the crowd into the hall, where we all stood, milling around, looking one way and then the other, waiting for somebody to tell us what was going on and what we should do.

"Eugene's gun room," a man's voice shouted. "Down here."

The crowd shifted and headed to the left. Me and Meemaw were two of the first down there, joining the half circle of men listening at a door, then talking to one another, calling out Eugene's name.

Other people pushed up behind us. "Door's locked," one said, for something to say, I supposed.

"Can't get in and Eugene's not answering."

Justin pushed through the crowd. "Gotta break it down," he said to the men who'd put themselves in charge. There were head shakings, agreement, and then three of them put their shoulders to the door and pushed again and again until the center panel gave way with a loud, ugly crack. Justin, youngest and strongest, stepped through the broken door into the room beyond as we all held our breath.

I heard my brother say, "What the hell!"

He was back in the doorway. "Call the sheriff," he shouted to the men. I could tell it had to be bad. Justin's face was whiter than I'd ever seen it, under a deep, outdoor workingman's tan. Meemaw pushed past me to go put her hand on his arm and ask what was going on.

"Bad, Meemaw." He shook his head. "Real bad."

And then all hell broke loose as Elizabeth Wheatley and Jeannie came tearing through the crowd blocking the hall. Jeannie was big eyed and scared. Elizabeth moaned.

Meemaw got ahold of Elizabeth and stopped her from going into the gun room. She turned her around and passed her into waiting hands, and then off through the crowd.

Jeannie was faster. I got in the room right behind her, trying to grab ahold of an arm in all that yellow fluff, but she was too quick for me. She stopped where her husband lay slumped across a mahogany desk. You might have missed the hole in his back with only a single stream of blood running from it, but you couldn't miss the huge pool of blood on the desk where he lay facedown, arms stretched wide. A gun lay on the floor beside him, and papers were scattered around as if a huge wind had blown through the room.

Jeannie threw her hands to her mouth. For a second—not long enough for me to grab her—she stood frozen, then leaned down, arms wide as if to save him, trying to cover his back with her body. I pulled her away though the yellow dress was already covered with blood. A book was pushed out in front of him, stained terribly with spreading blood and spatter.

More men ran in behind us, one hurrying to open a heavy metal door in the back wall, letting in fresh air and clearing out the awful stench of gunpowder and fresh blood.

I held Jeannie away from Eugene, my hands locked on

her arms. Still she stared at him, eyes wide open as shock froze her face and body. I wanted to get her out of there, but at the same time, I felt her need to be with him.

The pistol lying on the floor near Eugene's feet was odd looking. Accident, ran through my head and I was almost relieved. The man was cleaning the gun. So many gun tragedies in Texas.

There wasn't time to be thinking all the things I was thinking. Jeannie was my main concern. Her eyes got huge and glazed, as if she was protecting herself from what was there in front of her. Her hand hovered over Eugene's back, but I stopped her from touching him again. Better we didn't touch anything. I knew enough, because of Hunter, about crime scenes and how mad the sheriff got when things got messed up before the cops got there.

Talking quietly, I pulled at Jeannie's arm. She felt limp now, like the life was going out of her. She came with me easily, back out into the hall. When she stopped and tried to turn, I blocked her from looking back at what was left of Eugene Wheatley.

Chapter Four

"Suicide!"

Some jerk was yelling at the top of his lungs. People hushed him as I led Jeannie back through the crowd. Hands reached out to pat her shoulders. People said nothing, or murmured words at her as we moved forward. I hoped I was going in the right direction, toward the main stairs.

"Accident," another man shot back, trying to make things better. "That's his gun room. Must've been cleaning a gun."

I don't think Jeannie heard any of it.

"I want to be with him . . ." Jeannie looked around at me as if we were alone. "Are they sure he's dead?"

Justin came up and held her gently—the way my older brother seemed to do in any emergency; this big sturdy farmer with a rough look to him but a heart ten times bigger than he was. He helped me direct her toward the front hall where a woman in a maid's uniform beckoned toward the upstairs.

It seemed only minutes before Sheriff Higsby and Hunter

Austen hurried in, to my great relief. My arms were still around Jeannie, whose whole body felt empty. We stood at the bottom of a wide staircase leading up from the grand foyer. I was never so happy to see Hunter, my tall, broad, buzz-cut friend, in my life. The sheriff ran back toward the crowd and the gun room, ordering the two deputies rushing in behind him to round up the people and take names then get them out of there.

Hunter stood with me for just a minute, his large hand squeezing my arm.

"You all right? Is this Eugene's wife?" He nodded toward Jeannie. "You taking her to her room? Good. She doesn't want to be here with everything going on."

He hurried off after the sheriff and the others, down the long hall toward the gun room. The investigation would take over now; the routine following a death. The coroner would be there soon. When he was through, the body would be brought out on a stretcher and taken to the morgue. The techs would move in and things in the house would get quiet as routine took over.

Jeannie didn't need to see the aftermath. Hunter or Sheriff Higsby would talk to her, but probably not until morning. The big house already seemed to be echoing—voices coming from around corners; a shout from out in front. There was the black-draped feeling of grief sinking across the front hall. The front door, behind us, was wide open, the darkness beyond the door shot through with bright flashes of strobe lights.

"Let's go upstairs," I said, prodding Jeannie.

She stood with one hand on the banister, her eyes closed. I put an arm around her waist and looked for Meemaw, a woman a lot better at soothing people than I was.

Jeannie's shoulders bent forward. She lifted one slow foot at a time, then stopped, and put her face down into her hands, crying.

I had her halfway up the stairs when there was a rasping shout from the entrance hall and a woman rushed up toward us. She was in a frenzy—yelling Jeannie's name, hands flopping in the air above her head. The woman seemed to float in a cloud of many-colored scarves, a halo of tight, way-too-blond curls, and a mask of colorful makeup. I stepped in front of Jeannie, protecting her from whatever was coming at us.

"My baby girl!" the older-than-she-wanted-to-be woman screamed and threw her head back in a wild, theatrical cry, showing teeth that were large at the back and overlapped in the front. "Mama's here. I'll take care of you."

Then came a tussle as the woman elbowed me aside with one of the sharpest elbows I'd ever felt. She snaked her arms around Jeannie, getting in between us. She began pushing Jeannie up the stairs although she protested, "Mama, don't. You—"

"Hey!" was my only contribution to the nutty scene.

"Mama?"

I looked around the now empty hall. No help. If the woman was her mama, I had no right to interfere. But . . . where the heck had she come from?

I couldn't handle everything at once. Too much going on. I felt useless now. Maybe it would be better to head out to my truck and get on home. Still, there was a dead man back in that room. I knew Hunter would want to talk to all of us. I stepped around, into the long hall, then back where I'd come from, opening another doorway leading out of the foyer and finding myself in a kind of morning room, or something dainty and half lighted where I could sit down a minute on a damask settee standing in front of a dead, stone fireplace and try to figure out what the heck had happened. Somehow I was flashing back to the day I heard that Sally had been shot at a game ranch over near Austen. I had the same feeling as I'd had then. Sadness and emptiness and thinking how here was another tragedy visited on the Wheatleys.

I was going to go look for Meemaw or Mama, though I figured Meemaw was with Elizabeth and maybe Mama was up there, too. I needed to know what Hunter wanted all of us to do—he'd want names of the guests. Maybe they'd be interviewing some of us yet tonight.

And more than anything, I needed Hunter to tell me what had just happened in this place.

He stuck his head in at the open door. "Looking for you. Thought you went upstairs with the new wife."

He walked over and patted me on the back—all the sympathy I was going to get from him though, come to think of it, I wasn't the one needing sympathy.

"Awful thing," he said, not sitting, ready to turn and get back to the crime scene.

"Her mother came in. She took over."

He raised his eyebrows. "Heard the woman was in town. Thought they weren't exactly close, was what I heard. Surprised, that she'd be at the party."

"She wasn't. Came running in and took over. Pushed me right out of the way." I let a little of my pique show.

"Good to know. It looks like an accident, though. Probably cleaning his gun. Should be able to clear everybody out pretty fast. Coroner followed us right in. He's in there now. Techs waiting. Not too much more we can do besides talk to a few folks."

He shook his head and let out a long sigh. "Just want you to know that your meemaw's upstairs with Elizabeth. Your mama and the rest of 'em are in with the other guests. Staff's staying until they can start cleaning up. Could be a couple of hours yet. You can go on home. Or you can wait for your family. You need a ride back to town?"

"I'll wait," I said and looked hard into a pair of concerned blue eyes. If anybody could make me melt back into being a kid, it was Hunter. I kind of teared up for a minute. I never knew why this happened. I can be strong as a general and then, when it's all over, turn into a baby.

"Poor Jeannie," I said. "I just met her. This is so sad. I mean, Eugene's first wife was shot and now him. What happened in that gun room?"

Hunter ran a hand gently over my hair, brushing it back from my face. He was going to reduce me to a puddle of salt water.

To Hunter's credit, he didn't say a word about the burlap and white powder. I'd ditched the noose.

"Happens. Guy forgets the gun's loaded. It goes off . . . Like I said, you can go. I know where to find you."

"I'm almost glad to hear it was an accident. Somebody was saying suicide. Can you imagine what Jeannie would feel like if that's what happened? A new bride . . ."

Sheriff Higsby stepped into the doorway and called out to Hunter. He turned to leave. But not without first touching my cheek. For a big cop, he had a very soft touch. "Death's never pretty, Lindy. You should know that by now. And it never gets any easier to take."

He was gone and I was left alone in a strange house with only the sounds of official voices and rushing footsteps coming from different places.

I sat awhile longer, wondering if I'd done the right thing, letting that woman take over with Jeannie. She didn't seem to welcome her. There was no reaching out to her mother.

"Are you Lindy Blanchard?"

The tall man coming into the room startled me. He was maybe in his mid-thirties, with fine blond hair—a little long at the neck. He was dressed as a doctor, with a stethoscope around his neck and a white jacket with an embroidered name over the pocket: DR. FRANKLIN. The name was familiar, but I didn't know him. I was confused—every uniform in the place could be a costume or he could be the real thing.

"Doctor?" I looked up. "For real?"

"Not medical." He leaned down and stuck his hand out. I shook it. "Dr. Peter Franklin," he said, bowing his head in a formal gesture. "Guest. I sent you a letter. Did you get it?"

"Oh, yes. You're with that biogenetics group in Italy, right? You want to see my work."

He smiled and nodded.

"Global Plant Initiative. I've been hoping to talk to you all evening. And then this . . . terrible . . . thing." The rather thin man shook his head. He had the look of a professor—hair a little too long by Texas standards, wire-framed glasses sliding down his nose.

"May I?" He indicated the sofa, beside me.

I nodded. He sat, sinking into the overstuffed cushions.

"I met Elizabeth in town. We got to talking and I told her I'd made a stop in Riverville to visit you, take a look at your work."

"I don't really let people into my greenhouse. Everything's still too tentative. You understand." I wrinkled my nose. "Maybe after I finish the article I'm working on. If I'm right, there could be significant changes coming to pecan agriculture."

He gave a light laugh. "Don't worry, Lindy. I didn't come to steal your work. I wanted to meet you. Elizabeth said you'd be here tonight and invited me to the party. She pointed you out, but before I could get over . . . well . . . you know what happened. I didn't know what to do. Stay or go. I don't want to impose on anyone. It's not like I'm an old friend or anything."

"If you give the sheriff your name and a way to get ahold of you, I think that's all they'll need tonight."

"Lord, Lord, what a truly awful thing for the new bride."

I agreed.

"Still, it would be good if we got to talk a little. I'm in the same line of work. Drought resistance. I'm staying a few days more. I suppose I should go to the memorial. I mean, I did accept Elizabeth's hospitality." He looked sadly at his hands and, with a deep sigh, stood. "I know this isn't the time, but could I take you to dinner? Maybe tomorrow night? I don't often find people in my field to talk to."

I had to smile. I knew what he meant. Not too many of us nutty scientists around to talk trees. He'd been nervous up until then. I guessed I'd be pretty nervous, too, in a strange state, with a lot of strange people, dressed up in a strange costume, then a man getting shot. I almost felt sorry for him.

"If you don't mind . . . I mean, I overheard Elizabeth going on about your costume. What was that all about? She surprised me. I wouldn't have identified her as an emotional woman, but she certainly did light into you. Actually, I think a lot of us were embarrassed. And right at that moment—a gunshot. At first I thought it was just something Texans did at weddings—shooting guns off."

Peter threw up a hand, stopping himself. "Ah well, I can see by your face this isn't something you want to discuss right now. Eh . . . could I give you a ride home?" he asked.

"I'm waiting for my grandmother. I've got my truck."

He nodded. "I'll call tomorrow, if that's all right. I don't mean to be pushy, but I'd really like to discuss what you're doing. I've been hearing some very good things. And I have such a short time in Riverville."

I was saying "yes" just as Hunter walked back in, striding into the room and stopping near us, looking hard at Peter Franklin.

The men nodded to one another, then shook hands as they exchanged names.

"Officer, I assume it's all right for us to leave. I've given one of your men my name. I'm staying in town, the Columbus Inn." Peter gave Hunter a slightly arrogant smirk. I watched Hunter bristle. The one thing you didn't do to Hunter Austen was act like you were better than he was.

Hunter wasn't the kind of person who looks down on anyone, and being a cop led him to discover, he told me, it wasn't the clothes people wore, it wasn't how much money they had, it wasn't where they lived or who they came from that made good people. It was what was inside and how they treated everybody around them. "Real simple," he'd told me many times. "Golden Rule's all it takes."

Hunter's voice was coldly professional when he answered. "You might as well go. We probably won't be contacting you. Pretty straightforward thing, what happened to Mr. Wheatley. Can't say it's a rare occurrence here in Riverville."

Hunter avoided looking straight at Peter Franklin.

"And Miss Blanchard? I've offered to take her home. This has been a very rough night for all of us."

"'Specially Eugene Wheatley." Hunter's response was sharp and out of character. I could hear the anger stuffed into his words.

"Was it really an accident? So unfortunate."

Hunter shook his head, still not looking at the man. "That it is. Maybe you should get going. We'd like the house cleared out so our techs can work the areas they have to work. And then there are the two grieving women upstairs. Don't worry about Lindy. She's waiting for her family . . ."

Peter Franklin gave a half snort. His face was red. "I'll 'get going,' as you say, as soon as I've finished my conversation with Miss Blanchard. I assume that's all right with the police?"

Hunter's face was red, too, and Hunter pissed off was a sight to see. The red went straight up into his hairline and his ears looked like a pair of red earmuffs. His bottom lip came out the way I remembered back when we were kids swimming naked in the Colorado and he got his foot tangled in the rope and swung back and forth over my head while I laughed at him.

"You wanna leave, Lindy. Go on," he said, stressing my first name. There was a kind of male claiming territory note in his voice. "I'll take Miss Amelia back to Rancho en el Colorado when she's finished with Miss Elizabeth."

"I think my mama can handle it, Hunter."

He nodded and turned slowly back to Peter Franklin. "You're a stranger here, aren't you?"

"From Boston, originally. A friend of Elizabeth Wheatley's and now, I hope, of Lindy's."

Hunter made a face. "Never saw you around before."

"I suppose you wouldn't since I was never here before."

"You staying in town?"

"Yes, I'll be in town awhile. As I said, I'm at the Columbus Inn if you need to reach me, but I won't be of much help. I was at the buffet table when I heard the shot. Awful thing. I'll probably stay a few more days."

"You don't need to, you know. Long as we've got a number where we can reach you."

To put an end to what should have been a flattering male display of power, I said, "Think I'll get going. I'll call Mama and Meemaw later."

"Walk you to your truck," Hunter said to me while looking pointedly at Peter Franklin. He stepped between me and the other man, taking me by the elbow.

"Lindy . . . eh . . . Ms. Blanchard, I'll call you tomorrow. I'd like it very much if we could get together for dinner. Be to both our benefit."

Hunter's hand was on my back and pushing until we were out the front door and across the drive. I stepped aside, looked up, and glared at him, forcing him to back off. "Hey," I said. "I'm going to trip on this thing." I held up one corner of my shroud.

"Dumb outfit," he half growled.

My truck was parked back behind a clump of mesquite trees. I got in then turned to thank Hunter for walking me out.

"I'll be over to the Nut House in the morning. After I get through here, I've got to find a place for a mongrel I picked up out on the highway. He's in my car. Pound's closed. You don't want to take him with you, do you?" He motioned toward where he'd parked, in the circular drive.

I gave him a "not on your life" look.

"Didn't want to say in front of that man, but I've got to interview you. You were in the gun room—wish you hadn't gone in there. Even though it was probably an accident, people rushing in messed up the scene." He shook his head at me and rested his hands on the car door after I slammed it shut. I knew he had more to say. I turned on the motor and waited.

"I don't like that guy." He gave me one of his narrow stares that usually warned me not to push back.

"He's a scientist," I said. "I don't get to talk to many people in my field."

"You going to let him into your greenhouse?"

Feeling I was being manipulated, I made a noncommittal face. "Maybe."

"You don't let anybody in there."

"He's not just anybody."

"That mean you're going out to eat with him, too?"

"If he's buying."

He shook his head and stepped back from the car door.

"Don't forget your dog," I yelled out the window and drove off a little faster than I should have. I was mad. An old friend just died—well, somebody I used to know. Two women were suffering. And here were two men playing silly mating games over me.

I started back toward Riverville and my apartment, trying not to let myself take even a little pleasure in the spectacle I'd left behind.

Chapter Five

The Nut House was full of Rivervillians when I came down from my apartment over the store, dressed for a day back at the farm in torn jeans and an Alamo T-shirt. I was looking forward to not thinking of much beyond investigating a specialized genome I'd read might work with my trees. The feeling of a day to myself was like tasting freedom and I was ready for it.

Tongues were wagging up and down the aisles of the store; aisles filled with sugared pecans and Pecan Sandies and pecan brittle and boxes with all kinds of good pecan things in them. And, of course, bags of our supreme Texas pecans all by themselves.

I thought a tour bus must have stopped, something Miss Amelia depended on for a good season, but the faces were familiar: neighbors and pecan farmers standing in circles, whispering away at a great rate. Ethelred had her own little clique around her. Freda Cromwell, Queen of the Riverville

Gossips, stood beside Ethelred with a frustrated look on her quirky little face.

No question about the cause of all the heated gossip. Like anywhere in the world, death brings out speculators and spectators. I imagined a little bit of sorrow, some regret and sympathy, a dose of fear, and a smidgen of relief in all that talk. Relief that it wasn't one of them, cleaning a gun, getting distracted, and being taken out by their own bullet.

Meemaw saw me and left her assistant baker, Treenie, in charge of the cash register. She rolled her eyes and took me by the hand, leading out to the kitchen, while she huffed and puffed and mumbled under her breath. When the doors swung shut behind her, Meemaw went to one of her bottom cabinets without a word and pulled out a couple of industrial-sized stainless steel pots, got a gigantic spoon from a utensil drawer, and gathered the ingredients to make a batch of filling for her pecan pies.

"See what's going on out there?" She gestured with her spoon, her pale eyes rolling. "Like a war starting up. Most of it's about jealousy. Just 'cause the Wheatleys got so much money. Makes me sick to my stomach. Disgusting. Every mouth going a mile a minute. I suspect some are talking just to hear themselves talk."

She banged around the stove then got out her measuring cups for the sugars and spices, measured everything, poured things into the pot, added a whole lot of Karo Syrup, melted butter, and a bunch of beaten eggs. She turned the fire low and started stirring like mad.

"Special pies?" I asked because she wasn't saying anything, just stirring like her arm could fly off.

"'Course it is. Everybody in town will be wanting one. Especially all the good church folks. Just to get 'em through this terrible thing that's happened to 'em."

"Want me to break out the Garrison Brothers?"

She nodded to a cupboard that surprised even me when

I opened it. Bottle after bottle of Garrison Brothers Texas Straight Whiskey. I pulled one down and took it to Meemaw, who measured out the whiskey, poured it in the pot, and then added an extra dollop straight out of the bottle.

She followed that with a pile of pecans, stirring until the filling was ready for the pie shells she'd made earlier, all waiting to be filled and baked. I helped her fill the unbaked shells then get them into the industrial-sized oven.

"There." She shut the door with a loud thunk. "Pie for any Texan's soul. Going to only those people who deserve it."

She looked over at me and gave me a smile that was full of the devil. "None for Ethelred and none for that Freda Cromwell. They may be friends of mine, but there's no solace going to either one. I don't care if Ethelred begs. The thing about Ethelred is, she won't get any nicer all liquored up so no use wasting the Garrison's."

I dug in for the cleanup at the big, deep sink. I was used to helping. Been in the kitchen since I was a kid when I stood on a chair to wash dishes. I had all her recipes memorized though baking wasn't something I'd ever be good at. I wasn't a baker, nor a chef, and had little interest in working with anything other than dirt. The only thing I loved smelling was fresh water coming out of my overhead sprinklers in the greenhouse; and my trees; and sun on the bare earth in my test garden; and maybe the smell of the muddy Colorado River in the spring.

And what I liked seeing best wasn't cooling pecan pies but the catkins hanging from the pecan trees and then the little green blossoms that meant there was going to be a bumper crop of nuts.

And what I liked best of all was being around my family and Hunter and standing out in the groves, under trees that towered over me, and feeling the cool shadows they made on warm fall days.

That's who I am and Meemaw tells me it's all right to be

the way I am and to love different things than other people love. Mama just rolls her eyes and says, “Whatever, Lindy,” to me. Bethany says I’m nuts myself. But Justin, my quiet brother, knows. He knows that loving pecan trees and the land and the river can run right through your blood.

Meemaw pushed her steely gray hair back from her face with her wrist, finally took off her Rancho en el Colorado apron, hung it on a hook, and looked hard at me. “We’ve gotta talk.”

I nodded. There would be no getting away early.

Meemaw motioned for me to go sit at the enameled table at the back of the kitchen. I knew I’d get a slab of pie for breakfast and a cup of coffee. The one thing about Meemaw, she never remembered I was a tea drinker. Tea for breakfast wasn’t right, to her way of thinking, so I got coffee—strong, black coffee, and I didn’t say a word.

We sat over our pie and coffee. She pushed the milk pitcher toward me, knowing I was one to pour an awful lot of milk in my coffee, hoping to kill the taste.

“Hunter was here first thing this morning,” she said, leaning back in her chair. “Before I even opened the store. He thought you’d be up. Had some things to tell us, and some questions to ask. Then he got a call and left. Should be back anytime now.”

“What’s he want? What kind of questions? We don’t know any more than anybody else there.”

“You went in the gun room.”

“So? All I touched was Jeannie. Trying to get her out of there.”

She gave me one of her long, thinking looks. “Said he’s feeling a little bit out of his depth here. Especially with Elizabeth Wheatley so ready to come after them and all that money behind her. Sheriff’s feeling the same thing.”

“Over an accident? We get lots of gun accidents around here. What are they worried about?”

"Think now, Lindy." She raised an eyebrow at me. "There's that pistol he must've been working on, down by his feet. First of all, that little gun didn't make the big hole in his body like Hunter told me about. Second, you saw where the bullet went in and where it came out. Shot through the back, am I right? Can you tell me how, or why, Eugene reached around and shot himself in the back? Hunter said it was straight through—where arms don't reach.

"Me and Hunter talked for half an hour or so. What we came up with was that someone with a powerful rifle shot him. Could've been from the back doorway—a gun like that. The forensics people are looking at trajectory, but I think that's clear enough. Hunter's thinking the same thing. He's pretty shook up. Talked to Elizabeth and I guess she won't take anything but accident as the reason her brother's dead. Makes you feel sorry for her. Been through an awful lot. Still, truth is truth. Hunter's worried about her bringing in her own specialists and lawyers, the way she's threatening. That's gonna muddy everything they're trying to put together."

I wanted to moan. Poor Jeannie. Poor Elizabeth. But then I took back the "poor Elizabeth" because I didn't like the woman and she'd embarrassed me—but what the heck. This was about a man dying, not about a catfight.

"Elizabeth's going to have to face facts," I said. "Can't cover up a murder and, I'll bet anything, by this morning she won't want to."

She shrugged. "You know Elizabeth. Enough to scare any man when she's on a tear, and I'll bet anything the idea of her brother being murdered isn't something that's going to go down easily. You know she idolized the man."

"Too bad she never got married. Been better for Eugene not to have his sister running his life the way she does . . . eh . . . did. Better if she got married and ran that man's life. Not a bad-looking woman. I never understood—"

"Maybe Elizabeth's been around more than you think. And I don't mean 'around' here."

"Gossip?" I gave Meemaw a wicked grin.

I sipped the coffee and felt the chlorogenic acid hit my gut. I'd be in the bathroom soon.

"I think Hunter and the sheriff are gonna need my help, Lindy," Meemaw was saying. "I got a feeling . . ."

"You mean you're going to get mixed up in this mess? Wheatleys are Wheatleys. I'd stay away, if I was you."

"Tough, sometimes, for the police to get answers. But you know how it is with women my age. People talk to us like we can't really hear, or they think nobody will listen to us anyway. A habit for listening's not a bad thing."

"I don't see you getting involved. Just end up with Elizabeth mad at all the Blanchards and, Lord knows, you know she was mad enough at me to start with. And remember what happened when the historical society wanted to erect that plaque on Carya Street? Honoring the ranchers and farmers? Mad as a wet cat because they didn't put her name on it."

She shrugged, thinking. "A lot of those people there last night weren't even from Riverville. I probably don't know any more about them than the sheriff does. Still . . ."

She stirred her coffee and looked past me, one of her faded blue eyes moving off a little, as if on a thought of its own. "I told Hunter I'd do what I could. Maybe just stand back and look at what he digs up. You know, for the most part, I see good things in people. And then sometimes I see the evil, too. Not that I like it, but an eye for evil comes in handy once in a while."

She waited until I nodded, as I knew I had to.

"And wouldn't you say that an eye for evil is the very thing lawmen need when it comes to murder?"

I nodded again.

"And an ear. If I can listen to somebody talking and know they're lying, or look into their eyes and see the cruelty there? Wouldn't you say those are good things to have on your side?" She took a deep breath. "So what would you have me do, Lindy? Not help when I know I can?"

I nodded because I knew she wasn't really talking to me but to herself. If she wanted to use her eyes and ears, and maybe her nose, to help find a killer, that was fine with me. Just as long as Hunter kept her safe.

"I wasn't saying not to—"

"You expect me to be like these people who keep their heads in the dirt and don't say anything because they don't want to hurt somebody's feelings or don't want anybody mad at them? Well, just forget that. I know what I know and I see what I see and I put things together maybe other people don't know to put together. And I'm gonna use these very fine abilities I've got for good." She nodded fast, winning this argument with herself.

"So you're jumping in, and taking me with you, I suppose. My Supermeemaw. 'Truth, Justice, and the American Way.'"

We were both laughing when Hunter came back, stuck his head in the door, and frowned hard at us.

Chapter Six

Hunter walked in looking bent and tired and quizzical. I supposed he hadn't been laughing much so far that morning. His face was drawn down into a deep frown. The usually sharp crease in his uniform pants was blurred. Even his well-shaven chin and bright blue eyes looked dark and kind of out of it.

Before he shut the door behind him, I heard the big, deep huffs of a barking dog from somewhere in the parking lot.

We exchanged terse good mornings, last night's hard feelings still hanging on though I was looking at our little spat as just another one of those games we played, kind of showing what we felt about each other without having to put it into words.

"That your dog out there barking?" I asked, needing something other than Eugene's murder to break the ice between us.

"Not my dog." He threw a leg over one of the chairs and

sat down without looking at me. “Still gonna take him to the pound soon as I can get done here.”

“What’d you do with him last night?” Meemaw asked.

He looked down at the table. “What could I do? He stayed at my house.”

“No wonder you look so tired. Keep you awake all night?” I asked.

“What do you think? Couldn’t keep him off my bed so I slept on the couch.”

“Well, good luck getting rid of him now. You know what they say, ‘Sleep with a dog and he’s yours forever.’”

“Funny.” He wasn’t in the mood for humor, or at least not from me.

“Gettin’ hot out there. Hope you left the windows down,” I said.

He nodded. “All of ’em.”

Miss Amelia got up heavily, leaning on the table, and went to cut him a piece of pecan pie from a cooled pie in the big refrigerator. She poured him a mug of coffee and brought it all over to the table.

“Awful, there at the house last night,” was the next thing Hunter said after thanking Meemaw for the pie.

“Yeah, especially for Eugene.” I threw his own words back at him.

“Think I should start this early with your ‘special’ pie?” Hunter ignored me and grinned up at Meemaw.

“Nothing in there gonna get you, Hunter, but the sugar. Rest’ll sharpen your mind.”

He dug in then narrowed his eyes at me, setting his fork down slowly. “Who *was* that dude you were with last night? Sure thought a lot of himself.”

“I told you. He’s another plant scientist. He heard about my work. We couldn’t talk there . . . I mean . . .” I looked hard at him. “It wasn’t a pickup, if that’s what you’re thinking. I don’t pick up men at murders.”

When Hunter opened his mouth to come back at me, Meemaw jumped right in. "Terrible thing, about Eugene."

Hunter turned away from me to speak to Meemaw. "Talked to Elizabeth again. She's in a state, but keeps saying it had to be suicide if it wasn't an accident. Seems he wasn't happy about marrying that Jeannie, according to Elizabeth. Said he'd been shattered—that's the word she used. Shattered about making such a big mistake. Said she didn't know how to help him. Then comes this."

"Suicide?" I scoffed. "Don't believe a word of it. He seemed happy enough to me. I saw how they looked at each other. They were in love. Come on, now. Nobody believes it was a suicide, do they, Hunter? You've got the same problems as saying it was an accident."

He didn't answer, only pushed his mug around on the tablecloth.

"Be suicide magic if it was. No man can shoot himself in the back with a little pistol and have the bullet act like a high-powered rifle. Don't know how she plans on explaining away the evidence."

"Eugene said he was going to go set up his gun collection for people who wanted to get a look at it," I said. "Somebody had to have come in by that back door. Somebody he was expecting or why go sit down at his desk after he let the man in? Maybe a gun dealer who came to pick up a gun he bought earlier. Maybe there were bad feelings . . ." I was speculating.

He looked at me briefly. "Tell that to his sister."

Hunter was thinking hard. "I asked a couple of the regular servants about that back door. The cook—you know her, Chantal Kronos—well, she told me that door was always kept locked and only Eugene had a key, as far as she knew. That collection of his is supposed to be really valuable. Frank Tolliver, from the co-op, said he was the one opened the back door last night after the murder. Didn't remember if it was locked or not, but he thought it had to be. One of those automatic locking things. Said the smell in there was awful. Had to get air in somehow."

Frank Tolliver. Nobody in town wouldn't trust Frank's word. He was a member of the pecan co-op. Vice president back when my daddy was the president. Frank owned a ranch bigger than ours and a house twice the size of the one my daddy built. He was a man well thought of in town and not somebody to be caught aiming a killing gun.

"Did he say it was unlocked or open a little bit when he pushed it?" Meemaw asked.

Hunter shook his head. "Didn't remember. He'd just seen Eugene and knew the smell had to be cleared out when he saw Jeannie rushing in the way she did."

"Murderer had to come in that door then. The only way. But Eugene sure wouldn't have been handing out keys . . ."

"So what it all boils down to is a locked-room mystery." I threw it in because we weren't getting anywhere, going in circles.

"Hope not." Hunter almost growled the words as he looked from me to Meemaw and back. "Don't say a word to anybody about what we've been talking about. Me and the sheriff have got to think about all of this and come up with a way to handle Elizabeth Wheatley while we're finding a killer. No accident. No suicide. Don't leave much."

"What about that pistol on the floor?" Meemaw asked. "Why was it even there, do you think?"

"That's the gun he was cleaning, polishing the handle and stuff. Found out this morning it's what's called a presentation piece. You know, guns given to famous people—like Winston Churchill. Heads of state, like that. Gun companies give them out sometimes. That gun is a Schwarzlose, given to Emperor Wilhelm the Second of Germany. We found it listed in Eugene's catalog. Goes back to the early nineteen hundreds. Eugene has the value as near a million dollars at auction. But the thing is, Miss Amelia, that gun's never been fired. Wasn't meant to be.

"Sniper rifle, is what the lab people are saying," Hunter went on. "Found the cartridge by the door. Aim was straight. Wasn't an accidental shot."

He thought a moment. "They tested Eugene's hands. No gunpowder residue. Might have expected some, if he was cleaning guns that actually fired."

He narrowed his eyes at us. "Somebody was in that room with him, is what I'm thinking. Shot him and went out that back door."

"What I don't get is why," I said. "Right there, in the middle of his wedding party? What murderer wants two hundred people around when he commits his crime? Oh, and a lot of servants. Throw in a DJ."

"What you've got to do is look at what's possible and leave the rest out," Meemaw said.

"Still scrambling to catch up with the guests, now that we know it's a murder, not an accident. Deputies from other counties coming to help. Understand there was a list. Maybe Elizabeth Wheatley can help us out with that. Sheriff wants to see who was invited and who came, and then who was still there at the end, after the gunshot."

"You know who had the list?" Meemaw was thinking hard and fast. "Roy Friendly. He's over to the Barking Coyote usually 'bout three o'clock. He'll be stone-cold sober then. You don't want to wait too long after that. Tell you the truth, Hunter, I'd rather be talking with Roy any day of the year than Elizabeth Wheatley. But that's just me. And Elizabeth Wheatley dealing with the death of her brother . . . whew . . . worse than anything I can imagine."

Hunter took a small notebook from his pocket and wrote down shorthand-like notes.

"We're going to get a rare-gun dealer in there today," he said when he looked up, "if Elizabeth will agree to let him take a look. The collection was cataloged so maybe something is missing. Something a lot more important to somebody than money. Or maybe there's a gun so rare even Eugene didn't know the value."

"I suppose that back door was fingerprinted?" Meemaw said, raising her eyebrows at Hunter.

He shook his head. "That's one of the problems. Everybody thought the shooting was an accident. They weren't as thorough as they should've been. Techs are back in there now going over the whole room, especially the doors: front and back."

"The back door's the only one that'll tell you something." Meemaw stood as the oven timer pinged.

Hunter touched the stiff hat he'd set on the table beside him then pushed his dish and mug away. "That poor wife. I can only imagine what she's going through. New bride and now a new widow. Wish this wasn't so urgent. Sheriff's going over to talk to both of them again. Jeannie and Elizabeth. Not going to be a happy day for either one of 'em."

He turned to look me squarely in the eyes. Nothing friendly in the look. "You knew Eugene, Lindy. Anything you can tell me about him?"

"Knew him from high school, is all. Just like you."

"I didn't know him. Wasn't interested in me. Not from a ranchin', or pecan farm, or oil family."

"Well, I knew his first wife, Sally. Sally and me even got together a couple of times. Supper. Things like that. I liked her. It was really sad, what happened to her. Geez—stop to think about it. That was a shooting, too."

I couldn't help but shiver. Some families went through such deep pain. It didn't matter how much money they had. In a way, that was just like our family, with my daddy and even my uncle being murdered.

I had a question for Hunter, something still bothering me. "Who was the woman who ran in and took over? Jeannie didn't seem happy to see her."

"Turns out that really is her mother."

"Not invited to the party? Isn't that strange? Where was she? Hanging around outside? Looking in the windows?"

"One more question I've gotta ask, Lindy." He put his hand up, stopping my questions as he set the stiff hat on his head. "Any reason you were there looking like death last night? Was that really your costume? Couple of people mentioned it."

"Yup. That was my costume. But I wasn't there predicting a death at the feast. And I don't see dead people. I was supposed to be— Oh well, never mind. It was kind of because I was mad and didn't want to go to the damn party to begin with."

He nodded, knowing me. He twisted his head from side to side then put his arms up to stretch.

The three of us were sitting still when a noise started, a kind of raspy scratching at the back door.

"What the devil . . ." Meemaw got up to see what was happening beyond her door.

Hunter jumped up fast, scraping his chair along the tile. "Gotta be that damned dog. I'll go."

He opened the door and an animal bounded in. Too big. Too black. Too curly-haired. With round black eyes going from side to side and from me to Meemaw and back to Hunter. The dog took one leap at Hunter's chest and they both went down.

Meemaw and I helped Hunter to his feet with Hunter swearing at the dog and Meemaw chastising Hunter. "You put the windows all the way down?"

Hunter brushed off his pants while he held up a hand to keep the leaping dog off him.

"Halfway. Thing's got to be Houdini." He grabbed for the dog's scruff and held on. The dog yelped and threw his head back and around, long pink tongue coming out, aimed at Hunter's face. The beady eyes leaked love.

"So he came after you rather than run," I pointed out, standing out of the way. "Dog's nuts."

"You sure do have your hands full, Hunter," Meemaw said from back over at the stove, where she was taking one hot pie after another from the oven and setting them to cool on a long metal table. "Better take him out of here before the Board of Health gets after me."

Hunter nodded and practically rode the dog through the door and out toward his squad car. I watched and yelled back at Meemaw, "That dog's in love. Hunter's got himself a big, crazy dog for life."

"Guess that's how a woman'll have to hook him, too. Chase him hard. Lick his face. And knock him out of bed." Meemaw was looking real innocent as she stepped back to admire her pies.

Chapter Seven

I washed up the cups and plates and put things away for Meemaw, who then blocked my way out of the kitchen, hands at her waist, a tough look on her pretty face.

"What in the name of heaven is going on between you and Hunter?" she demanded. "Why are you treatin' the boy like that? And why's he so cold to you?"

"Oh, Lord, Meemaw. There's nothing wrong but in Hunter's head. It was a man there last night. In the same field I'm in. Heard of me, he said, and asked me to dinner tonight. Guess Hunter didn't take to him."

"Did you?"

I had to stop and think. Sure, I was flattered. With Meemaw I knew better than to lie.

"Guess I liked him well enough. I don't often get someone who understands what I'm trying to do, let alone be interested, even maybe wants to come in and take a look."

She didn't say a word. She didn't have to.

I frowned hard at her. A woman who preened when the

press came to cover her store; who liked being called a "master baker" in the local paper—and her judging me? There was sin enough to go around for the both of us.

"Hmmm." She turned away to start a new dough. "Think you two better settle what you feel about each other and decide if you're right together or not. Sometimes people let it get away, thinking there is always time. Don't let that happen to you, Lindy. I've seen plenty of mistakes in my day. Ethelred Tomroy being one of them. Turned her back on a man she didn't think was good enough for her. Now you're taking the same kind of chance, maybe losing somebody you really want in your life. You do that and you'll end up being sorrier than about anything else you ever did. Won't be like not having one of your trees turn out right or not getting one of your papers published in some scientific magazine. This will be real. Be awful. I just don't understand why the both of you can't be happy . . ."

All of this while she was banging drawers closed and plunking things down on a metal table, pretending the only thing on her mind was her next batch of Pecan Moon Cookies.

"It's not that easy, Meemaw."

"Nothing's easy with you. Lindy. I'm still saying, there's no reason why you and Hunter have to act like enemies."

I pushed my way through the swinging doors to the store, turning back to say only, "And don't compare me to Ethelred Tomroy. Bet it wasn't her broke up whatever they had."

So why was she the first person I ran into as I tried to get to the front door and out to my truck? And just after Meemaw compared me to her, probably hoping I'd develop a kinship with a lonely old woman who, like me, had turned away the only love she'd ever known in her life.

None of that worked. I took a long look at the tall, broad woman with a sour face and scraggly hair, and got ready to go after her. *Say one word wrong to me, Ethelred. Just one word.*

Her big hands were in the air, one finger crooked, peremptorily calling me over to where she stood in the pecan candy aisle, surrounded by an enthralled audience.

"Lindy, here, was at the party last night, same as me." She nodded fast, until tendrils of steel gray hair were shooting up and weaving around like Medusa's snakes. "She can tell you about that new wife. Shame. That's what I called it."

I nodded to Freda Cromwell, short and elderly, in a dress too long and too washed-out to do anything for her. Freda, who usually had the gossip market cornered in Riverville, was looking mightily put out now that Ethelred had the floor and was an insider on this particular story. The others were neighbors and town women.

"The whole thing was a scandal," Miss Ethelred was saying to the circle around her.

"What's a scandal, Ethelred?" I asked, smiling my "cat's got you cornered" smile and vowing to lighten up whatever outrage she was spouting.

"You know very well, Lindy Blanchard."

"Man's death isn't a scandal. That's called a tragedy."

Ethelred frowned hard at me and leaned in, ready for a fight. "You ask me, that man's death was no accident, the way the sheriff's saying. Just take a look at that new wife."

"Jeannie? Seemed real nice, you ask me. Poor thing."

"Nice! You must've had your eyes closed—all that flour on your face. Why, that woman was advertisin' who she is, all night. You see that yellow dress? You tell me, Lindy, what famous person wore a yellow dress and was known for what she did with that General Santa Anna?"

"Yellow Rose of Texas. A true patriot. Kept Santa Anna busy in bed while Sam Houston was beating his soldiers in an eighteen-minute war." I gave a self-satisfied nod to the listening circle the way people always do when they're talking patriotism. "Why, Ethelred, all kinds of songs've been written about the 'Yellow Rose of Texas.' I remember, in school, we learned that even our men in the Civil War were singing about her."

I looked at the others and broke into a lusty version of one of my favorite songs ever.

> *"She's the sweetest little rosebud that Texas ever knew. Her eyes are bright as diamonds. They sparkle like the dew. You may talk about your Clementine and sing of Rosalee. But the Yellow Rose of Texas is the only girl for me—"*

"Now, Ethelred," I said to the red-faced woman when I figured the listeners had enough. "What on earth's wrong with that?"

"That's not what Jeannie Wheatley was about. I asked her and she refused to answer. And why on earth didn't Elizabeth know to stop her before she outraged so many of us? Pretends to be a historian, that woman. Don't know much of anything about Texas, you ask me." She nodded hard and fast, making some around her nod in return.

"Coming dressed as a woman who was no better than a . . . well . . . I'll come right out and say it: no better than a prostitute. And to her own wedding party? She's no Wheatley, I'll tell you. That Jeannie. Flaunting who she is right in your face."

"*'Who she is'?*" I was getting a little red in the face myself. "What in the name of heaven is that supposed to mean?"

"Things been going around."

"What things?"

"I'll bet you know very well, Lindy. You heard about her mother coming to town. Terrible woman. Heard Eugene wouldn't let her up to their house."

"You sure hear a lot, Ethelred."

"Well, she wasn't invited to the party, was she? Yet she showed up anyway, right after Eugene died." She leaned down to those closest around her. "She's been hanging out at the Barking Coyote. Bragging who her daughter just married. Saying how she was going to be rich. Why, even Finula, who everybody knows is only as good as she needs to be, has been talking about it."

Meemaw came up behind me and put a warning hand on my shoulder. I knew she was afraid I was getting too mad and about to blurt out what Hunter told us that morning, adding fuel to Ethelred's fire.

"Think that's about enough gossiping here in my store," Meemaw said. "Poor woman just lost her husband. I'd say, let's have a little respect and wait for the sheriff and Hunter to make their conclusions, what happened out there last night."

I heard a deeply angry Meemaw in her pronouncement and felt it as her fingers dug into my shoulder.

There wasn't another word spoken as the group, led by Ethelred Tomroy, turned and took their ugly talk out to the store porch, where they'd soon be sweating in their limp cotton dresses. Nothing like a good dose of Texas heat to fry out meanness.

Chapter Eight

I was on my way out to the ranch and back to work. It was great, doing nothing, playing things through my head: what I was going to say to Ethelred the next time I encountered her; how everybody would know what an idiot the woman was. But then I put all that aside: murder, and Hunter being jealous for no reason on this earth, and me enjoying his jealousy a little too much.

It was a beautiful spring day. The road ahead was empty. I didn't want to waste time thinking badly of myself so I rolled down the window and let the wind blow at my face and through my hair, as best it could since I'd thrown my hair into a ponytail that morning.

I was singing along with KULM, 98.3, playing an old Miranda Lambert song, then bouncing in my seat with Tyler Farr's "Whiskey in My Water."

But like always, my ringing cell phone brought me down to earth, like Mary Poppins at that sad tea party.

Jeannie Wheatley. I didn't recognize her voice at first.

She sounded kind of beaten down. No laughter here, but who could blame her? I wondered fast if Hunter'd been out there yet; if she knew Eugene was murdered.

I figured I'd have to be careful.

We got through the "so sorry for your loss" and her saying how she was still in a daze, not believing Eugene was gone. We talked like that for a couple of minutes before she got down to what she was after.

"You know, Lindy, I got the feeling last night that we might become friends."

"I sure hope so," I said and found I really meant it. I liked Jeannie Wheatley. "What can I do to help?"

"Well, it's just that I don't have anybody here in Riverville I really know. No friends, not like back home in Dallas. I guess what I'm saying is I need to talk to somebody. Get away for a while. Things are moving so fast . . ."

"Sure. Be glad to help out. But you know the word's around already. Everybody in Riverville will be wanting to give you their condolences—we shouldn't be in public. Won't get a minute's peace. I'm on my way out to the ranch, but with Justin and the men in and out; with Bethany there talking to her clients—well, might not be a good idea." I thought a minute. "How about a ride? Maybe out to see the Chaunceys? You met them last night. The girls are great if you need a shoulder to cry on or just a listening ear. And there won't be anybody else around to make you uncomfortable."

"That sounds good. I was supposed to go with Elizabeth later to pick out an urn and make . . . well, you know . . . memorial arrangements, but she's been saying out loud she'd rather do all that alone."

"Really? You're his wife."

"Not something I want to fight over."

"Hunter been out there yet today?"

There was silence. "Yes," she said. "He's back in with Elizabeth now. I hate to think . . ."

"He told you both what they found out? What they think about Eugene's death?"

"He did. You can imagine . . . Elizabeth was already blaming me for his suicide. I don't have a single idea what she's making of murder."

"I know she watched out for her brother—maybe too much, but that's not fair. She can't be blaming you."

"Could we talk when I see you? I really need to get away from here."

I figured it would take me fifteen minutes to get to the Wheatleys'. It was past our ranch—which made me groan. I'd probably have to fight myself, wanting to turn in and get back to my own life, but not able to . . . one more time.

I told her I'd be there as soon as I could.

She said she'd be waiting on the front portico.

I hoped Elizabeth Wheatley would be nowhere in sight. The last thing I wanted was another fight with that woman.

Jeannie looked different. I'd seen her around town and then at the party, but she seemed smaller today, shrunken. Her hair wasn't so big—done up in a messy blond knot at the back of her head. She had on a kind of loosely knit blue sweater over white shorts, with white sandals.

Not Ethelred's idea of widow's weeds, I was willing to bet, and vowed to take Jeannie nowhere near Riverville.

I'd called Miranda Chauncey on the way over, asked if it would be okay to bring Jeannie out for a little while. I said she was upset and feeling all alone and needed to talk to somebody.

Miranda said she was going to make sandwiches since it was close to noon, time for dinner anyway, and sure as anything nobody but her around their place was going to get busy cooking since Melody was sulking out in the shed, only the Lord knew about what.

I got it, that there was a dispute going on between her and Melody, so I hung up fast and hoped the girls would be civil once Jeannie got out there.

Then I called my meemaw, to let her know where I was going.

"And you were upset about me getting involved." She cleared her throat, gave a little cough. "You know, Lindy. We don't know who did that to Eugene. I'd say everybody's a suspect."

"Not Jeannie."

"Everybody. Watch yourself. Promise me that much. Let me know where you're going at all times. Deal?"

I agreed it was a deal as I pulled up to the Wheatleys' mansion.

Jeannie was waiting and hopped in my truck. I peeled out of that driveway before she had the door closed behind her.

"You okay?" I asked, needing to come up with something as I turned on to the highway toward the Chaunceys' ranch.

She gave me a weak smile. "Wish I was. It's just been . . . awful. I can't believe he's gone. Eugene was so good to me. Like nobody ever was before. I can't stand the thought—"

She didn't cry, just fell silent.

"I knew somebody murdered Eugene." She rested her head on the back of the seat and turned to look at me. "I knew it first thing last night. I can't tell you why or how I knew. I just did. All along, ever since we came back here, I just knew nothing was going to be okay."

"What's the problem with Elizabeth?"

"Everything. She turned on me like a rattler. Right from the moment Eugene died, I'd say."

"I got the feeling last night that everything was all right between you two. I mean, she lit into me 'cause she thought I was insulting you. I thought you two were pretty close."

"I don't know where that came from. Maybe she was

protecting me. Nice enough at first, then all of a sudden she started making comments about how I didn't have the taste to help with the party and asking Eugene to keep me out of her hair while she was setting things up. I don't know if she meant to hurt me, but she sure did. Eugene saw it and promised we were getting out of there soon as the dumb party was over. He'd already seen to having his guns packed up afterward. Eugene changed his mind about staying in Riverville once Elizabeth told him she was going to live here." She took a deep breath. "I guess Elizabeth always looked after him when they were kids. You know, their mama and daddy traveled a lot on business and, well, just kind of left them both with servants. Eugene said she was a little rough on Sally, too. But then, after Sally was gone, she told him she just wanted him to be happy. Said she hoped he'd find somebody else, and when we met and he asked me to marry him, she acted happy. Now he's gone and neither one of us have Eugene.

"Thing is, Lindy," she went on, "I can't stay in that house another minute. That's where Eugene was murdered. Can't get it out of my head. And then with Elizabeth treating me like I was . . . trash. She doesn't want me in there any more than I want to be there."

"The house belonged to Eugene. Just about everything did, is what I was told years ago. So it must be yours now. Could be a family trust or something. Still, whatever he had should come to you."

"I don't want it. She can have it. All of it. If I have money, it will only bring more trouble."

"This about your mother?"

"Guess you heard about her. I didn't even know she was here in Riverville. Eugene told Mama, back in Dallas, to stay away from me. There's already been times—"

She shut her mouth as I turned in at the Chaunceys' long, dusty drive.

"They know I'm coming, these women?"

"Said they were happy to have you. Fixing sandwiches or something. Don't get your hopes up for a good meal. Just be as gracious as the girls will be to you."

The road in was long and winding, ending in the hard-packed, dirt turnaround in front of the ancient, low-roofed ranch house. Beyond the house were the girls' pecan groves, a bunch of tired-looking trees with weeds growing between the rows.

The twins, in their usual getup, met us on the porch, both hugging Jeannie and giving their condolences. Melody was the first to invite us on in and warn Miranda not to keep us standing out there in the heat.

We were led straight to a table set for four in the long, low main room. Miranda told us to sit while Melody fussed with a plate filled with white bread and some kind of meat.

"Don't know what this is, to tell the truth." She poked at the meat. "Miranda did the food today. Can't vouch for anything."

Miranda grumbled but passed the platter of mystery meat and bread without apology.

We were told to eat and nothing more was said for a while as the girls passed hot sauce our way, along with a bag of taco chips.

Melody got up and scurried around the table, filling our tall glasses from a sweating pitcher of sweet tea.

After we'd eaten, Jeannie got tears in her eyes, thanking the girls for their kindness. Melody got tears in her eyes right back at her and mumbled all kinds of things about the sorrow of losing a husband and how life goes on, but never the same, and all Jeannie could do was hold on tight to that love and hope to join him one day in heaven and . . .

Miranda couldn't take another word and blew up, telling Melody to keep her trap shut. "You don't know a thing about losing a husband. You never had one to lose. And if you did, bet anything you'd be happy to be shut of 'im."

"Why, Miranda Chauncey!" Melody's buxom chest swelled up like a couple of balloons. "What a thing to say in front of a newly-made widow. Least you can do is have a little respect—"

That went on for a while. Jeannie and I avoided each other's eyes and sipped at the tea.

When things settled down, I filled the girls in on what we'd learned that morning. Miranda took it easily. Melody moaned and reached over to pat Jeannie's hand, murmuring her sorrow at such a sad state of affairs. Soon Miranda was shrewdly asking Jeannie, "How're you getting along with Elizabeth? She gets bowed up at the best of times. I can only imagine—losing Eugene. The apple of her eye."

Jeannie took a while to answer then shook her head. "Not very well. Soon as she heard Eugene'd been killed by somebody and that it wasn't an accident after all, she kind of looked at me and I think she decided I had something to do with it."

"Wha' the hell—" Miranda stopped herself, looking disgusted.

"Terrible." Melody took over. "When's the memorial? You know me and Miranda want to be there. Especially now that we know you need people to kind of line up on your side."

"Elizabeth's seeing to everything. But she can't set the day yet. Hunter says the coroner's not through with Eugene's—"

"You're not going back there, are you?" Miranda blurted out. "To that house?"

Jeannie said nothing.

"Seems like an awful thing. You in mourning and being picked on by your sister-in-law. I just knew that woman was going to cause trouble, one way or the other. But I didn't expect this."

"What about your mother?" I asked.

Jeannie shook her head and threw both her hands into the air. "Like I was saying, I don't know where she came from last night. Eugene told her when we first got married to stay away from me. That's what I wanted. My whole life . . . if she thought she smelled money, she'd come around, wanting to be a mama to me and carrying on. Last night—said she was driving by and saw something going on and just ran in. Driving by! I didn't even know she was in Riverville and here I'm told she's been around over a week."

"That bad between you?" Miranda asked.

Melody added, "What a shame. Think of it, yer own mother?"

The two of them clucked and shook their heads.

"Mama's . . . well . . . she's different from most mothers."

"You an only child?" Melody asked.

Jeannie shook her head. "Got a brother. He's the one Mama's always trying to get money for. Some kind of—I don't know. Maybe she feels bad she was so awful to the both of us. She's been after me before to help him out, but I never had much. I put myself through nursing school. You know how much nurses make . . .

"This time, though, when she heard I was marrying Eugene Wheatley . . . whew! Even in Dallas the name means something." She looked down at her plate and stopped talking.

Melody finally reached over and touched Jeannie's arm. "It's okay, ya know. You don't have to tell us anything you don't want to."

Eyes red, Jeannie looked at Melody and then around at the rest of us. "Billy just got out of prison. He was in a fight. The man died. Elizabeth knew about it, and right in front of that deputy and me, she said she thinks Billy killed Eugene 'cause he thinks I'll get all the money. She told me right then I'm not getting anything and right after the memorial I'd better get out."

Melody sat back with a thump of her hands on the table. Miranda's exasperation matched her sister's.

"Then don't go back there." Miranda stood and started clearing the table. "You need to be someplace where none of them can get at you. I'd say that's right here with us. Got a nice spare room I can clean out in an hour or so. Lindy, you take her back there, to the Wheatleys' an' get all her clothes. She'll be safe enough with us. Seems we got ourselves a killer in Riverville. Had 'em before. I took out one myself once, with my twenty-two. Sheriff said I must've been shooting at a snake, but I knew darned well what I was doing. Sheriff didn't want me going to jail over a skunk like that one, so he comes out here and tells me to just forget about it. I did. Not even a guilty conscience. That was the biggest snake I ever plugged. And the worst of all of 'em."

"No—" Jeannie put her hand up. "I've got to get myself out of this."

Miranda shook her head. "You get yourself out of the next mess you get into. I can smell this one's going to be bad. You got people coming at you from all sides and no middle place to rest. You're staying here."

Miranda turned to me. "Don't you think that's best, Lindy?"

I nodded. I did think that was for the best. I could see why Eugene fell in love with Jeannie. Not just the fun and sweetness, but a real need for somebody to love her and care for her.

I took Jeannie home to get her clothes, then back to the Chaunceys'. Elizabeth was still at the funeral parlor, the housekeeper said.

I got back to Rancho en el Colorado too late to get out to the greenhouse, and when I told Meemaw where I'd taken Jeannie, she wasn't happy.

"This is a murder, Lindy. We don't know who did it and we don't know who else they're after. Hunter's not going to like you getting in the middle of things. And the Chaunceys are sometimes too helpful for their own good. They could be in for trouble they can't handle."

"Just don't tell anybody where she is, okay? I've got the feeling it's going to be one awful thing after another with those families. And I mean the Wheatleys, and Jeannie's family."

"Hunter's got to know where she is."

All I wanted to do was get back to my apartment and sleep. I called Hunter on my way into town. He was curt. Not happy with me hiding Jeannie away like I did, he said. But then Hunter wasn't happy with much of anything I did lately.

I figured it was time to go home, lock myself up in my apartment, and let the Garrison Brothers put me to sleep. Which I did, forgetting all about the dinner I was supposed to have with Peter Franklin.

Chapter Nine

When I woke the next morning, I wondered, for just a minute, if there was something wrong with me after all, as Meemaw was implying. I had Hunter, and now Meemaw, mad at me. Ethelred probably hated me, along with Elizabeth Wheatley, and I wasn't even that pleased with myself.

I got out of bed, checked my phone, and saw I'd ignored three phone calls from Peter Franklin.

It was only eight o'clock. Too early to call him back. And now I was the one at fault here, too. He'd probably planned our dinner last night and I'd stood him up. I figured I'd call in an hour or so and we could make plans. Someplace nice. Someplace out of town where nobody would see me and pass the news to Hunter.

I opened the small living room windows and let warm morning air rush in to clear out all that air-conditioning. It would be hot later, but for now the air still felt heavy with rain that hadn't reached Riverville though it had been announcing itself for a couple of days. We needed the rain, as usual, what with the trees blossoming and the pecans setting. Justin was digging the irrigation ditches deeper and keeping the pumps going, but nothing took the place of a good hard soaker.

I brushed my teeth and made myself a pot of tea. I was thinking about breakfast but came up with a great idea. My friend and town librarian, Jessie Sanchez—the daughter of our ranch foreman, Martin—wouldn't be at the library yet. Wasn't due there until ten. I called her to see if she wanted to meet me for breakfast at The Squirrel, coming right out and telling Jessie I needed a friend right then.

"Sure, Lindy. Know the feeling myself. Meet you in . . . how about twenty minutes?"

Since the Sanchezes lived at the ranch and their house was a ways down the road from ours, I figured twenty minutes was cutting it close for her, but I said I'd be there.

"You think Cecil's got those awful kippers and knockers this morning?" She was laughing.

"I don't think it's called knockers."

"Well, whatever he calls that stuff he throws together. Awful."

"Don't order it."

"He makes me feel like a hick when I don't know what the heck he's talking about."

"That's your problem. I'm getting good old American fried eggs and bacon."

So we were on and I'd proven to myself I still had at least one friend in the world.

Next I called the Chaunceys to hear that Jeannie slept well and was having breakfast and then was riding out with Miranda to shoot rattlers, which made me wonder if I'd put Jeannie in the right place after all. Then I figured if Miranda wasn't worried about going shooting with Jeannie, everything would be fine, and Meemaw was wrong about her being a suspect.

I got to The Squirrel first. And, just my luck, Hunter was there with a couple of other deputies. I waved and smiled. He waved back halfheartedly.

"Still got that awful dog?" I called over, but he didn't hear. Or he didn't want to hear. No answer. He went on eating and never come over when I sat down in a booth by myself and picked up the scuzzy plastic-covered menu with a hand-typed card clipped in one corner. I kept the menu in front of my face though I could barely see the words.

Jerk, I thought. See if I care. Who needs you?

The man didn't have the courage to talk to me. Coward. First cousin to Moses Rose, the guy who fled the Alamo. That's who he was, I decided.

I smiled really big at Cecil Darling when he meandered over to see what I wanted to eat. Not that I usually smiled big at Cecil Darling, a misplaced Englishman come to Riverville, he said often enough, to bring couth to the savage. Cecil was a small man with pale eyebrows that could jump up near his meandering hairline when he found somebody to be beyond his understanding—which he seemed to do with most of us Texans.

"Lindy Blanchard, of all people. I thought you'd be out there showing up the police, taking on a killer, at least getting your nose in the middle of things the sheriff's got to warn you away from."

Word sure traveled fast in Riverville. I could only imagine the gossip going on at the Nut House. Since I'd skipped out the back door that morning without stopping to talk to anybody—not even Meemaw—I'd missed it all. I was willing to bet there were a lot of disappointed people still waiting to corner me with questions.

"Good to see you, too, Cecil."

He sniffed and turned toward Hunter's table to see if they were watching. They weren't.

I told him I was waiting for Jessie and would have a cup

of tea before I could settle my stomach down enough to look at his menu.

"Bag or loose?"

"This about you?" I asked and smiled big.

"Your tea, Philistine. Do you want a bag floating in a paper cup of hot water or do you want it the English way?"

"Bag. Sounds more sanitary."

Jessie blew in before I got the tea. And I mean "blew in" because she's a beautiful woman with dark, long curly hair, and a flair for color. Like today, with her wide skirt in reds and golds, her blouse in red cotton. She had a swish to her I could only envy.

When she leaned over to kiss me on both cheeks, I smelled sweet soap and something like rosemary.

After settling across from me, Jessie gave a flick of her hand, pushing her hair back behind her shoulder. "So you need a friend. Guess that's me? Am I the last you've got?"

"Is everybody talking about me? I had to get Jeannie out of that house. Elizabeth's decided she had something to do with Eugene's death and is on a tear. Would be hell if she stayed there."

"Guess the sheriff and Hunter are trying to get a handle on things, too. Jeannie's gone and Elizabeth's not cooperating. That's all I heard so far this morning."

"Truthfully, I felt it was the best thing I could do, get her out of there. You know, Jessie, there's a murderer here in town and I don't think it's Jeannie."

"Heard it was murder. Everybody's speculating who could have done it. They're making guesses. Ethelred Tomroy's telling people that she and Freda, since they know people so much better than other people do, are taking it on themselves to solve the whole thing and bring the killer to justice."

I moaned. "No wonder Meemaw's so cranky with me. Now Ethelred's taking the competition from who bakes the best pecan pie to who can catch a murderer first! Whoa. Hunter better put those two in their place."

"Seems he's sitting right there." She gestured toward Hunter and the other blue backs, all bent over plates of eggs and bacon. "Go talk to him."

"Let him come over here. He practically ignored me when I came in."

She was winding up to say more, but Cecil was back, pad in hand. He wrote down our regular orders then smirked at me.

"I've got black pudding to go with the eggs. Just made it. I know you'll love it, since you seem to be a little bit above an uneducated dolt."

"Black pudding! What is it?" I was always wary of Cecil, and used to his insults.

"Actually it's a very fine sausage. Very popular in London, where I come from, you know. I imagine you've heard of London. I make the pudding myself. A true treat for people with such . . . eh . . . limited tastes."

I ordered the pudding against my better judgment then got down to why I'd wanted to meet Jessie.

"Have you heard anything about Jeannie's mother? She's here in town and Jeannie wants nothing to do with her. I figured that the library is a center where people meet and talk, like they do at the Nut House. Ethelred was saying she's been hanging out at the Barking Coyote since she got here, maybe a week or so ago."

She shook her head. "I don't know who you're talking about. I heard something last night. I think it was Sandy Thompson came in to get a book on French cooking." She leaned in close. "Guess Cecil insulted her yesterday because she's French—well, back a couple of hundred years ago her people came from France. She's going to show him up, she says. Getting ready for the county fair. He won some prize last year and she doesn't want it to happen again."

Jessie sipped at the coffee Cecil set in front of her.

"Anyway, she said Elizabeth Wheatley was at the beauty salon this morning hinting that Jeannie had something to do with Eugene's death. Awful, for all the women there. Some of them met Jeannie and liked her. You know how it is—somebody you meet personally can't go around killing people."

I got my breakfast: one egg over easy, wheat toast, and a circle of something black I figured had to be his black pudding. It didn't look too bad. Kind of like a patty of overdone sausage.

"What's in it?" I looked up at Cecil. He smiled, putting me on guard immediately.

"Don't be a child. Taste it. Wonderful." He leaned back on his heels and smirked.

I put a fork into the dry sausage, cut a piece, and put it in my mouth.

I didn't spit it out—that would be uncouth. I chewed it, swallowed it, and congratulated myself on getting it down.

"Hmmm," was all I said. "So what's in it?"

I got the smirk again. "Oh, nothing untoward. Pig's blood, pork fat . . . Hmmm, let me see . . . oats and barley. Things like that. I mix it all together and stuff it right back into the pig's intestines. Absolutely pure and tasty."

I felt my throat close and my stomach jump, but I got ahold of myself and didn't let him know he'd gotten to me. When we were through eating, I wrapped the rest of that awful black thing in my paper napkin and put it in my purse so he'd think I ate all of it. Next time I'll bring him something to taste, I vowed. Though I didn't know what it would be yet, I figured Meemaw would come up with something. Maybe *huevos de toro*. Yeah, I told myself and could hardly wait.

"One thing I want to tell you, though," Jessie was going on. "One of the high school interns—we've got a couple helping check out books this summer. She told me something a couple of days ago. Somebody came in and wanted to know about your family. I think she said the person seemed especially interested in you."

"Hmmm. I wonder what for?"

She shrugged. "Probably another one of those historians working on Texas history. Family stuff. We get 'em about once a month. You'd think by now everything that ever happened in Texas would be well recorded. Guess they're still finding new things."

"Man or woman?" I asked and stopped when the door to the restaurant opened and I wanted to shrink down in the booth. Of all the awful times for Dr. Peter Franklin to show up. I glanced over at Hunter and saw he'd noticed the man. His eyes narrowed as he watched Franklin close the door behind him and look around the room. When he spied me sitting in the booth with Jessie, Peter Franklin smiled big and walked over, as if he were expected.

I'd forgotten to call him back. Another mark against me.

I greeted the man, and moved over in the booth, offering him a seat beside me as I introduced him to Jessie, who gave him her hand, then looked over at me and raised one eyebrow.

"I'm not staying." He spoke only to me. "Elizabeth Wheatley asked me to join her. More memorial planning, unfortunately. And Jeannie seems to have disappeared. You wouldn't know where she's gone, would you?"

I shook my head again and then again.

"I called you . . ."

"I know. I saw the calls this morning. I haven't had the time . . ."

"Then tonight? Seven? Shall I pick you up at that store, or out at the farm?"

"Probably the farm. I have things to do. I'll be there all day."

"Seven then. I'll find you. I'm really looking forward to

it, Lindy. It's not often I meet a beautiful woman who has a mind to match."

I colored up. I knew Hunter was watching. Maybe Peter Franklin knew he was watching, too, and played to the audience. Again, there wasn't much I could do about it. All I could hope was that Peter would be on his way back to Boston soon and Hunter would get over whatever the heck was bothering him.

Hunter was gone by the time Jessie and I had finished eating. Not a word to me. Didn't come over. I was getting madder and madder at him—carrying on this silly business. And over what? That I talked to a man who spoke the language of genomes and acids and nucleotides?

If that's the way he wanted it, with no trust left between us, then let it be. I spent a few minutes, after he left, hoping he'd get stuck with that mangy dog.

On the way out to the ranch, after Jessie and I hugged and kissed good-bye, a deep, empty feeling hit me. Maybe I was getting exactly what I deserved, I thought: a long and lonely life which, at the moment, didn't seem like the kind of life I wanted after all.

Chapter Ten

Martin Sanchez came into my office as I settled down to work, record books piled in boxes around me. Five years of them.

My office isn't a place anybody would envy. The floor is gray cement. The ceiling is high—with red pipes running across it, pipes that sometimes dropped sweat on my head. But I did have a metal desk and a corner with a small kitchen so I could make tea in the morning or have a cold Coke-Cola in the afternoon. And rows of file cabinets. One for each year since I'd started keeping track of the experimental cultivars.

"Wanted to show you something out in the test lot," Martin said, his dark and well-lined face crunched up from coming into the shade of my greenhouse after the bright sun outside.

I immediately felt guilty—the way I always did. Something was wrong, I told myself. Because I hadn't been watching the way I should have been, the trees had been attacked by some awful virus. *Mea culpa! Mea culpa!*

I followed Martin outside and over to my fenced test grove—an acre set up in the sunniest place we could find. The gate to the grove was always kept locked—to keep out curious ranchers and jealous destroyers—one had actually broken in and tried to ruin my work, but that one was in prison now.

This was truly God's Little Acre. Just opening that gate and stepping inside, looking down the perfect rows of trees—some fairly tall, some barely more than seedlings—made my heart thump. Each little tree had its own bucket watering system. A mound of soil ringed each with gauges stuck in to monitor acidity, the level of dampness, even temperature. I knew everything about each specimen.

Martin led me to the last row where we'd put in a cultivar that was really experimental. This was a rare and very old pecan cultivar combined with a genome I'd never worked with before. I had a lot of hope for drought resistance with this new seedling.

Martin pointed to a row of tiny trees I'd set out about a month before. At first they'd been disappointing—the few leaves on each turning yellow and dropping immediately.

"I stopped watering, the way you told me to. Figured they were a total loss," Martin said. "Now look."

The trees were about two feet tall. Not just sticks anymore, but showing full leaf budding. They'd come back from the dead. A few of the buds were swelled to bursting.

I looked back at Martin, mouth hanging open. "Same ones?"

He nodded.

"But we gave 'em up for dead."

He smiled and nodded again.

"No extra water?"

"None at all. I quit with the irrigation when I saw they were dead."

"Must have been early dormancy—and here they are.

Oh, Martin. This might be what we've been waiting for. This could be the centerpiece of my work."

He smiled from ear to ear, this wonderful Mexican man who came to the farm as a young boy, under my grandfather, and was still here, now with his wife and daughter.

He lifted and dropped his heavy eyebrows a few times—the closest thing I'd ever seen to celebration in this stoic, hardworking man.

I could have hugged him, but it wouldn't have been seemly. Instead we shuffled around, looked at each other, and smiled a few dozen times.

It was only the sound of voices on the other side of the gate that broke our happy spell and wiped the goofy grin right off my face.

I walked from the garden and shut the gate tightly behind me. When I turned, not knowing who to expect, I saw Peter Franklin, with Elizabeth Wheatley sailing behind, her sturdy, made-up face set and ready and aimed straight at me.

Elizabeth Wheatley was as different from most of the women in Riverville as an ostrich is from a robin. I'd always kind of admired her—all that attention to how she dressed and how her hair was fixed and how she applied her makeup. Today she wore white pants and a pink flowing top with a lot of gold at her ears, wrists, and around her neck. From the wide smile on Elizabeth's face, you would have thought she'd never said a single unkind word to anybody on the face of this earth, let alone me.

"There you are, Lindy. Your mama said she didn't think you were out here. Maybe she was just trying to fool me."

I smiled one of those half-frozen smiles I smile when forced to be nice. "She knows I don't like to be disturbed when I'm working."

Elizabeth waved a hand at me. "Peter said you two are having dinner together tonight so I thought you must be friendly enough not to mind us barging in on you."

She was wrong. It was a mark against Peter. And another one against her.

"Anyway, I'm not here to see a bunch of little trees. How on earth you keep them straight—one from the other—I'll never know. What I do want to know is where you've taken my sister-in-law. The servants said it was you who drove away with her. I know she's probably distraught, but we do have things to discuss. Urgent things. There is the matter of the family trust, you understand. Eugene's will is tied up in that. Never changed, as my attorney informed me. Jeannie and I really have to talk." She stopped to look around. "So? Is she back up at the house?"

None of your business, was what I wanted to say. This was going to be a knock-down, drag-out battle, I figured. I made no offer to take them inside the much cooler greenhouse. Be easier to get rid of her out here when she starts to melt.

She waited, one eyebrow tilted up. "Well? Are you going to answer me or do I have to go speak to your mother?"

"She's not here." I leaned back, crossed my arms in front of me, and drew a long breath. "Jeannie's very upset. She says the two of you got into it over Eugene's death and she wasn't ready for a thing like that. I'm not taking sides, mind you, Elizabeth. I just figured the poor woman's going through a lot and could use a couple days off by herself."

"Where is that?" she demanded, nose headed into the stratosphere. "Where'd she go, 'off by herself'? You shouldn't have interfered. Jeannie comes from a very different background than the Wheatleys, hope you recognize that. Eugene married her knowing there were things . . . well, unsavory things about her family. She has no idea of the protocol surrounding the death of a wealthy man. She needs to come back and hold up her end of this memorial, as his wife. People are calling to express their condolences from as far away as New York City, and here she is, nowhere to be found."

"When she's ready, she'll be back."

"I'm afraid I can't wait for that. Will you please give her this card and tell her to call him today?" She dug in the huge straw handbag hanging from her shoulder. "He is our attorney. He needs to hear from her. She's going to be unhappily surprised with what's due her. I understand that. But I'm prepared to be generous anyway—you, know, to honor Eugene's memory. I can only imagine that mother of hers going through the roof and causing her trouble. And that brother . . . well, I understand he's out of prison now. Second-degree murder, I heard. I've passed that bit of news on to Sheriff Higsby. If he's looking for suspects, that's the place to begin, I told him."

I took the business card she handed me and stuck it in the pocket of my jeans.

She turned and left, stepping high across my rutted parking lot.

Peter Franklin cleared his throat. He didn't follow her but stood, squinting into the sun, watching as she made her way to a black Mercedes.

"I'll be back later." He turned to me, his face unhappy. "Sorry about this. She demanded that I bring her out."

We left it at that. I wanted to get inside fast and call out to the Chaunceys' ranch, pass on my news, see how things were going, and maybe go there, give Jeannie that lawyer's card, and tell her what Elizabeth was saying. She had to know where she stood and what Elizabeth planned for her.

Chapter Eleven

When I called, all Melody did was whisper for me to get out there as fast as I could. I asked her over and over what was going on, but then she'd go off into saying how wonderful it was to talk to me and how "We'd love to see you someday, soon as you can find the time to come on out. Hope it's as soon as you can make it." And then she was sort of laughing like I'd said something funny and then carrying on about "How nice it is to have people dropping by, even when you don't expect them. But isn't that what Texas hospitality is all about? Welcoming unexpected visitors with open arms and hoping they'd take you just the way you are . . ."

I thought I was never going to get off the phone. I got it. Something was going on out there. Why she couldn't come right out and tell me meant it was a situation the Chaunceys weren't used to handling.

I stuck my phone in my purse and hesitated about a minute and a half. I should call Hunter—in case whatever was happening was more than I could handle. I was mad, but not mad enough to be stupid. Hunter could drive on out—say he came about something or other. Just to be there.

He wasn't at the sheriff's department. The deputy said he was on a call, that maybe I could catch him back there in an hour. But I didn't have an hour. I called Meemaw and told her the Chaunceys seemed to be having some trouble. She said, in a voice that meant business, to get ahold of Hunter. When I said I tried and he was out on a call, she said to pick her up on the way back through town. She was going with me.

"Not unless you're packin'."

"Just do what I tell you, Lindy. There's no time for playing games. Anyway, those girls got enough guns out there already."

And so I was on my way out of Riverville with Meemaw sitting upright in the truck beside me and the both of us trying to figure out what in heck was going on at the Chaunceys'. We talked over a lot of things. I guess Meemaw's mighty brain had been going full speed since I'd seen her that morning, but to be honest, I wasn't paying much attention right then. I'd heard Melody act kind of lighthearted and playful before. Maybe that was all it was. Still, I was grateful to be pulling into their long, dusty road leading toward the ranch house, going as fast as I could go with a big cloud of dust shooting up behind me and a couple of cottontails scooting faster than they'd ever scooted, getting out of my way. Poor things. Out enjoying a day that wasn't windy, 'cause wind does something to their hearing, and here I come like a crazy roadrunner.

I stopped in front of the house and leaped out of the truck to get a face full of my own dust and grit. A blue Ford was parked farther up, pulled alongside of the house. Meemaw looked at me and I shrugged at her.

Melody was on the porch as fast as we were hurrying up to see her.

She put a finger to her lips and rolled her eyes back toward the house.

"So you got company, Melody?" Meemaw was smiling real big, but at the same time wiggling her eyebrows.

"Yes, ma'am. We do."

"More than just the lady Lindy brought out yesterday?"

"Yes, ma'am. I'd have to say it's more than yesterday."

"And just who would that be?"

"Well." Melody licked at her lips. I'd never seen one of the girls this nervous before. I guess I'd always figured if anybody could take anything the world wanted to throw at them, it would be the twins. "Whyn't you come on in and meet these folks. Think you heard of one of them: Wanda Truly. Jeannie's mother. You met the woman."

She made an ugly face, wrinkling her skin up like a potato doll, telling me what she thought of "the woman."

"Probably never met her brother, Billy, I'll bet. Got quite a story he's been telling Miranda and me. But you two come on in. Jeannie'll be happy to see you."

So that was it. I gave Meemaw a look. From what I'd seen of the woman at the Wheatleys' that night, I couldn't say I was looking forward to meeting her again. And what about this brother, Billy?

The two visitors sat at the big, cluttered table in the shadowy main room. The woman sat up straight, hands clasped in front of her. She had a big red smile pasted on her face over big crooked teeth. I recognized the blond hair, the makeup: blush put on with a paintbrush; bright red lipstick outlined with dark red; musky eyes and lashes so long they looked like awnings.

The man, maybe in his late twenties but somehow older looking, sat slumped forward at the table, head down, hands clasped in front of him like he was praying. He didn't look up when we walked in.

Jeannie sat across from her brother, her back to us. She turned and I could see the anguish written big all over her face.

Miranda was just coming from the kitchen with a metal coffeepot in her hands. There were already mugs set around the table. A plate of cookies sat at the center. Looked like an afternoon coffee klatch in progress.

Miranda, her face scrunched up as bad as Melody's, hailed us and pointed to chairs.

"What's going on, Jeannie?" I asked fast, sitting down next to her. Better to be in control of a situation like this than to let somebody else grab it and start going off on us.

"This is my mother, Wanda Truly," she said, gesturing toward the woman staring back at me like a made-up doll left out in the rain.

"How'd ya do." Wanda nodded.

"And my brother, Billy Truly."

I looked hard at Jeannie, who licked at her lips and took a deep breath.

"Thought you were in jail, Billy." Meemaw spoke up before I had a chance to catch what was going on here.

His mother sputtered and blinked hard across the table. Billy turned slowly to look over at Meemaw, then back down at his hands. "Got out," he said.

"Glad to hear it," Meemaw went on as if she were having a happy conversation with a new acquaintance. Like she actually knew him. "Hope things'll go better for you from now on. Must've been awful, being in a place like that. Where were you?"

He glanced up again and I could see Meemaw was getting to him. Maybe it was the look about her—an older lady, grandmotherly, kind voice. "Huntsville," he said then cleared his throat and said it louder, "Huntsville, ma'am."

"Well, it's nice to meet you. How long you been out now?" She slid into the chair next to him, grabbed the heavy coffeepot, and began pouring out mugs of coffee for all of us. Billy dumped three spoons of sugar in his cup and passed the bowl to Meemaw.

I could see they were getting along fine though the smile was gone from Wanda's face and Jeannie looked on in amazement.

"Been out two weeks," he muttered then shook his head over and over. "Hard, being out. Six years in a place like that . . . ya kind of lose . . . well . . . you know, like how to make small talk and stuff."

"Bet you do," Meemaw agreed and passed him the plate of cookies, as Wanda let out a harsh, brittle laugh.

"Small talk!" She blew out her puffy lips in exasperation. "Living with a bunch of killers all that time. I'll bet you anything you didn't sit around making 'small talk.'"

"Mama," Jeannie warned from across the table. "Don't start on Billy."

"I'm not starting nothing," Wanda spit back, ignoring the rest of us. "Just saying. He's been through some terrible times. That's why I came to tell you to get back to that house of yours. You could help your brother back on his feet, you know. Think about somebody besides yerself. That woman's already stealing things belonging to you. You're the wife. She's only his sister. Got no claim and here you are running off like this. For once in yer life you gotta stand up and be a woman. You gotta fight. I been fighting all my life and what do I have? Nothing. Nothing to show for it."

So that's why the mother and brother were here. They smelled money and the possibility of Jeannie coming into a fortune. Sometimes I just wanted to pretend people like this mother didn't really exist. Or they existed only in fairy tales where the wicked stepmother always got it in the end, like being cooked in an oven, or melted, or run through with a brave warrior's lance.

"How'd you find Jeannie?" I stepped in the middle of the mother-daughter battle.

"None of yer business," Wanda spit back at me.

"A man at the Barking Coyote told them." Jeannie turned to me. "He saw you bring me here yesterday. Just driving by."

"Should've known. Not many secrets around Riverville. Hunter Austen will be coming out soon, too," I lied. "He's a local sheriff's deputy." I added this last part for Wanda.

I saw Billy shiver. "Rather not be here to talk to him. I'm not ready for something like that . . ." He shot a pleading glance at Wanda.

She made a face at him. "Not about you, Billy. It's about Jeannie's deceased husband. Talking all over town how he was murdered, didn't commit suicide. No accident."

She turned to Jeannie. "They'll pay the insurance, long as it wasn't you who killed him. And you'll get all the rest, too. But you can't sit out here and leave that sister of his to grab everything. You go back there too late and I'll bet you anything the place is stripped clean. I seen women fighting over flowerpots after a man dies."

I didn't know if it was the right time or not, but I pulled the attorney's card from my pocket and handed it to Jeannie. "Elizabeth stopped by my greenhouse, said you should call this man. The estate has to be settled."

Jeannie took the card and looked at it, then at me. "I don't want anything from her. Tell her she can have everything. I loved Eugene. But I shouldn't have married him. Awful things happen around me. People die. First my father . . ." She shook her head. "It's all my fault."

Her eyes welled as her mother scoffed and her brother cleared his throat. I had to say, the man looked miserable.

Melody leaned over and patted Jeannie's folded hands. "I want you to go ahead and call Ben Fordyce." She nodded along with her words. "He's the lawyer everybody around here goes to. Ben'll help you."

Wanda pushed her chair back and stood, one hand shooting to the hip she stuck out. "Go get your stuff, Jeannie. I'm taking you back to that house right now. You've got nothing to be afraid of. I'll be staying right there with you. Billy, too. She won't go starting nothing with us there."

Miranda was on her feet. I could see her chest puffing up and her chin sinking down.

"She's not goin' anywhere she don't want to go."

The words were growled. Melody said nothing though I thought I caught a smug smile cross her lips.

"Well, yes, she is." Wanda didn't bother to look around at what she thought was a useless old lady. "I'm her mother."

"And Jeannie's a grown woman. Let her talk for herself. You want to go with these two, Jeannie?"

Jeannie shook her head.

"Then that's settled." Miranda reached around and grabbed Wanda by the back of her neck and lifted her around the chair as the woman squealed and flailed out.

Miranda tapped Billy on the shoulder and lifted her head, letting him know she wanted him up and out of there, too.

Wanda went cursing and kicking out the front door. We ran to watch as Miranda prodded a squealing and cursing Wanda over to the blue Ford. Billy walked along behind, doing nothing to help his mother. When they were both in the car and turned around, headed back out the road, we all watched, hand up over our eyes against the sun, until we couldn't see them anymore. Miranda swiped her hands together, and walked back to the house, offering everybody more cookies.

Chapter Twelve

"We're going to the Barking Coyote," Meemaw said on the way back from the Chaunceys'.

"Can't. I've got a dinner date with Peter Franklin. He was out to the greenhouse this afternoon, along with Elizabeth Wheatley. I think I'd better get it over with or he might never go back to Italy or wherever the heck he's from. I don't like people coming to the greenhouse. Seemed, I don't know, like he was invading my space. Best that man left town as soon as possible."

"I'd say you're right. Get him moving and clear thing's up between you and Hunter."

I made a disgusted noise. "Me and Hunter! He acts like there is no 'me and Hunter.' Over something I didn't ask for—that Dr. Franklin coming here. So now he's mad. Let him stay that way. I'm going out to dinner with Peter Franklin and I don't want to mess up again tonight, like I did yesterday."

Meemaw looked at her watch and then at me. I couldn't read her expression. "You going this early?"

"Not until seven, but I've got to change and—"

"Won't take long. I just want to talk to a couple of people out there at the saloon."

She used a voice that scurried up and down my spine and told me there was no way out. She was on a mission.

Still, I had to groan and whine a little—because she expected it. This was our way of being with each other and kept the nasty little girl inside of me alive and miserable.

"You got plenty of time. A couple of hours yet. I heard that woman, Wanda Truly, has been hanging out at the Coyote for the last couple of weeks. Morton Shrift will tell us what she's been saying and what they think about her there. You know—that good ole boys' thing isn't all bad. Won't say much, even to one another, but you can bet your boots those people have been judging her and will have a thing or two to say to me. Might know something about Billy, too."

"You sure took to him. He perked up like nobody's said a kind word to him in a long time."

She nodded. "Probably nobody has. That mother of his is a piece of work."

She rolled down her window to let in some real air. I snapped off the air conditioner because I knew she didn't like it much. "Bet that boy hasn't been spoken to kindly in his whole life. Greedy, grasping, evil mother. Bet anything, if you took that boy back and put him in a decent home, with decent God-fearing folks, he wouldn't have been in prison. That's what's wrong with our system. We punish the wrong people. You ask me, if we made a few parents do time with their kids, you'd see a lot nicer group of people raising children. And you'd see a lot fewer children landing up in jail."

"And a lot fewer children being born if people were made to look after them right."

"True enough," was all she said, ending that discussion then starting a new one. "So what are you thinking? I mean, about Wanda Truly?"

"I don't know yet. Just that if she was my mama, I'd run like Jeannie's running to get away from her."

"Yes, well, bet you would. But I'm talking about what she was saying there at the Chaunceys'."

"You mean about Jeannie going back home? Wasn't like she cared much what Jeannie wanted."

"It's the estate. She's been hanging around town like she was waiting for something to happen."

I thought a minute. "You think she's got something to do with Eugene's death?"

I looked over as she shrugged. "Somebody did it. Got to find out who wanted him dead. That usually starts with 'who benefits.'"

"That could be Jeannie," I said.

"Or that awful mother."

"What if Jeannie's been in it from the beginning? Marrying a wealthy man. Seeing that he died pretty quick. Mother hanging around in the wings 'til it's over. And that brother. Guess we were looking at a man who could kill, all right. Huntsville, he said." Meemaw was hot on a trail. "Why don't you ask Hunter to look into what Billy really did to land up there?"

"Why don't you ask him?" I said.

"Wish you'd get over this silly business with him."

"Tell him to get over it . . ."

And we were at the Barking Coyote, parking under the half-lighted sign with a dancing coyote's feet going at a great rate and the rest of him dark.

Not too many trucks there yet. It was early in the day for most of the regulars. Finula Prentiss, who waitressed, should be around. She was a big talker and not one to sit on an opinion. Morton, the owner, would be behind the bar. Roy Friendly, I'd been told, usually came in early in the afternoon and hung around 'til closing. We'd get a lot of information the sheriff, or Hunter, would never get out of these people, who were wary of blue uniforms and stiff hats.

"No line dancing," I warned Meemaw on the way in. "I'm still living that last time down."

"Nothing wrong with a dance or two. Good for the circulation," she said and outmarched me up the dry hill.

The inside of the saloon was the same—day or night. Dark, loud with twangy music, and smelling the way, I suppose, a saloon should smell. The smoke was dense, like a swamp in a horror movie. It took a while for my eyes to adjust from the light outside; people slowly taking shape—all looking at us. But no Roy Friendly.

There weren't too many there. A few of the tiny tables had couples seated at them. A few more had one man with one long-necked bottle of beer in front of him or one short shot of whiskey. Meemaw was waving to people she knew—since they all came for "special" pecan pies on occasion. I waved to a few people I'd graduated Riverville High School with.

Morton Shrift was behind the scarred mahogany bar, wiping away, then crouching down to admire the shine he was getting. He smiled as we walked down to him.

"What'll it be, ladies? Ain't laid eyes on you since that last time you come in. Still talking about your dancing, Miss Amelia," he said.

"Thank you, Morton." She settled herself on a high stool. "You could get me a Coke-Cola, if you don't mind."

"Sure thing. What kinda Coke you want?"

"Dr Pepper, I guess."

I had the same and we sat and looked around, drinking our sodas until Morton was free again to lean on the bar and pass the time of day.

"Morton . . ." Meemaw began, sitting up and squinting through the smoke at the man.

"Here it comes." He chuckled. "Knew you came in for a reason."

"Since I'm not a drinker . . ."

"Except all that Garrison's in your pies."

"I don't know what you're talking about. Shame on you, Morton Shrift, implying I push alcohol on—"

"So," he interrupted. "What can I help you with today? And before you start in, Miss Amelia, I'm betting anything it's about what happened to Eugene Wheatley."

"I heard his mother-in-law was hanging out here ever since she got to town."

"Got to be a regular fast."

"Can you tell me what you think of her?"

He smiled and shook his head. "If I went around telling what I thought about any of my customers, the Barking Coyote would be closed in a week."

"She's no regular, Morton. And this is a murder we're talking about. I just met the woman."

"Where? Wondered why she ain't here yet."

"Never mind where. I'm telling you I got very bad feelings about her."

"You should talk to Finula, you want to talk about bad feelings. Never once tipped her. Finula won't wait on her anymore. Says only the devil thinks he's hot enough not to tip a hardworking woman."

"She here?" I looked around but didn't see her walking through the tables, or passing the time of day with an old cowboy.

"In the back. I'll get her."

"I'm asking you first." Meemaw drew him back to what she was after.

"Well, I'll tell you, Miss Amelia, I've seen worse. But not much worse. From the first time she came in, she started bragging how rich she was going to be. Daughter married into the Wheatley family, she said. Soon her daughter was going to buy her a house and a building so she could start up a beauty parlor in Dallas. She'd go on and on for hours. The more she drank, the bigger that house got. The beauty parlor got to be a spa in one of the swankiest parts of town. By midnight she was mumbling and nobody was listening."

"Did you meet her son, Billy?"

He nodded. "Came in only the last couple of days. I could smell prison on him, but he turned out not to be so bad. He didn't drink and he'd pull his mother out before she got stumbling drunk."

"Have they been in since Eugene died?"

He nodded again. "Last night."

"They talk about it?"

"Not him. But you couldn't shut her up, how her daughter was a rich woman now. Just that kind of thing. Nobody was listening. They left pretty quick."

"Was she saying anything about who killed Eugene?"

"Tried to. Said the police would find out that Elizabeth, that sister of his, had something to do with the murder."

"She say why?"

"Only that she bet anything Elizabeth had some kind of different will to spring on everybody and that's why her kid, Jeannie, was going to fight her right from the beginning."

Morton motioned us to turn around. Finula was standing behind us, listening.

I've heard men say a certain kind of woman looked like she'd been rode hard and put away wet. That was Finula. Early in the afternoon, but Finula was already looking smudged and sleepy.

"You and Hunter working together on this?" she said, her black eyes burrowing into me. "Heard you two aren't getting along so well. Surprise to see you here. You know he called me the other night."

"Bet he wanted you to watch his dog."

Finula looked flustered. I would have bet anything she was going to come up with some other story. "Well, yeah.

But I was working. I told him how much I love dogs and am willing anytime he needs me . . ."

Right then I was wishing I'd had a shot of bourbon or two and that I had the nerve to reach out and pop the lady right in her nose. I knew Finula'd always been kind of sweet on Hunter, but if she thought she had a chance with him, with me out of the way, she was barking up the wrong cop.

"They're asking about Wanda Truly, Jeannie Wheatley's mother," Morton told her.

Finula flicked her hair, as dark and dyed as a cheap fur coat, back over her shoulder and sniggered. "That one. Thinks she's gonna be rich now that Eugene's dead. I hear she's in for a surprise. Somebody found an old trust or something leaving everything to Elizabeth. Not that I like that one either."

That was about all Finula had except for calling Wanda Truly tighter than the bark on a tree. Meemaw was off her stool, telling Morton to let Roy Friendly know she'd like to talk to him if he had the time to drop in at the Nut House. We thanked Morton and Finula for their time and were out of there, back to town with my cell ringing and Peter Franklin's name coming up as the caller.

Chapter Thirteen

I got into my tiny shower and let the water run as long as I dared. Even after I shampooed three times and rubbed my head dry, I could smell booze and smoke in my hair, but I was running out of time. When we got back to the ranch, Bethany and Justin and Mama, whom I hadn't seen since the party, wanted to talk. Everybody had a different idea of what happened at the Wheatleys with Justin standing firmly behind "an accidental shooting" despite everything the police knew to the contrary. Mama wanted to know if I'd talked to Hunter about it and I said "yes," I had. Then she said that was a good thing, considering what she'd heard in town.

"Anything new?" Justin asked.

I shrugged.

"You're not talkin' to him, are you?" This was Mama, probing as hard as she could.

"Got other things to do."

"What other things?" Mama demanded, giving me that

arms behind her head stretching thing that only meant she wasn't believing me.

"Things like my work, Mama."

"You ask me, I'd say there's something wrong between you and Hunter, like people are sayin'."

I was too tired to take on all three of them so I hurried back to my old room and found a good enough outfit in the closet. I spent most of the time in the shower talking to myself. I was mad at every one of them.

"Enough is enough," as Meemaw liked to say.

I decided I didn't want to go anywhere in Riverville with Peter Franklin, especially not to The Squirrel, where Cecil would start in with the snide remarks and be telling everybody who I came in with so it would get back to Hunter. I didn't want that, not now that I'd decided me and Hunter were going to make up and be friends again—or whatever we were to each other.

There was a little barbecue place over in Schulenberg. Everybody who comes to Texas wants Bar-B-Q so I knew I couldn't miss, though once we got there and settled in, Peter wrinkled his nose at the menu and picked at his plate of ribs as if he were going through dirty laundry.

"I still hope I can at least get a look at your test grove, or even take a look at your records. We are working on similar problems, as you know." He sat back and wiped his mouth so hard the paper napkin stuck and I had to point out places where he had dots of white paper around his mouth. I finished my plate of ribs and slaw and even gave a greedy glance over at the last of the ribs Peter had left on his plate. I reminded myself—as Meemaw often told me—to act like a lady. So I delicately wiped sauce off my chin and smiled, thanking him for the wonderful meal.

There wasn't a whole lot to talk about. He didn't seem

interested in discussing things I'd read that other scientists were doing, nor saying much about his own work, so I figured I'd jump right in. "You know what Elizabeth's up to? You seem to know her pretty well."

He shook his head, seeming to be startled. "Hardly at all. I'm afraid I used her to meet you and now she's taking a proprietorial interest in me. I'm very sorry about bringing her out to your greenhouse without your permission this afternoon. Not my idea, I can assure you. But she seemed so worried about Eugene's wife and where she'd gotten to . . ."

"You call that worry? More like a posse after a bank robber." I shook my head. "I'm not giving Jeannie up until she's got a lawyer of her own. Melody Chauncey told her to go see Ben Fordyce. He's been our family lawyer since before my daddy died."

"If she thinks that's necessary. I don't think Elizabeth's that bad a person."

I shrugged and pulled my feet back from under the table. That was enough of that. I was ready to head home.

"What I meant was . . ." Peter leaned toward me from the other side of the table. He reached over and laid one of his hands on top of mine. I pulled my hand away slowly, getting a creepy feeling. His smile didn't help any. Smarmy, I'd say. Nice-looking man, but he could sure ruin it with his trying too hard.

I was leaning down to pick up my shoulder bag when the restaurant door opened across the low-ceilinged room from where we sat. I wasn't ready for who walked in and wasn't ready for him to look at me, register who I was there with, then turn right around, put his big hand on the back of the pretty blonde he'd come in with, and almost push her out the door.

Any idea I'd had about making up with Hunter washed right out of my head. Didn't take him long, I was thinking, as I sat kind of open-mouthed, not knowing what to tell myself I should be feeling.

"Wasn't that the deputy I met the other night after Eugene's death?"

I didn't look at Peter. I nodded.

"Didn't seem so friendly now."

"Wasn't then. He didn't like you."

"Didn't like me? He doesn't know me. If you mean he thinks I had anything to do with Eugene Wheatley's death—why, that's insane."

"No," I said and felt mean enough to add, "he wasn't thinking that. He just said he didn't like you."

Peter made a kind of disbelieving noise and got up, pushing his chair back under the table. "Not exactly a wonderful example of Texas hospitality."

I followed him out to his car and sat in miserable silence. All the way back to town, and my apartment, where I hopped out of the car and didn't ask him in, Peter was lost in his own thoughts, repeating again and again, "Doesn't like me," as if he found such a conclusion impossible to believe.

Chapter Fourteen

That night was bad. In the morning I showered and washed my hair, bundling it into a rubber band while it was still dripping wet. Sounds from down in the Nut House kitchen were actually welcoming. People nearby. The world was still spinning the way it was supposed to—only I'd been dropped off somehow, going back again and again to the minute when Hunter and that blonde walked into the restaurant.

I self-talked all the way through dressing and getting on my hands and knees to dig out a pair of sandals from the back of the closet. I could've made a cup of tea for myself, but there was still nothing to eat. I opened the fridge and found a bottle of water and a piece of hard-looking cheese. So much for being on my own and responsible—all the things I'd argued I was going to be when Mama got mad that I wanted to move out of the ranch house and come to town. Which was silly, when I thought about it now. My greenhouse. My trees. My work. All of it was out there and here I was, having to run the gauntlet of relatives and neighbors before I could even get out the door to my truck.

Everything was wrong with my life, I decided. I hoped Peter Franklin would just leave town and let me be. There was no spark between us. I didn't want a spark of anything between me and any man but Hunter. Now I'd fouled that up, playing games. Ego games, I realized. Good he's jealous. Serves him right. Let him suffer . . .

Only he didn't suffer long and here I was the miserable one. I had to call him, I told myself. That's what I'd do, call him like I did since we were kids. Ask him who the blonde was and what was going on. Maybe demand to know how he really felt about me . . . and then I'd burst out crying and act like an idiot and lose any power I ever had over what we were to each other.

Still, I could call. About the murder. Tell him what I'd found out about Jeannie's mama and brother. But he probably was way ahead of me on that. Then what I knew about Elizabeth and her plan to leave Jeannie with nothing—if she could help it.

I had one thing—he needed to talk to Jeannie and she'd be more relaxed with me there.

I picked up my cell, determined to be nice and friendly and pretend I hadn't seen him with that woman. The phone rang in my hand. I didn't look to see who was calling. I was so into thinking about Hunter I let my magical thinking tell me it was him.

"Lindy? Peter Franklin here. How are you this morning?"

"Fine." I forced out the lie.

"You did say I could come out to your office this afternoon. I hope you haven't forgotten."

I did forget. I didn't remember saying anything about him coming to my office. I must've been deep into my own head and not listening.

"Okay . . ." I hesitated. "But I don't know what I've got on this afternoon."

"Could we make it about threeish?"

Ugh. I hated when people talked that way. What was it about this man? Maybe that he wasn't Hunter. He was interested—that's a thing every woman can tell right off—and I had no interest in him.

We made it "threeish."

I groaned as I hung up and the phone rang again.

Miranda Chauncey. "Ya think you could come out here?"

"What's up, Miss Miranda?"

"Had a little trouble last night."

"What kind of trouble?"

"Nothing I couldn't take care of myself. Just think you should come on out. First thing I got to tell ya, Lindy, is that Melody took Jeannie into Ben Fordyce's office yesterday. Kid doesn't know which way to turn—with that mother of hers. And Elizabeth Wheatley on the other side, beatin' her up. Ben's getting ahold of Elizabeth's attorney today. Says he'll let us know what's going on. What else I called about is I think Jeannie's going a little stir crazy, just sitting out here with us two old coots. I done everything I can think of to amuse her. Two rattlesnake hunts. Fence building over there by that big wash where I been having trouble. Miranda taught her how to make biscuits, but they don't want to raise up for her. I'll tell ya, Lindy. We're out of ideas. Not that we don't want her here, it's just that we don't like seein' her down, the way she is."

"She just lost her husband, Miranda. In an awful way. I don't think she needs much entertaining . . ."

"Well, what me and Melody were wonderin' was if you could come on out. Maybe take her into Columbus for the day. I think she needs somebody younger to talk to. Just maybe a couple of hours away from here. Take her out for a ride. Get some dinner someplace. We want to keep her, don't get me wrong on that. But we'd like to see her cheer up a little bit."

Reasonable enough. I'd dumped this grieving widow everybody wanted a piece of on them and kind of turned my back. "I'll be out. Tell her we need to talk and we'll go someplace, or I'll take her to the ranch with me. She'll be safe there and I do have a lot of things I want to talk to her about. I don't know anything about how she met Eugene. When they got married. What their plans were. I'll be out in a couple of hours, if that's okay."

"Well." She hesitated a minute. "Should tell you about last night, I suppose. Probably just Melody being nervous the way she is. I took a shot at somebody looking in Melody's bedroom window. Melody came out screamin' for me to get my gun. Not the first time the woman saw a man hanging around the house. 'Bout ten years ago same thing happened. Never saw any evidence of him, but she swears it was a man looking in her window. Don't know if this is the same kind of thing or somebody after Jeannie. Guess I had to tell you. Hope you come on out pretty quick."

That took me right out of the mood to call Hunter. Somebody hanging around the Chaunceys' place. Have to be the dumbest cowboy God ever put on this earth—to skulk around where Miranda would shoot you as soon as holler. Or somebody really after Jeannie. I was putting my money on her brother. I should've told her to call Hunter, but I was mad at him all over again. He wasn't sharing what he knew about Eugene's murder so neither would I. Me and Meemaw, that's all it took. We'd find out who shot Eugene and why and we'd have the man locked away before Hunter could get his boots on. Strange blonde, huh? Trying to make me jealous, was all it was. Two could play that game.

Meemaw, making her pies and pecan sandies, took time to fry me an egg, make Texas toast, coffee, and sit down with me while I ate.

She eyed me pretty close. "What's going on?"

I shrugged and shoved egg in my mouth.

"You and Hunter, I'll bet."

Damn the woman. Like she could see inside my head. And all that made me do was tear up and choke on my egg and have to tell her everything that happened the night before.

"Blonde? You know her? Somebody from around here?"

I shook my head.

"He was taking her to a restaurant out of town, same as you did with Peter. Doesn't seem like he was flaunting her. Not trying to make you jealous, or anything. Like you were doing to him."

"I did no such thing. The dinner was about work. I mean, after all, the man's from an Italian institute. I mean, they've heard of me over there. That's a good thing, Meemaw."

"You check him out? Make sure he's telling you the truth?"

"Meemaw! Why would he lie to me?"

She shrugged and set her coffee cup down in the saucer. "People do all kinds of things, Lindy. Long ago I gave up trying to figure reasons behind some of the things people do. Like Eugene's death. First we have to find out why somebody wanted him dead. Then we'll find the 'who.'"

"Meemaw! I'm telling you about my heart being broken and all you can think about is a murder."

She waved a hand at me. "You and Hunter will be back together before you know it. In fact, I'd say call him up and ask him who the girl is."

I pretended to be outraged, not admitting I'd had the same idea.

"Why would I want to do that? When he saw me, he hurried her back out of the place, like he didn't want me to see her."

I stood and threw my napkin on the table. Normally I'd clean up after myself, but I was feeling a little ashamed for not rushing out to the Chaunceys'. Seemed like there were too many places to rush to and so many people needing me to be where I didn't want to be.

"Forgot to tell you," I said. "Miranda called. She took a shot at somebody hanging around their house last night. Asked me to come on out. Guess she wants me to take Jeannie away from there for a while. Thinks Jeannie needs somebody her own age to talk to."

"That girl's years younger than you."

"Sure thing. Thanks, Meemaw. It's like four years. All Miranda's been doing is trying to entertain her and now she thinks days filled with rattler slaughter aren't keeping Jeannie happy. I'll see what happened last night and then take her out for a while. Think I'll bring her over here, let Bethany show her around."

"Good idea. I'll try to get home for dinner, leave Treenie in charge. I've got to talk to Jeannie, too. Got a couple of questions I think only she can answer."

"About that mama and brother?"

"Well, yes. And a couple of other things." She slapped her hands on the table and prepared to get back to work. "Still want to talk to Roy. I've got some questions about that system—him checking off people. Hunter said they checked out everybody supposed to be at the party. A couple of people left before Eugene got killed so they weren't on the list of names they collected after the murder. Hunter and the sheriff already talked to most of them, is what Hunter told me. Nobody hiding anything and nobody saw anything strange or odd at the party. Hunter says there doesn't seem to be anybody unaccounted for and nobody skulking around, sneaking out of the house and back in later."

"You sure talk to Hunter a lot. So if they saw to everybody, why do you still need to talk to Roy?"

"Got a couple things going around in my head, is all. Need to check it out for myself. And Chantal Kronos."

"The Greek lady?"

"Yup. Her. She's the cook over to the Wheatley place. I want to find out about the waitstaff that night. There was a waiter I didn't recognize as anybody from Riverville."

I thought a minute. "Yeah. A tall guy with curly black hair. I didn't see anybody else I didn't know."

Meemaw nodded. "Think maybe tonight? Could we get over there?"

I wanted to groan. Everybody was filling up my time and I didn't have a thing to say about it. "You mean back to the Barking Coyote?"

"I'll give Roy a call. Ask him to meet us outside, in the parking lot, about nine."

"Make it eight. Otherwise he'll be too far along in the bourbon to remember much of anything."

"Okay, eight. We can see Chantal on the way. She lives out there. I don't imagine it will take much time to get answers from her."

"What do you mean, 'Won't take much time'? That woman can talk the leg off a buffalo."

"Now, Lindy." Meemaw stood, drawing herself to full height, leaning back and crossing her hands in front of her. Meemaw's battle stance.

I knew where I was going to be spending the whole day and evening, none of it of my own choosing. But then, maybe I needed lessons in saying "no." And meaning it. Which was a thing that was never going to happen between my beloved grandmother and me.

"Do you know that Ethelred and Freda have been going around town saying they've almost got the murder solved? Have you heard about that? Crazy old ladies. Making accusations against this one; hinting it was that one. Talking to everybody like they know what they're doing." She made a face at me.

"They out there?" I motioned toward the store, beyond the swinging doors.

"Not yet. I had to throw them out yesterday afternoon when I was closing. Still going at it. Loud as could be. You ask me, I think it's part of poor Ethelred's jealousy. Those ribbons at the state fair I get every year just about do her in. Nothing I can say about it. I'm not going to mess up my recipes to let her win." She shook her head as if she'd been having this argument with herself. "Now, just because I've had these little successes solving murders here in town, why, she thinks she's got to beat me there, too. Very sad day, I'd say. When a person can't find something for themselves to be proud of."

I was leaving, halfway through the swinging doors, when Meemaw said behind me, "Call Hunter. Make some excuse. Be nice, Lindy. That boy loves you, and you can't tell me any different."

Chapter Fifteen

The first thing I saw was the blue and gold parked in front of the Chaunceys' low ranch house. One of the sheriff's cars. So I was facing Sheriff Higsby, or Hunter. I didn't know which one I was pulling for and wondered why Miranda didn't tell me she'd already called in the big guns.

I stomped hard up the long wooden steps and across the board porch. I knew I wouldn't have to knock. Melody was on the other side of the screen door, the way she always was, watching me.

"Mornin', Lindy. Good to see ya. Thanks for comin' on out." She opened the door wide.

It was Hunter, sitting over in a corner of the low-ceilinged room. I looked around at everybody watching me and suspected there was more going on here than just me coming out to get Jeannie. Something told me Meemaw was behind this and I set my face hard and still. People had to learn to stay out of my life and out of my business. My blood was doing a slow boil.

Jeannie walked into the room, dressed in tight jeans and

a checkered blouse. She looked tired, dark circles under her eyes. I thought, considering what she was going through, she actually looked pretty good, all that hair piled up into some kind of cascade, a little pink lipstick, a pretty smile. She came over to hug me and say her own thanks for me coming out to rescue her.

"You see Hunter?" Miranda demanded, as if directing whatever was going on here.

"Hunter." I turned to where he sat in a wide, handmade chair, notebook in his hand. I nodded.

"Lindy," he said back to me just as stiff. "Guess you heard about the break-in out here last night."

I looked around at Miranda. "Nobody said anything about a break-in."

"Turned out to be more than I thought," Miranda said. "Guess whoever it was already broke the lock on the back door, off the kitchen. I didn't notice it. Just grabbed my shotgun and ran outta the house when Melody screamed. Don't know if he was in here or just about to come in."

"Was it your brother, you think?" I turned to Jeannie.

"I don't think Billy would be breaking in. What for? All he's got to do is call me if he wants to come out. I've got nothing against Billy. Just when he gets near Mama. She's got some kind of hold on him. I still think he wouldn't have gone to jail for manslaughter except it was some man bothérin' Mama."

"Seen plenty of it in my day," Miranda said. "Mother's bring up their sons to be like good little boys all their life. Listenin' to Mama. Got a lot of 'em in trouble, I'll tell you."

"Anybody else you can think of that would want to get in here? Maybe it's got nothing to do with Jeannie." This was Hunter, his official voice in place.

Melody nodded. "Maybe thirty years ago some man Miranda got mad at over a land deal swore he'd get even one day. Coulda been him."

"Fool's dead, Melody. Ninety-six when he died."

Melody shrugged. "You never know. Could be a son."

Miranda groaned and slid way down in her chair.

"Looks like it has to be about Jeannie. Everybody seems to know where she is now. I tried to keep it quiet." I was trying to help.

Jeannie turned dead white. "You really think it was about me . . . I mean, out here, at the end of nowhere?" she said. "I was thinking—somebody roaming the hills and saw lights is all."

"You ask me, you couldn't stay at a better place than here. No matter what." Melody turned to Jeannie. "I know how to handle a gun same as Miranda. It's just that I don't go around braggin' the way she does. Unless Hunter here sticks you in a jail somewhere, I can't think of a safer place for ya."

"I don't want to put the two of you in danger. You've been so good."

"What do you think, Hunter?" I turned to him because he was, after all, the law in the room.

He thought awhile. "Seems Miss Melody's right. I can't think of a better place. And after Miss Miranda shooting at 'im last night, I don't think anybody's going to be coming back around too soon."

"Still, let me take you back to our place for the day," I insisted. "Bethany's getting things ready for a wedding tomorrow. Maybe you could lend a hand out at the tent. Justin's got lots of men working in the groves right now. I think you'll be safe with us. Somebody'll bring you back here tonight. Probably Justin. He'll take a look around."

"I'll be waiting," Miranda put in, patting the holster she wore on her hip.

"Don't go killing anybody, Miranda. You don't want to get mixed up in some legal wrangle," Hunter warned.

"You know how old I am, Hunter?"

"Never thought about it," he answered, though I could see he was holding back a smile.

"Eighty-eight. Old enough to handle myself and the law and anybody else wants to stick a finger in my business."

"Just tellin' you, ma'am."

She nodded at him. "Now what I'd say has to happen is Jeannie here goes and fixes that hairdo of hers while you and Lindy go on outside and talk about what we've all gotta do next to put an end to whatever's going on." She looked around. "And I don't mean just with a killin'."

The look I got was meant to be profound and knowing. On Miranda it just came across as mad and unwilling to put up with any more from me.

I guessed I was being sent to the woodshed—for daring to turn against my man. And from one of a pair of ancient spinsters. I wanted to laugh but wouldn't, not in front of Hunter, who, like most men, didn't have a clue what was really going on.

Hunter got up as instructed.

With a sigh I followed Hunter outside, to go stand by his car in the bare, late-morning sun. I knew I looked nervous, sweating already, but Hunter wasn't looking at me so it didn't matter.

"Guess we should share information better than we've been doing," was all he said as he opened the door to his car and stood there, squinting hard into the bright light.

"Might be best."

"You got anything?"

"Just what Meemaw knows. I hear the two of you have been talking."

He nodded. "What do you think about what happened here? You really think it's safe for Jeannie to stay? Seems maybe back at that big Wheatley place would be better."

"Not with her sister-in-law after her. The man's not even buried and Elizabeth's called out the lawyers. Anyplace else, her mother and brother will be at her. To tell you the truth, I wouldn't want to be Jeannie Wheatley about now."

"The funeral's day after tomorrow, from what I heard. Coroner released the body, but I hear she's having him cremated anyway. Just be some kind of memorial. She's having another one back in Dallas."

"Geez! And Elizabeth didn't even let Jeannie know?"

"Didn't know where she was, is what Elizabeth said. I told her I was going to tell her. That didn't sit well with the woman. But now I'm thinking that memorial might not be the safest place for Jeannie to be."

I thought hard a minute. "So what's going on, Hunter?"

"What do you mean? With us?"

That took my breath away. I wasn't ready for some big showdown.

"I mean with what happened here last night. You think it was some random thing or somebody out to kill Jeannie?"

He shook his head slowly. "Got to protect Jeannie until we know. Things are moving pretty fast. I've got work to do . . ."

Hunter made as if to get in and close the door.

"I saw you last night, you know." It was something I had to get out of me, as close to the "us" thing as I could make myself get.

"Thought that was you," he said, not even embarrassed. "With that Franklin guy. I'm thinking you better watch yourself with him."

"Watch myself? He's a scientist, not one of your . . . criminals."

Hunter shrugged. "Do what you want. I'm just saying I don't like his face. Wouldn't trust him far as I can throw him."

My back stiffened. "Guess you just trust cheap blondes. But that's your taste."

That was my last word. I turned and hurried back into the house. His car door slammed harder than it had to. I tried the same thing with the twins' screened door and missed.

Chapter Sixteen

Bethany was thrilled to show Jeannie around the farm. Justin was acting like a schoolboy, shuffling his feet, head hanging down. All I could think was "Oh no, Justin's smitten." Which was something I never thought I'd see in my lifetime, this hulking man so into pecans and business. Never, never had I imagined Justin—the tough, sometimes scowling brother who almost never approved of what I did—acting like a lovestruck twelve-year-old. I figured I'd have all kinds of fun teasing him later.

Since it was almost three o'clock, I had to get out to my greenhouse. I'd left it unlocked so Peter didn't have to stand outside waiting for me. But I wasn't looking forward to talking biogenetics today. With everything going on, it just didn't feel right. And not with my mind whirling in all directions. Not a little of the whirling being a growing fear somebody might be after Jeannie and I didn't know what to do about it. I supposed Hunter could put her in jail to keep her safe. The sheriff didn't have enough men to put a full-time bodyguard on duty. And anyway, Melody'd only "thought" she spotted somebody outside. The door could have been left open. Could have been one of them—forgetting to lock it. Who knew if it was about Jeannie, or just some transient wandering through, seeing a house, and thinking it might be empty and coming up to see.

I parked next to Peter's car in my rutted lot under some of the biggest, oldest trees on the farm. Beautiful day. Texas hot but with the sun coming through a haze. I could smell the trees and the river. And wouldn't I be happier if I was running into the water, barefoot, and yelling back at Hunter, who started throwing sticks at me, and if I reached down into the slow-moving water and pulled up a big mud ball and threw it back at him? Then he'd get mad at me and swear and come after me while I was yelling at the top of my lungs and Daddy would come running and give Hunter a lecture on how to treat a girl while I snickered, knowing full well I deserved everything I got.

I hurried in as if I was just so eager to see Peter. Something Southern women do, I think, to buy time and get the real measure of the man.

"Sorry I'm late. Busy day. Real busy." I put out my hand to shake his though he was seated in my desk chair and held on to my hand a little too long. I felt those old creeps running up my back and pulled my hand away, wanting to wipe it along my jeans but knowing that would be tacky.

"No, no, don't apologize, Lindy. It's been great, sitting here, taking in your surroundings. I see you keep your test grove locked. Think I could take a look?"

I pretended not to hear and offered tea or coffee, like some lame stewardess, though I resented making it for anybody in a place where I'm supposed to be left alone and working and not having a party where I'm showing off my home-baked cookies . . .

Grrr . . . I wouldn't have wanted to be anybody visiting

me right then when I'm that crabby and not just crabby but feeling violated by this man who probably didn't mean me any harm, just wanted to be a friend.

He took the mug of coffee I handed him and got out of my desk chair to take a folding chair across from me. He picked up his briefcase and laid it on top of the desk, knocking some of my magazines to the floor, which irritated me even more than I was already.

"I'm staying until the memorial," he said. "Elizabeth insisted I remain at the Wheatley place. I really need to be back in Europe, but considering what she's been through, well, I decided I'd stay on awhile."

"Terrible thing. All this."

"And with Jeannie out of the house, too. And Elizabeth really needing her back there to get some legal things settled. She with you? Elizabeth thought maybe."

"Jeannie's got problems of her own. I think wherever she is, is the best place for her right now. Seems this whole thing is going a lot deeper than it looked at first. I mean, now it's murder. Isn't Elizabeth worried about that?"

"Well, of course. Horrible thing. She can't imagine anybody who would want to hurt Eugene. That's what she said."

"Did you know about Sally, his first wife?"

"I heard what happened to her."

"Makes all of this so strange. Both of them killed by gunfire. Talk about coincidences—"

"By the way, Elizabeth said to tell you the memorial is day after tomorrow, if you can get the news to Jeannie."

I said I already heard and would make sure Jeannie got there.

"I know this whole thing is making Elizabeth look bad, but you have to understand, Lindy. There's Jeannie's awful mother. And her brother—fresh out of Huntsville. You ever see that mother of hers? Elizabeth wants the legal business right out on the table so she won't be harassed by the woman.

Very low class—all of them. I can see why she's afraid the whole lot of them will be coming after the Wheatley money."

"You know, Peter," I was angry and bored with the whole subject of Elizabeth Wheatley, "Jeannie's Eugene's wife. Bet anything Eugene took care of her or would have wanted to. I'd say let them fight it out in court."

"Well, of course." He moved nervously in his chair. Seems he wasn't used to direct women.

"So." I sat forward and slapped my hands on the desk. "What can I show you?"

"You mentioned something new that looked promising. Maybe start with those trees and then how you came up with the crossbreeding or whatever. Would you mind?"

I thought a long while. Maybe the trees—well, saplings. I'd show them to him, but something was telling me to keep my mouth shut about my process. I looked around my desk for the propagation book for the new genus and was happy that for once I'd been diligent about putting it back in the file where it belonged.

My fingers didn't want to open the lock on the gate to the test grove. I wasn't feeling like a geneticist at the moment, more like a kid about to show off her hidden treasures and not wanting to.

Peter did make over the small trees, the way I wanted anybody allowed in here to do. The buckets were full; the little hose coming from the bottom leaking a steady, slow supply of water into each mounded circle around the weak-looking saplings. Weak, maybe, but very much alive and looking like miniatures of the stately, tall trees in the main grove.

"Interesting. Congratulations. I hope they're all you say they can be."

And then he reached for me and hugged me tighter and longer than was necessary across a line of fragile saplings.

When I pushed him away, his smile was artless. Just a grin of happiness for me. But I wasn't that stupid anymore. I'd fallen for that bull a couple of times in college—young guys grabbing a feel under the guise of wishing me well after a test.

He immediately acted offended at the push. "Oh, Lindy, I didn't mean . . ."

I smiled, the way I was supposed to, and headed for the gate and, I hoped, the parking lot.

"But I haven't seen your work in the greenhouse," he protested as I led him straight out to his car.

I shook my head. "I'm really sorry, but I've got appointments." I looked at my watch as if appointments were written on my arm. "Maybe another time."

"May I ask one question?"

I laughed a little, knowing I was giving him the bum's rush, and feeling a little silly now. A hug is a hug is a hug, after all.

"Which journals have you contacted? Your work will be of interest to geneticists everywhere, you know."

"Only one. I told them I'd get something to them by next fall."

"Oh." He raised his eyebrows. "Which journal? You don't want to settle for anything less prestigious than *Genetics Now*."

"Propagation," I said. "Best place for what I'm doing."

He sniffed and blinked at me a time or two. All he said was, "Well, if that's what you want to do."

If I ever heard a snobby huff in anyone's voice, his sure had it. So he'd studied at Harvard—that's what he'd said. Who cared? I certainly didn't like being instructed by this man who didn't seem to know as much about my field as I did. Maybe he wasn't even working on drought resistance. Maybe he was working on finding a rich wife like Elizabeth.

He leaned forward, both hands on my upper arms, and

kissed me first on one cheek and then the other. "You're very nice—for a scientist." He smiled when he was still close.

How European of him. But I knew a move when I saw one and this was his second today. I pulled away and fixed him with a hard look.

"By the way, where were you when Eugene was killed?" I asked bluntly, which immediately changed the temperature around us.

He shook his head. "I suppose you mean, where was I when we all heard the shot?"

I nodded.

"Ha! Like that old game: Clue. I was in the ballroom. As it happened, I was with Elizabeth at the buffet table. Elizabeth fairly flew out of the room when we heard the shot. Thank God people stopped her before she got into that gun room. Poor woman, bad enough as it was, imagine if she'd seen . . ."

He gave a shiver, then recovered fast. "By the way, Lindy, I can help you, you know. I have contacts all over the world. With my help you will be asked to symposia and conferences everywhere. I could set you on a path to renown in this field."

I nodded and made a face. Here came the offer. Whatever it was he wanted from me—this was it. I narrowed my eyes and watched his face.

"I could do that for you. Up with the big guys."

For a minute I saw me on a stage pontificating on genomics, molecular-assisted selection, transgenic crops; or surprising molecular markers; maybe bioinformatics. All things I got excited about and my family rolled their eyes at.

All I had to do was be nice to him. Very nice, I supposed. Been there. Done that. Even a college professor had offered things he shouldn't have.

A couple of good, solid curses came flying through my head. But like a good girl, I didn't say anything. Just smiled and waved good-bye—which could have ended in another gesture had I not been such a well-trained lady.

All I could do right then was get my mind cleaned out the only way I knew how.

I called Hunter and asked him who the blonde was.

Chapter Seventeen

"I called Hunter," I said.

I was with Meemaw on our way to Chantal's house. Her smile was bigger than I expected. It was too bad I had to burst her bubble. Hunter and I weren't close friends again, just talking, still with a chill snaking back and forth through our words.

"What about?"

"About the blonde."

"Oh." She turned to look out the window. I could see she was dying to know what was said, but I was going to make her wait a little while; make her suffer for coming down so hard on me over Hunter. As if our cold war was my fault. "What'd he say?"

"Not much. Like he's got this big secret."

"Who is she?"

"He wouldn't tell me. I told him I thought we knew all the same people and I've never seen her before. He said he knows lots of people. I asked him where he met her and all he'd say was through his work."

Meemaw's eyebrows shot up at that.

"So I asked him if she was a felon. He got mad."

"I can see why. You've got a smart mouth on you sometimes, Lindy."

"Well, how do you think I feel? I mean, our whole lives and now he keeps secrets from me?"

"You do realize he's investigating a murder?"

I nodded. "You mean he's probably taking a suspect to an out-of-the-way diner to grill her."

"Did you mean that as a pun?"

I was mad all over again. Just that voice he'd used with me: "I do know other people, Lindy." Like he was clucking his tongue.

"Now, before you go off gettin' mad all over again, stop and think what he saw when he walked in there. You and Peter Franklin—in an out-of-the-way restaurant as if you didn't want to be seen. Seems to me this is a case of what's good for the goose is good for the gander."

"You don't like him, do you? Peter."

"Not much. Don't know him. Just what I hear."

"What have you heard?"

"Justin looked him up on the Internet. Just curious so don't go off yelling. It's because of him coming on so strong and everything. We didn't find a thing on him at that Italian website you told us about. What we did find makes it look like he's mostly on his own. Last time in Africa, not Italy."

"Sometimes the Internet's not up to date on these thing. Could be his latest place—Italy."

"Well, I'd be careful," she said, her stern look in place.

"Of what, Meemaw? Not many scientists out to do more than snoop into somebody else's work. Some are known for that. You've got other things to worry about. Like Ethelred and Freda stealing your thunder."

"Humph. All that pair knows how to do is stir up trouble."

I was watching addresses. The houses this far out of town could be down a dusty trail with no road sign out on the highway. Usually I just steamed right on past them, not seeing the mobile homes set in clusters or the tiny square block houses under old, dead live oaks. Beyond the houses, the dry earth ran up small hills and then away to blend with a sky that today matched the earth—kind of pale yellow at the horizon.

I was thinking, too, the way I could think when I looked at the Texas landscape and let myself be a part of it, that I did love this country. I almost never had to wonder about people's motives. Usually I knew those within five minutes of meeting somebody. This was different. Maybe to some people my research could mean a lot of money. I didn't have any patents on my trees or on the processes. Didn't think I needed them. For the first time I thought how lax I was on the business end of things.

Chantal lived down a long driveway leading to a small house set in the middle of some tall bushes. The house was covered with vines. Dead vines and live vines. It looked like something caught in the roots of a tree. Chantal Kronos got up with difficulty from a rocker on her pitched-roof porch. She stood at the top of her steps, waving as we got out and waved back. While we climbed the front steps, she greeted us again and again, then pointed to two other rockers. We turned down sweet tea, saying we weren't staying long, which brought a look of sadness to her heavy face, eyes disturbed under thick brows; lips pursed in a pout. She steepled her hands together and shook them at us.

"You never come to my home before, Miss Amelia. Now you refuse my hospitality!"

So, of course, it was sweet tea and cookies so light they almost lifted off the plate by themselves.

"You want to know about the staff at the party," Chantal said after a lot of town gossip and talk about the weather.

"Only a couple of strangers. Well, strangers to me. One man who said his name was Curly, though he didn't look like any Curly I ever saw before. He was tall—like a Greek man. Dark, like me. Didn't say much the whole evening. Anyway he was a bad waiter. I'd see him standing at the side of the room looking around and I'd send Willy Mason out to get him moving with his tray."

"Anybody else?" Meemaw asked.

"One woman came in. I didn't like her. Ms. Wheatley must have hired her. I thought we had plenty of people from town there for the job. But I guess she thought different."

She shrugged, lifting her shoulders high and rolling her eyes.

"Did you see the man after the murder?"

"Yes." She narrowed her eyes at Meemaw. "I think so. But you know what? I wasn't watching anybody after that. What we had to do and do fast was take down the buffet table and clean up the house. Then we couldn't clean the ballroom and some of the other rooms until the police left. The police wanted to talk to all of us first, so we waited for that. I didn't get home until three o'clock in the morning." She thought hard. "No, I didn't watch out for anybody. Too busy."

"What about the woman?"

She shook her head. "You ask me, she was out of there before the police came."

"What'd the woman look like? You remember?" I asked.

Chantal settled back in her chair and rocked hard a minute or two. She was working up a sweat, her forehead shining. I figured she was struggling with getting somebody in trouble.

"I don't want this getting back to anybody." Chantal frowned over at us. "I didn't know the woman, but still, maybe she wasn't supposed to be there. People have got all kinds of reasons for not wanting to deal with police."

"Somebody shot Eugene," Meemaw said, her voice slightly scolding. "Anybody having anything to do with that should be worried. Anybody who didn't, well, they've got nothing to worry about from me and Lindy."

She nodded, agreeing. "She was kind of funny. I mean, started telling some of the girls I had helping me what to do and how to do it. I told her more than once to butt out of their business and then she'd look at me like she was outraged. Like who did I think I was? You would've thought it was her house or something."

"She wear a lot of makeup?"

She shook her head. "Yeah, sort of. Probably hiding bad skin. I do remember two crooked teeth at the front. One overlapping the other one. Kind of skinny. Blond hair, but coarse and curled up."

"You don't remember her name?"

Chantal shook her head slowly. "Didn't listen, I suppose."

"You ever see Jeannie Wheatley's mother?"

"Why?"

"Well, nothing, I guess."

"Never saw her that I know of. She was at the house a couple of times, causing trouble I heard, but I didn't see her."

"Was this woman out in the ballroom at all? I mean, setting up the tables or anything?"

She shook her head again. "Kitchen help was all she was supposed to be, but I caught her peeking out there, looking at the people."

"Did you have to check out with anybody after the party?" Meemaw asked. "Were you paid by the hour?"

"I'm paid weekly. Extra for big parties like that. I'm not like that fly-by-night help she brings in. You ask Roy Friendly about the man and that woman. You ask Roy. See if he knows anything."

She stopped a minute, putting a crooked finger to her lips. "You know, your friend Ethelred Tomroy came out to see me. She says they're looking into gun runners from South America."

"Who's looking into gun runners? And for what?"

Chantal shrugged. "That's what she said. They think Mr. Wheatley's gun collection had something to do with his murder. Like maybe he made a deal to sell guns and then he didn't go through with it."

"Most of the guns didn't even fire was what I heard. They're collectors' guns."

"Don't know about that. That's what she said. That they're getting close to solving the murder. Sure hope so. Poor Miss Jeannie. I like her—Mr. Wheatley's second wife. Just as nice as that first wife, Miss Sally." She looked around and lowered her voice. "I'm gonna tell you something. Maybe I can get in trouble, but I've been thinking hard about that family of Miss Jeannie's."

I sat up straighter, maybe something real at last.

"For a week that mama and her son came to the door and asked Mr. Wheatley to see Miss Jeannie. Martha, the housekeeper, told me Mr. Wheatley said never to let them in the house. And never to let Miss Jeannie know about it. I guess Mr. Wheatley didn't like them, and when Martha said they were threatening him, I didn't blame him."

"What kind of threats?" Meemaw was quick to ask.

"Martha said it was mean things. Things like he took their girl away from them and owed them something. Well, this was that mother talkin', you understand. Something else about getting a lawyer after him if they didn't get in the house to see Jeannie. I felt so bad when I heard. That poor Miss Jeannie's as sweet as can be. What a terrible mother! But it's not my place to have human feelings in that house. Miss Elizabeth wouldn't like it. Now, from what I'm hearing almost every day, there's trouble with Mr. Wheatley's will, or a family trust. Something like that she keeps talking about on the telephone."

"What about Dr. Peter Franklin?" I asked.

She shook her head. "Never saw him before the party. But he's at the house almost every day now. Kind of—what do you call it? A hanger-on or something. I heard her talking to somebody on the phone today, saying after the memorial 'that man' was leaving town or else. I thought she meant Dr. Franklin. It was, like, maybe he made a pass at her, or something."

So I was right—the rich wife thing. Then why me? What a letdown if I married him and he had to share my near-poverty existence. Well—free room and board, I guess. Maybe that was all it took to entice the good doctor.

After we left Chantal, and I agreed that the woman didn't talk our heads off exactly and had been very helpful, we headed farther out the I-10, toward the Barking Coyote. Almost nine o'clock and getting dark fast. Roy Friendly had promised Meemaw he'd meet her outside the saloon. All I worried about was if Roy was checking the time, or could still see his watch by then.

On the way out to the Coyote, I called Jessie Sanchez and asked her to talk to her summer intern about the man who'd come in asking about the Blanchard family. "Just curious," I told her.

"I did already. I asked Mindy what he looked like. She said he was average looking. Not young, not old. He had a Boston or Eastern accent. That was all she remembered. And she said he was stuck-up, like not looking at her when they were talking, not saying thank you for her time. Things like that. Sounds like that man who came in The Squirrel the other day. That Peter Franklin."

"Could be. Maybe checking me out. Seeing how I'm thought of around here. I mean, if I was a serious scientist or not."

"Mindy said she got the feeling it wasn't the oldest families he was interested in so much as the richest."

"That sure isn't us."

"Well, land and business rich, I guess you could say."

"Poor guy. Better he concentrate on Elizabeth Wheatley."

We agreed to meet for breakfast in the morning—the only way we ever got to talk without family around.

Meemaw'd been listening. "Not what that Franklin man made himself out to be, I take it."

"Well, scientists are always looking for money to keep their labs going. Once he met Elizabeth, I'll bet his eyes popped open. One look at the Wheatley mansion would do it. But why he had to go to the library to check on me is a mystery. What I'm doing is all over the Internet. All he had to do was look."

"Really?" she said. "Your work, huh? You still think that's what this is all about?"

Chapter Eighteen

Nine o'clock and there was Roy Friendly coming out of the Coyote, shutting the door on the sound of a whining guitar. He stood still, in silhouette, cowboy hat pushed to the back of his head. He looked like every tired cowboy ever resting out on the range. A heroic stance for a guy who'd been drinking for hours.

Roy glanced around, saw us, and took the bright stub of a cigarette out of his mouth and threw it to the ground. He stepped on that butt again and again, grinding it into the dirt before ambling over to my truck.

"Evening, ladies," he greeted us through Meemaw's open window. He wasn't drunk or anything, just smelled of whiskey and cigarettes and that other thing the Coyote always smelled like. Meemaw didn't open the door. Just left him standing there, leaning on the truck.

"Mighty happy to see the both of you. Fine weather, don't you think?"

We agreed it was a fine, almost cool, evening. Then we

agreed that the stars were brighter than we'd ever seen 'em before.

Here was the man from the party, dressed up in a tuxedo, standing formal and cool in that front hall, demanding to see invitations. I couldn't help but wonder how humans, more than any other animals, could change color and who they were whenever they needed to. Which brought me back to that extra woman helping in the kitchen at the party. Those crooked teeth couldn't be anybody else but Wanda Truly. Probably getting as close as she dared to get, keeping an eye on things. Or as close as she could get to be in on the killing of Eugene Wheatley, leaving Jeannie a wealthy widow.

"What I wanted to talk to you about was the party," Meemaw started the conversation when she figured they'd socialized enough.

He closed one eye and grimaced. "What'd you want to know that I ain't told the sheriff?"

"I was thinking." Meemaw knew how to talk to cowboys. Don't push 'em too fast or they get nervous. Drag out what you want to know so you both could chew it over and over like a cow's cud. "Was there anybody coming to that party that you didn't know?"

He thought awhile. "Sure. Lotsa people. Wasn't exactly my crowd."

She looked out the window over his head. "Anybody come who wasn't there after the murder? I mean, you see anybody leave, go out the door, around that time?"

"Couldn't tell you, Miss Amelia. They was coming and going all night. After a while, I just gave up checking off names."

"What do you think happened out there, Roy? You're a pretty good observer of human nature, I'll bet."

He took a while then nodded. "You gotta study 'em. People come in just a few types. Those people there were all rich and don't care a damn for anybody like me. Didn't even see me. Some, I heard, were nasty about Miss Jeannie though I liked her good enough. And Mr. Wheatley, too. Good man. Too bad he's the one they got. Now, that sister of his—"

"You think she could have been in on killing him?"

"I'll tell you one thing. She loved her brother. Maybe too much, some said. Trying to run his life and all." He shrugged and pulled another cigarette from a squashed pack in his shirt pocket. After feeling around in his back pockets, he brought out a matchbook, lit the cigarette behind cupped hands, and blew smoke off, away from the car window.

"Still, you never know about women. Saw one in here . . ." He moved his head toward the Coyote. "Long time ago. Always quiet. Nice. Took a lot from that husband of hers. Ya seen the kind. Drunk and insulting her in public. Like that. One night she just up and stuck a steak knife in his chest. Missed the heart, but she went to jail for it. Came out and went right back to him. Like I say, you never know about women."

"And what about the staff? Anybody different?"

"I was never there before. It was Chantal, the cook, called me, said they needed somebody like a butler to check invitations. You know, keep the riffraff out."

"Was the staff on your list?"

He shook his head. "Some of 'em didn't know no better and came in the front, by me, but all they did was tell me what they were there for."

"Did you see anybody who was working that night that you didn't know? I mean, people not from around here."

He thought awhile as he blew out rings of smoke. "Maybe one, I'd say."

"Do you know what Wanda Truly looks like?" I asked.

"You mean that woman who says she's Jeannie Wheatley's mother? Yeah, I know her. Been hanging around for a couple of weeks. Not anybody you want to be too friendly with."

"Did she come in past you?"

He shook his head slowly. "Didn't see her there. Suppose that was funny, her being Miss Jeannie's mother and all, and not invited to her daughter's wedding party."

"What about a tall, dark man? He was one of the waiters."

"Yup. That's the one I was talking about. He came in the front door. I sent him 'round to the back, where he was supposed to go. Never saw that one before."

"Did he give you his name?"

"Didn't ask. Too much going on. That was just about the time all the other people started walking in and I was busy."

"Do you have any suspicions who did this terrible thing, Roy?" Meemaw asked.

He shook his head. "Heard about gun runners from South America. That's all."

We thanked him and got out of there before Meemaw split a gut.

I still had to take Meemaw out to the ranch and then get back into town, to my apartment. I had to find something presentable to wear to the memorial service the next day. Supposed to be about seven o'clock in the evening. Be a long time in church, I was willing to bet. Then some small dinner or something afterward. That was the usual thing.

Back at the farm I could tell Miss Amelia was tired. I shooed her right off to bed then went looking for Justin and Bethany. I hoped one of them had taken Jeannie back out to the Chaunceys'. I was too tired for that long trek—out and back to Riverville.

I could've groaned when I saw the three of them sitting at the long trestle table in the kitchen. Justin was nursing a glass of whiskey. Jeannie and Bethany had clear glass cups of tea in front of them. They gave me relieved smiles.

"Wondered where you got to," Bethany said.

"I called Miranda," Jeannie said. "They're worried about me. Especially coming back after dark. And I guess my mama was out again, looking for me."

"You want to stay here?" I asked immediately.

"My clothes are all out there. All my personal stuff. Even some of Gene's things I brought with me."

"I'll take you, if that's what you want," Justin offered, and I could see he meant it, wasn't just being nice.

"Eugene's memorial service is tomorrow evening," I said, not apologizing for how late I was because I didn't think apologies were in order at this point.

"I heard. Miranda said Mama was in a state, insisting I be there." Jeannie shook herself. "None of it will be about Eugene. I wish I could . . . have a moment in that place. You know, alone with his ashes. Ever since he died, it's like he was spirited away from me. No time to say good-bye. We were just getting to really know each other and then it was over. I feel . . . I don't know. Cheated, maybe? Or just mad at whoever did this to him. So mad!"

She shook her head. "Nobody's going to scare me away from the memorial. Last thing I have to do for Gene. Ever. This wasn't the way it was supposed to go. He wanted us to get away from Elizabeth. Move to Dallas, if we had to, or wherever we could be left alone. That was why he was going to sell that gun collection once we got back there. Just get rid of it. We were going to buy a condo—not too much to have to look out for. Travel. That's what he wanted to do. Take me to Europe and Asia, is what he said. He painted word pictures of where we were going to go. I think Gene was more excited about showing me the world than I was to see it."

She smiled a sweet, sad smile, and took a deep breath.

"So he was going to sell the whole collection? How much is it worth, if you don't mind my asking?"

She shook her head. "We didn't talk about it. I don't know a thing about guns. I guess his collection is a rare one. One time he said he was having an appraiser come out."

"Are we talking millions?"

"I . . . think so. Gene told me after Sally was killed, he needed something to fill his mind. That was when he seriously began collecting—just about every rare gun that came on the market. Like, if he owned them all, nobody could kill somebody he loved again."

"Who does the collection go to? I mean now. Will it be yours?"

"I talked to Ben Fordyce today. Guess he's your family lawyer, too. He called back with some information. He's looking into all the rest for me. But I just don't care. There's nothing I need that much money for. It was all about Eugene. He said he was glad for the first time he was so rich, because of me."

I believed her, about not caring for the money. Maybe not caring about anything—with people after her, people accusing her of things, people letting out their meanness in her direction. The more I thought about it, the more I wondered how the poor woman could stand on her feet.

Bethany said Jeannie had been a big help with the wedding that afternoon. "She's a natural at this business. If I ever need a helper—" She blushed, probably thinking it was inappropriate to be talking about giving a new widow a job.

"I don't suppose you feel like talking more about what Ben said." My curiosity overcame any pity I was feeling. All this had to be about the money. I couldn't come up with anything else.

Jeannie bowed her head and rubbed at her eyes.

Justin gave me an angry look.

"Why don't you leave her alone, Lindy. You can see—"

"No, no." Jeannie put her hands up, then looked directly at me, her eyes shining—maybe with tears, maybe fatigue. "He said there's a family trust that Elizabeth claims Gene didn't change after we got married. I thought I remembered Gene saying he went to Dallas to do that very thing. The current trust is only held in Gene's name and Elizabeth's. At least that's what Elizabeth's lawyer said. I guess she'll get almost everything, except what isn't in the trust."

"So the gun collection might still come to you?"

"Ben asked for a copy of the trust to be faxed to him. We're getting together tomorrow evening so we can go over everything and see what I have to do."

"After the memorial?" I asked.

She nodded and started to get up. "Think it's best I get back out to the twins' ranch now. Miss Miranda and Miss Melody really seem to worry about me. I don't want to cause them any more—"

"I'll take her," Justin said again, and it was settled.

"And maybe stay the night?" I asked, giving him a significant look. Better a young man in the house, though I couldn't really think of anybody better in a tough spot than Miranda and that shotgun of hers. "The girls won't care."

"If you think it's needed." Justin pulled out Jeannie's chair, like the gentleman he was, and they were off.

Chapter Nineteen

In the morning I waited until I heard Meemaw's key in the lock downstairs at the Nut House. Since the store wouldn't be open for another two hours, I hurried on down in the clothes I slept in: an old yellow T-shirt and a pair of pajama shorts. No shoes, which was the first thing Meemaw noticed and warned me fiercely about getting slivers from the old wood floor, which meant I had to run back up the steps and get a pair of sandals before she'd even talk to me.

I sat at the table, feeling like a little girl again, with my grandmother fussing over me, bringing out a fresh pecan bread to toast a slice. One slice, I told her since I was meeting Jessie for breakfast.

She poured coffee, which I drank without complaining. No use being ungrateful, especially when the pecan bread slice came hot out of the toaster, and I could use a little taking care of since I was feeling alone and unhappy with Hunter still being such an ass. I'd checked my cell first thing that morning and there was a call from Peter Franklin asking me to call him. Which I did, to get it over with. He wanted to know, he said, if I was going to the memorial. And Elizabeth wanted to make sure Jeannie knew the memorial was set for seven that evening, at the Rushing to Calvary Independent Church. And she wanted to talk to me, if I could find time in this sad day to come on over to the house.

"You understand, don't you?" he went on. "Elizabeth says Jeannie should make it a point to be at the memorial, otherwise everybody will be scandalized—the wife not there. I'm sure you can see what she's saying. Last thing Elizabeth wants is more scandal."

I said far as I knew, Jeannie was going to be there, with a lot of friends around her. He ignored that last comment and went on to say he'd love to pick me up, but Elizabeth requested that he go with her. She had a limo for the occasion. And she'd be in no state for conversation by that time.

I congratulated myself on not being compelled to go with the two of them. Just hearing his voice made shivers run down my back. My plan, from there on, was to freeze him out cold. Something I didn't like about the man—no matter how he kept trying to impress me. Two scientists, after all, he seemed to suggest, while all I could think was I may be a scientist but I wasn't a snob, and I didn't stick my nose into other people's work, and I sure didn't suck up to rich people.

No call from Hunter. That was a thing that was starting to hurt like somebody pulling a big scab off a sore.

When Meemaw settled at the table across from me, I got into what I'd hurried down to discuss. "Did you know Eugene was selling that gun collection of his?" I asked, my mouth still full of pecan bread.

She shook her head, eyes blinking a couple of times as she thought about what I said. "Kind of brings in another angle, doesn't it?"

"I thought so."

"Hope it's not Ethelred's angle. You know, that gun

runner business. You think about it, those drug people have a lot of money. What's a couple million more or less to them?" She yawned behind her hand and said she didn't sleep too well last night.

"Meemaw, think about it. Bet anything those gun lords want guns that work, not to hang on their wall."

Meemaw sort of giggled. "Just shows you how tired I am. But I'm just as happy to have Ethelred stuck on her theory. Keeps her out of everybody's hair."

"Justin took Jeannie home and stayed out to the Chaunceys'. Just to keep watch." I gave her a dubious look.

"You don't think he's smitten with her, do you? Poor soul just lost her husband. Justin needs a better sense of timing."

"He hasn't been interested in a woman since that Grace Prouty broke up with him," I said.

"Probably about time, but for heaven's sakes, the girl's in mourning."

"I don't think Justin would be dumb enough to start anything. But I kind of hope she'll hang around Riverville. At least for a while. Be good to see Justin happy," I said.

"What about you and Hunter?"

I shook my head. "That man's a complete ass."

"Well, bless his heart. I've got to speak to that boy. The way he's actin'! Dumb as a box of rocks. And, you know, we gotta work together. So much is going on, and from what he tells me, the sheriff isn't any more ahead findin' the murderer than we are."

"Guess you can put away that silver set you been saving for me. Don't look like I'm ever gonna use it."

"Pshaw! This is just one of those bumps in the road. He'll come back around."

"Not with that pretty blonde after him."

Meemaw made a face. "You just forget about that girl. I'm sure she doesn't mean a thing to Hunter."

I smelled a rat. "You know something you're not saying?"

"When I don't say something that could save my granddaughter's feelings, you know I've got a pretty good reason. That enough for you?"

"No, ma'am. Come on, Meemaw. What's going on?"

She shook her head hard two times, made a disapproving noise, and went back to talking about guns. "Somebody who wanted that gun collection and wasn't willing to pay for it wouldn't shoot Eugene and leave all the guns behind. They would've worked the whole thing different. Wouldn't pose as a buyer and come at a time when Eugene was in the middle of his own wedding party. Doesn't make sense if you look at it like a robbery."

"Worth a lot of money," I reminded her.

"Still and all, Hunter said they had an expert in to go over the collection. Nothing missing, according to Eugene's own records."

"So you're still talking to Hunter behind my back."

Meemaw colored up. "Not about you, Lindy. He's got the basics to the case."

"And you asked him about that blonde he was with the other night. Won't tell me what you know about her."

She shook her head. "Think it's up to you to ask. I'm your grandmother, young lady, not your fight manager."

Jessie walked into The Squirrel in a gorgeous turquoise silk blouse that wrapped around and tied at her waist. I had just one tiny minute of jealousy, thinking how I should go shopping and get some clothes that looked better than things a farmhand might wear. And if I was going to start publishing my work, well, who knows what conferences I'd be asked to? But that all flew out of my head as Jessie sat down and pushed a computer runoff at me.

"I looked up that Dr. Franklin of yours," she said. "Seems he did go to Harvard. Even lived in Boston—some of the time."

"What about the Global Plant Initiative in Italy? Did it say anything about him being connected there?"

She scanned her runoff then shook her head. "Nothing like that on here. Some articles on plant propagation. Wow—a whole list of them, but nothing current."

"Could be because he's been working in Italy."

She shrugged. "Or he doesn't have a job."

I laughed. "You have any background in the CIA?"

She shook her head. "No, just tracking down overdue library books."

Cecil was on his way over with his usual scruffy menus from which I would be talked into some awful English dish. I looked up and out the big front windows and around the enormous squirrel painted on the glass.

The man walking by on the sidewalk wasn't hurrying, but he still moved like a person with a purpose: long, thin body bent forward, head with a mop of curly black hair. He wore a muscle shirt, sun-darkened arms sticking out at the elbows, hands shoved into the pockets of dark pants. No waiter's tuxedo, yet I recognized him. The waiter from the party, who nobody seemed to know.

I didn't have time to say a word to Jessie. I got up and ran out of the restaurant, the door closing with the tinkle of the bell behind me.

Curly was taking long strides, getting along without seeming to be going fast. I walked behind him for a couple of blocks, almost down to the Nut House, when he turned to look over his shoulder. The look on his face was all shock. He knew who I was, or remembered me from the party. I expected him to stop, seeing I was almost up behind him, but he didn't.

"Curly?" I called out.

Faster than I could catch on to, he was off, loping around a corner, past the sheriff's department, and over into the park. I was too surprised to go fast enough to keep up. And what if I caught him? I asked myself. What then? I slowed down and watched as he jogged around the ice cream shop and ran deep into the park where people were sitting on benches, or standing with baby carriages, talking, fanning themselves because the day was getting to be a hot one. There was no use yelling "Stop that man," since I had no reason to stop him if he wanted to get away from me.

I turned back and ran up the steps to the sheriff's department. Greg Harner, new to the force, was on duty at the front desk. I asked for Hunter, but he said he was out looking for that dog of his.

"Thing won't listen to Hunter worth a damn," Greg said. "If it was me, I'd get him to the pound fast as I could. But Hunter says he likes the dog. Go figure that one."

I asked for Sheriff Higsby. He was out on a call, too.

No cop to help me. That was a pretty scary feeling.

Chapter Twenty

I pulled up and parked outside the Wheatley mansion—still stately and icy cold. I did some self-talking in my head about not feeling small in that huge place and then about not being intimidated by a woman with a lot of money and a look on her face like maybe I smelled bad. Which made me check both armpits and be happy that I smelled kind of like a pine tree.

Meemaw, riding shotgun as usual, gave me a worried look. I put up one finger, letting her know I needed just a minute to think before we went in . . .

When I'd gotten back to The Squirrel, and explained what happened, Jessie agreed I had better things to do than gorge myself on Cecil's Bangers and Mash. "I saw a plate of it go by," she whispered. "Looked like pig intestines curled over a lump of yellowish mashed potatoes. Let's get out of here."

"You tell Deputy Austen about the man?" she asked on

the way out the door, the tinkling bell letting Cecil know we were leaving without eating, for which I would pay—double and dearly—the next time I was in.

"I tried to, but nobody was around and that idiot new deputy was all wrapped up in Hunter's dog." I rolled my eyes the way women do after dealing with men who weren't raised the way they should've been. Jessie got it and gave me a sympathetic cluck and a hug.

"He kept that mongrel then?" Jessie was laughing to herself. "Heard the dog doesn't listen, doesn't like being touched, eats more than a cow, and never comes when he's called. Sounds like the perfect companion for Hunter. He's kind of that way himself, you ask me."

She smiled and so did I. It was good to have a girlfriend. Women knew about things men didn't even know existed.

"Guess where I'm going?" I said though Jessie could have no idea, not being in the middle of all the things Meemaw and I were in the middle of.

"Un-uh."

"Elizabeth Wheatley called and wants to see me. I want to see her, too. See what that Curly was up to and why he was at the party."

"Good idea," Jessie said, then kissed me on both cheeks and hurried off toward the library. At least somebody had the kind of job they had to get to—and people let 'em.

I called Meemaw and told her who I'd been chasing in town and that I was going out to see Elizabeth.

"You get ahold of Hunter, Lindy. I don't like you out doin' things on your own." Her voice was as stern as it gets.

"Tried. He's on a call."

"Then come pick me up before you leave town. I don't want you at that place alone. Seems so much is going on. People taking up sides. Jeannie's and Elizabeth's, and it's all wrong. Every bit of it. Eugene's murder wasn't an attempted robbery, so who benefits? I see a bunch of people standing in line for that one. Elizabeth, Jeannie, Jeannie's mother and brother. And somebody's helping whoever did it. Neither Elizabeth nor Jeannie could've done it alone. They were in plain sight at the time of the shot."

She hesitated when someone in the store asked a question. She answered then came back on the phone. "Last thing whoever's responsible for all of this wants is you and me looking into it. I think we have to make a pact, Lindy. You may not like it, being free-spirited the way you are, but I say we stay together as much as we can from now on."

"You mean I have to work in the store all day? Or you have to sit out in my greenhouse?"

Her voice froze a couple of degrees. "You know very well that's not what I'm talking about. I mean: You go to the Chaunceys'. I go. You go hunting down some dark man. I go. You go to the Wheatleys'. I go. So come and get me. Treenie's here now. She'll take over."

I wanted to groan, but I agreed, just to make peace and not stir her up more than she was stirred already.

On the way over to the Nut House to pick her up, I called Hunter again because Meemaw said I had to, telling me, "He's looking for that man, too, ya know. He has to know the man's still hanging around Riverville."

"You're sure on top of what he's doing," I came back at her, trying to keep a nasty tinge out of my voice.

"Humph. Somebody has to be."

She hung up.

I dialed the station number. "Deputy Hunter," he answered, his voice gruff and hurried, but achingly familiar.

"Hunter," I started right in, almost breathless, as if I had to justify calling him. "Are you looking for that dark waiter who was at the party? That Curly?"

"Heard about him, but I'm pretty busy right now, Lindy. I'm out here at the Chaunceys' ranch. A little trouble. Could I call you in, say, half an hour?"

"What kind of trouble?" I got worried right away. "Is Justin still there?"

"Yup. He's the one took a shot at the Trulys' car. And they're the ones called me out."

"Oh, no!"

"I guess there's fault on both sides, Lindy. Don't worry about Justin. Melody and Miranda back him up—the Trulys were asked to leave and wouldn't go. Justin kind of chased them out to their car and took a shot when they wouldn't leave. Warning them, Justin says. But say, I gotta go now. They're all standing around. Trulys met me on the highway and were damned and determined to come on back with me. Wanted to press charges 'til I pointed out that they'd been trespassing, and in Texas, that gave the owner the right to protect their property."

"Thanks, Hunter. I really appreciate . . . Oh, Lord, wait 'til Mama hears. Justin's out there because of me and Meemaw wanting to protect Jeannie."

"Heard about that. Tell you one thing, Lindy. I don't think those people will be coming back too soon to bother these folks. I kind of read them the riot act. You gonna be at that memorial service later?"

I said I was.

"Then I'll see you there. You can tell me about that Curly fella then."

"But I saw him . . ."

Hunter was gone. More trouble. Poor Justin, I'd gotten him into this. I took just a second to be grateful for Hunter, being nice the way he'd been, then I realized he was talking in front of other people and had to be at least halfway decent to me . . .

Meemaw rang the bell at the Wheatleys' house, and waited. Elizabeth Wheatley answered the door herself, dressed in what I supposed were riding clothes: narrow-waisted jacket, jodhpurs, and small, round hat on her head. I'd seen pictures in school of people "riding to hounds" that looked like her. All that was different on Elizabeth was the small gun holster at her hip.

She didn't say hello, just "Come on in." Striding across the wide, front hall, she turned to snap out an unpleasant, "See you can't go anywhere without your grandma."

"Don't pay me any mind, Elizabeth." Meemaw had her "You poor dear" face on, the kind of face Southern women have been joyously showing to bad husbands as they died of too big a dose of pecan pie. "Just wanted to get out of the Nut House for a while. You won't know I'm here, dear."

We weren't shown to one of the pretty rooms off the main corridor. We weren't offered sweet tea or a single cookie, though my stomach was growling by now, having had only one slice of Meemaw's pecan bread to eat so far. Made me wonder just how "Southern" Dallas was these days, that people didn't know the simple rules of hospitality.

I was feeling huffy when Elizabeth pointed to a settee in the hall. We sat. She decorously lowered herself to a brocaded couch set at an angle to us. She sat there like she had a broomstick down her back, hands together between her knees. I reminded myself, she's the one asked me to come by. I couldn't help but think how some people maybe had a whole lot of money and no idea how to treat other people.

"So." Elizabeth cleared her throat and raised her eyebrows at us. "Jeannie's coming to the memorial this evening, or so I've been told. I mean, Eugene was her husband, after all. No matter that it was one of the shortest marriages on record." She smirked at me, then at Meemaw.

I wished, for just a minute, I wasn't a lady so I could smirk right back at her, but I could see Meemaw was doing it for me: a smirk, with a sweet tip of the head, so you weren't supposed to notice how pissed off she was getting.

"Not her fault the marriage was short, Elizabeth." Meemaw's voice had that touch of pure Southern oil that could make me cringe. "Poor soul seemed to have loved him an awful lot."

Elizabeth snorted. "Love. Phooey, you ask me. You've seen those relatives of hers, pure gold diggers. If any of you people are still looking to solve my brother's murder, I hope somebody's taking a good long look at that Billy Truly. Just out of prison. I heard it was manslaughter they got him for. So here's that family not wanting to wait too long to get poor Eugene's money. And my money, by the way. You ask me, it was that brother. He's the one hanging around the house that night. And that awful mother of hers running in almost as soon as the shot was fired. What was the pair of them doing here at all? They weren't invited. Must've been hiding in the bushes. I can see that Billy Truly now, knocking on Eugene's door, maybe saying he was there to see Jeannie, and Eugene, being the pushover he was, letting the man in."

"Doing what then?" I asked. "Did Eugene go back to work with the man behind him holding a gun? Wouldn't he have taken him out to see Jeannie—if he let him in at all? He wouldn't have gone back to work at the table. Just wouldn't be the right thing to do."

Elizabeth shrugged. "Who knows what happened? To tell you the honest to God's truth, I don't see anybody but him doing this. I'll just say it again, right out loud. Those awful relatives of Jeannie's hope to benefit one way or the other. I think, sincerely, this was the way they took."

"Was there anything special you wanted to talk about," I asked because I didn't like the circle we were plowing.

Elizabeth made a face at me and looked down at her watch. "That was it. I just want to make sure the sheriff takes a long hard look at that Billy Truly."

"I'll pass on the word," I assured her.

"I want this over and that pair in jail. I'm telling you, I

can sense things like that. Like who can kill another human being. I just know. Feel it just by looking at them." She nodded hard. "And that other pair, Miss Ethelred and Freda Cromwell. Did you hear what Ethelred's spreading around? She thinks it's some gun runners from South America killed Eugene. As if my brother would have anything to do with gun runners or drug lords or what have you. I hope you can put a lid on what she's spreading, Miss Amelia. I imagine you're the only one who's got any sway with that woman."

Meemaw frowned. "Nobody has 'sway' with Ethelred Tomroy, Elizabeth."

"Well, now that you know, I hope you'll have a word with her and shut her up."

Meemaw had nothing more to say though I could imagine her thinking she wasn't in the business of shutting anybody up.

"I want to ask about something, too." I drew out my remark. "There was a waiter at the party. Tall man with dark curly hair. Heard his name was Curly. Chantal Kronos and Roy Friendly didn't recognize him. You hire that man, do you remember?"

She turned away to think awhile, and then back. "No, I don't hire staff myself. Usually Chantal does that. She's the one got Roy Friendly to check the invitations. Don't want just anybody wandering in."

"Looks like somebody did. The man was there and Chantal said he didn't seem a whole lot interested in doing a waiter's job."

"Really?" She leaned back and gave me a look.

"And there was another one nobody knew. A woman. Lots of makeup. Crooked teeth. Blond . . ."

"For heaven's sake! That sounds like that awful—" She didn't finish what she was going to say. I saw the look in her eyes. She was guessing the woman was Wanda Truly, but she wasn't going to come out with it. For whatever reason

Elizabeth had for doing anything, she was holding this one close to her chest.

"Anyway, I saw that Curly in town this morning. I called out his name and he ran away like his pants were on fire."

She leaned back. "You don't say! Well, if you ask me, you don't have to go looking for any 'dark man.' I just know that Billy Truly had something to do with this. And you all know he's just out of Huntsville. You can check it out with Hunter Austen. Manslaughter, for goodness' sakes. Now, if that doesn't give you pause."

I agreed it certainly did.

"Oh, another thing. My attorney called a while ago. You hear that Ben Fordyce is taking on Jeannie's case against me?"

I nodded.

"He's the Blanchards' attorney, isn't he?'

"A good friend of my daddy's," I put in.

"You people choosing up sides?" she demanded and reared back to give us a hard look straight down her nose.

"Why no. We're not against anybody. She needs her own attorney. You gave me that card to give her. Remember? Stands to reason she needs a lawyer on her side, too."

Her eyebrows flew up. "Heard you took her to the Chaunceys'. Imagine that. They were at our party, too. Always thought of Miranda and Melody as friends. Guess I was wrong."

"Sorry, Elizabeth," I said and meant it. Maybe we were all ganging up on her, because of her way with people. Still, she'd lost her brother just like Jeannie lost her husband. "It's just that Jeannie's grieving and maybe not up to dealing with estates and things like that on her own."

"That's too bad. I'm not up to it either, but when a family has money, that's what happens. If you're born to money, you know what to expect and do your duty. When you're not, well, you act like Jeannie's acting. Going around trying to get sympathy from everybody. Putting your problems on somebody else's shoulders."

With that, she stood. "Since you're Jeannie's friend now and not a friend of the Wheatleys', I guess I might as well tell you as tell Jeannie, or that awful mother of hers. She's not going to get millions out of me. I want to be fair and there are some things not in the family trust Eugene and I put together right after his first wife died so tragically. There won't be much that will go to her, you can tell her that for me. And tell her that she was only married a few weeks to a Wheatley. I'll be happy to see she gets a few weeks' worth of pay. But that's all. No use dragging me into court. The lawyers will be the only ones to benefit and she'll lose in the end."

I rose slowly and gave Meemaw a hand because the settee was soft and didn't give up people easily.

"I don't think I'll be passing on any kind of message like that," I said. "Money is between the two of you. I was a friend of Eugene's. I think I know what he'd like to have happen and it's not what you're planning. But he's not here to defend himself or his wife so I guess what's going to come of all of this will just have to come."

She sniffed and looked down her nose at me. "I'll have to ask you to leave. I'm meeting friends out at the stable."

I could see whichever poor beast she would be riding was going to get a workout.

"You take a gun out with you?" Meemaw pointed to the holster at her hip.

She closed her eyes and shook her head. "You know this wild country, Miss Amelia. Rattlers everywhere. Wild hogs. They scared my horse in the past. I take care of them first now."

"Must be a good shot." Meemaw shook her head, admiring Elizabeth's courage.

"Good as I have to be." Elizabeth smiled. "I'll see you

all this evening. Make certain Jeannie's there. As I said, I don't want people talking any more than they are already."

"Me either." I tried to smile. "Hope tonight's going to be about Eugene and that's all."

She hesitated, turning away from me, then back. "Maybe you'd like to stand and say a few words. I guess you're about the only person in Riverville who remembers Eugene from school."

I supposed being asked to speak at a Wheatley memorial was an honor, but I wanted to get up in front of those warring people about as much as I wanted to get up and sing *Madame Butterfly*.

She didn't wait for me to agree. "Peter will be driving to the church with me. I know you and Peter have gotten . . . well . . . to know each other, but I think I'd rather have a pleasant man at my side today and I imagine Hunter will be bringing you."

I opened my mouth because a decent human being would want to at least warn her about Peter Franklin and that he might not be completely as he presented himself.

I shut my mouth without saying a word. If Peter Franklin was what it took to keep her happy that night, she was welcome to him.

Chapter Twenty-one

The main sanctuary of the Rushing to Calvary Church was filled before we got there. It looked like every living soul in Riverville was hurrying to get good seats. I had a suspicion that not all of them knew Eugene but he was the talk of the town since being shot to death and, after all, going to church was free.

Or maybe I was wrong and all my neighbors wanted to pay their last respects to a dead member of an old Riverville family. Guess I do tend to be cynical at times, but then, in my defense, I'd lived in the area all my life and knew how folks liked a good scandal, especially one swirling around rich folks. Add in murder and you're sure to draw a crowd.

There was no body to make over, just a sealed urn of ashes sitting up front on a long table covered with an embroidered white cloth and a lot of photographs of Eugene from the time he was a baby on up until his wedding to Jeannie. I noticed, because I couldn't help it, that Elizabeth had put photos of his marriage to Sally up, too. Kind of mean, I thought, but what did I know about etiquette at the memorial of a man who was married twice. I supposed it was something that had to be acknowledged, just as when there were kids involved.

I liked Sally's smiling face and missed her all over again. When she died, we were already at the point where we told each other things we didn't need to say were secret, even though they were. I couldn't remember any of Sally's secrets, but I'd blurted out a few things in my time, like when I told Bethany she was adopted from Africa and she believed me. And how mad Mama got at that one. But how Meemaw asked Bethany if she really believed she came from Africa, with all that white skin of hers, and Bethany said, "No, but Lindy scared me. I'm afraid of lions."

And the times Hunter and me went skinny-dipping in the Colorado. Couldn't keep that quiet either. I loved reminding him. To this day he colors up so red you'd think he's on fire.

There was a line of people behind me so I moved on in. Elizabeth wasn't there yet, I noticed. Probably a grand entrance to make. I'd come with Meemaw and Mama, who stood at the back, talking with friends and neighbors. I saw Jeannie walk in flanked by the Chauncey twins in their very best old jackets and Stetson hats, which they removed as they entered the church, placing them over their hearts. They looked like bodyguards to me. If I ever needed a bodyguard, these were the people I'd choose. No matter they were eighty-eight or thereabouts.

Justin walked in behind Jeannie and the twins. He escorted Jeannie up front, found her a seat in the first row, then sat in the pew directly behind her. Jeannie looked small and alone, up there by herself. The blond hair was brushed down to her shoulders, not really neat, just there, like nobody cared. It looked like maybe Melody fixed it for her, claiming all her years of experience grooming horses. There was no bright yellow today. Jeannie wore a navy blue dress with a white collar. Her shoes were white and low-heeled. She looked like a librarian. Subdued. Not in deep mourning, just respectful, and sad. I started up to talk to her, but others surrounded her as they turned from the table with the ashes. I could see she was in good hands. No matter what Elizabeth had been spreading around town, people were there to support Jeannie and express their condolences.

Made me think I'd been hard on everybody in Riverville. Bet most of them had come because they thought Jeannie was getting a bad deal. That made me proud of our town. I often went back and forth like that, most of it having to do with how I was feeling about myself at the moment. Nothing like seeing bad in others when you're feeling it in yourself.

I saw Jessie with her parents, Martin and Juanita. She waved.

Hunter stood in the vestibule. When the inside door opened, he was just on the other side, in full uniform. He nodded as people walked past him and sometimes shared a word or two. The door closed and I couldn't see him anymore. I took a seat in a middle pew. I had a paper in my pocket with the few things I remembered about Eugene written down. I certainly wasn't going to talk about bullying him or picking on him because he let me do it. I remembered one time when we were in a play, a teacher had written about the Incas and Eugene had to carry a live parrot on his shoulder. The parrot bent down from time to time and bit his ear, causing him to yell out at one serious moment in the play, "Damn bird!"

Maybe that wasn't the kind of thing you said at memorials. I'd never done this before. Now I was nervous. I didn't have much else. Just that he walked me all the way home once, with his chauffeur driving slowly along behind and what a nice person he turned out to be and how sorry I was for what happened to him.

I stopped pretending I had nothing else on my mind, got up, and went to talk to Hunter.

First I had that dark man to tell him about. Then what Elizabeth believed about the Trulys. Then how Ethelred and Freda were stirring up all kinds of misery with their cockamamie theories. Then I wanted to know who the hell that blonde was and what he was doing with her at that out-of-the-way restaurant in Schulenberg, and just what the heck was he pulling anyway? Weren't we a couple? I mean, if you came right down to it, we'd been practically engaged for ten years now. All the time I was in college—seven years—I dated other men, but never thought much about any of them. I'd always supposed he dated other women, too. I'd just never seen real evidence of it before.

I leaned up, tugging on his arm, and said I had a few things to talk to him about and could he get away for just a minute.

Hunter frowned down at me, stiff and official in that uniform he loved so much. "Bad time, Lindy. Sheriff Higsby told me to stay in here and keep a watch on who comes in."

"Are you looking for that dark-haired waiter from the party?"

"One of 'em."

"I saw him yesterday in town. I followed him and he saw me. Took off like a bat out of hell, into the park. I wasn't going to chase him. Still, I thought I should tell you he's hanging around town. Can't imagine why. Nobody seems to know him. I asked Elizabeth Wheatley and she said she didn't do any of the hiring for the party. Chantal Kronos did. I asked Chantal but she said she didn't hire him. Oh, and she also said . . ."

I took a breath just as Morton Shrift and some of the waitresses from the Barking Coyote came in. Finula Prentiss's face broke in half with a wide grin when she saw Hunter.

"Why, Deputy Austen, I knew you'd be here, protecting all of us from that awful person who did it. Hope I can sit next to you in church, just so I feel as safe as I can feel."

She grinned up at him. I stared hard at her. Came to the

memorial in a black dress all right. Tight as the casing on a sausage. Short as one of Morton's Garrison's on the rocks. Made up like somebody was throwing makeup out a window when she passed by. And black hair—blacker than hair has ever been in all of time—tied up into some kind of knot on the top of her head and stuck through with a big rhinestone pin.

"Sorry, Finula." Hunter's voice had a lot of laughter to it. "I'll be busy with traffic and helping people. Keeping an eye on things, I guess."

She pouted up at him, reached out to touch the collar of his shirt, smoothed it down, and patted it a few times before moving on with the others.

My first instinct was to put a hand on Hunter's arm and pull him back a step or two, out of the crowd pushing into the church.

He frowned as he looked down into my eyes. "I'm on duty, Lindy," he protested, turning his head so as not to miss anyone entering or leaving.

"Well, so am I. I've kept my mouth shut since the other night. I want to know who that blonde was you were with."

He gave me a guilty look. "You mean in that restaurant over to Schulenberg? Weren't you there with that Peter Franklin? Seems like maybe you've got no right—"

"You know I was stuck with that man. I don't care what you say. And I found out something about him you've got to know."

He frowned. "What are you talking about now?"

"What I said. I had Jessie look him up. You should—"

The blonde walked in and Hunter didn't hear anything I said after that. He took her by the arm and walked her into the church. I watched as he saw that she got a good seat near the back and bent to talk to her. Solicitous. Her huge blue eyes stayed on his face. She nodded to whatever he said to her, looking up worried, like she was just going to be so afraid if he left her all alone.

He was being a jerk the way men are always jerks when a new pretty face comes to town.

As I stood fuming, Elizabeth Wheatley swept in on Dr. Franklin's arm, ignoring me. I went back to my seat. The service was starting.

First came the prelude and we were soon singing "Crossing the Bar," and then into Pastor Rogan's opening remarks. He was new to the church, a nice man with a sweet wife and two little girls. He raised his hands and began with a sermon on the brevity of life, tying it to scriptures.

Then we were singing again. I let rip on "There Is a Calm for Those Who Weep," since I loved singing in church and feeling all those other voices rumbling through me. Made me feel like such a good person.

But then I wasn't there to feel good. I was there to testify to the goodness and humanness of the man I knew, Eugene Wheatley. The pastor called on those of us who were speaking—one after the other.

I was the last. I figured I was stuck on after Elizabeth found herself one short.

The talks were all good. People talking about his charity and kindness. I pulled out my slip of paper again and read over what I'd written, wanting to change all of it. But then it was my turn and I went to the altar and took my paper out and spread it on the lectern—once, and then once more, before I looked up and out at all the expectant faces. Crap. How could I talk about the time I gave him a black eye just because he told me I was pretty?

I opened my mouth. I was going to wing it. What good friends we'd always been. Lie if I had to.

I didn't get out a single word. Loud noise came from over by one of the side doors, making everyone turn. I saw Hunter blocking someone from entering the church. Other men got up to help him. Everybody in the church turned to watch. People stood up to see. A quiet whispering spread across the room. I heard Elizabeth Wheatley barking orders from her place at the front and then Jeannie gasped. The organist began playing "How Sweet the Hour of Closing Day" but soon let the organ grind down with a painful squawk as a woman burst through the ring of men and dashed toward the altar.

Wanda Truly, of course. I knew enough about the woman already to recognize her sense of high drama. This wasn't a moment when she was going to be kept out of the spotlight, dressed so appropriately in a pink blouse with pink coral beads doubled and doubled again around her neck. Pink pants. Hair flying everywhere, away from the pink hairband she wore. Her elbows were pumping, knees stepping high, as she scurried to the front and elbowed me away from the lectern.

"I'm Eugene Wheatley's mother-in-law, Wanda Truly." The microphone squawked. "Jeannie, there, is my daughter. I don't know why Gene's sister, Elizabeth, didn't want me to get up here and speak, but she didn't, so I came anyway. You all understand, don't ya?" She looked around hard at the people, who stared back openmouthed. "My Jeannie was Gene's wife and she deserves a lot better than she's getting here in this town. My son, Billy, and I . . ." She gestured to the back where Billy stood with his head down, as usual. "We came to see that my little girl gets justice from the Wheatley family. I don't know if you all heard, but that Elizabeth is trying to keep my daughter from getting a single thing Gene would've wanted her to have. It's terrible, what's going on. And I thought people should know—"

I started back up the aisle, away from Wanda. Nobody paid any attention to me; they were fixed on what was happening at the front. Hunter and some of the others whispered together at the back of the room, guarding Billy as if he were the one to fear.

I ignored Hunter, the sheriff, other deputies, a group of

church leaders, and went straight to Billy Truly. He didn't look up when I said his name. He kept his head down, shaking it as I spoke to him.

Mostly I whispered. "Billy, your mother's hurting Jeannie all over again. You can stop her. Stop her right here and right now. You have to do something. You know, don't you, what she's put you and Jeannie through in the past. Don't let it happen again. Maybe she's right about the money and what Elizabeth is trying to do, but this isn't the place to fight about it. This is a man's memorial. He deserves better than the scene Wanda's making."

Billy thought awhile then lifted his head and looked me straight in the eye. Sad eyes. Kind of sorry eyes. He stiffened his back and moved his wide shoulders under the plaid shirt he wore. I said a little more of the same thing. Billy nodded only once before he started up the aisle.

Hunter reached out to grab him, but I knocked Hunter's hand away and warned, "Leave him alone."

Nobody realized who he was when he walked up the aisle, head down, fists clenched at his sides. When he got to the altar and started up the wide steps toward the lectern, Wanda noticed and frowned at him, but it was like stopping a charging bear. First he pulled at her arm, but she resisted. Then he tried to get his big arms around her. She ducked down between them, yelling at him to leave her alone.

I saw Jeannie get up. Justin tried to get out of the pew behind her, stepping on more than a few toes, I was willing to bet. Jeannie got to the lectern first, talking to Billy, ignoring their mother, who was struggling now in Billy's grip. He had his arms around Wanda's waist and lifted her into the air. Jeannie turned and grabbed at Justin's hands, then pulled him aside as Billy walked off the altar and up the aisle with Wanda struggling like a bug on its back, hands trying to reach back to scratch Billy's face. Feet kicking wildly.

He carried her straight out the door.

In a few minutes the pastor raised his hands for quiet and soon we were all singing a hymn of consolation as if nothing had happened. The only thing good about Wanda's show was that I didn't get to say a word about Eugene. And then I was sorry about that.

Chapter Twenty-two

One thing I learned right there in the church that day was how cool and kind Riverville people were. Outside, when the service was over, nobody stood around gossiping. Instead, they formed a wide circle around Jeannie, like they were protecting her. She was too busy to notice when Elizabeth and Peter exited, hurrying off to the black limo waiting at the front of the parking lot.

I heard Mrs. Vernon Williams, the Culinary Arts Supervisor at the county fair, asking if there was going to be a funeral dinner and somebody telling her no and her clucking that it was too bad, she'd heard the church ladies were great cooks.

There was no reason for me to wait for Jeannie. She had plenty of people around her to see she got back to the Chaunceys' safely. I'd come in Mama's car so I wasn't going anyplace until Mama and Meemaw came out of the church. All I could do was stand and watch. Mostly I kept an eye on the black limo idling at the curb, making no attempt to pull away. It seemed like an anticlimax, all of us walking out into the evening sunshine, long shadows falling over faces, and nothing to look forward to. Not even supper.

Hunter came out with the blonde. He was looking over to where I waited for the others and nodded. I turned my back. The parking lot emptied slowly. The black limo seemed to be waiting for everybody else to leave. Maybe protocol, for all I knew.

I was tempted to go in and hurry Mama and Miss Amelia along. They both could get to talking to the parson and his wife and forget I was waiting outside with no other way to get home. So I was just about getting mad when they came out and we were in the car—last in the lot, almost, and I was having a few words about leaving me standing alone outside.

Mama moved the car toward the narrow gates, letting me stew alone in the backseat.

The black limo with Elizabeth and Peter Franklin pulled out ahead of us and turned toward town. Mama pulled out right behind them then had to stop as they stopped dead. Maybe they were deciding where to go, or if Peter should be dropped off at the hotel in town, or whatever people have to decide after saying a final good-bye to somebody they loved.

One side of the road leading to the church was all trees—a thick woodland some people in town wanted to clear for new houses and others wanted left alone, maybe for a Texas botanical garden. I'd been out to look it over when Mrs. Beasley, from the local conservation group, invited me and I agreed with them: Let's save what we've got left.

I was looking at the pretty woods when I noticed a man standing between two of the trees. It was the dark man, Curly, from the party. He just stood there, like some kind of death's head, staring at the limo in front of us and then at our car.

"Meemaw." I tapped her on the shoulder. "That's him."

"That's who?"

"That waiter from the wedding party."

She leaned back and took a good look. "That him? I don't remember seeing—"

"Take my word for it. That's Curly. What the heck's he doing out here? Why's he hanging around?"

"Call Hunter, quick," she ordered. "I know he wants to talk to the man."

Which I did. But Hunter didn't answer and I was mad all over again and stammered into his voice mail that the man was right there at the memorial service and maybe he should get his mind back on solving this murder. I hung up, mad and wondering if we were ever going to get Eugene's death settled with our sheriff's deputies so busy with other things.

Elizabeth's limo started up right then and sped away. The dark man dissolved into the dark of the woods, and Mama took off, talking to herself about needing to get back to the farm and having had just about enough of the whole Wheatley family.

Since Mama had to drop me off at the Nut House, she drove straight up Carya Street, where there was more traffic that made her mad. I just held myself together, having had about enough of everybody for one day. I planned a couple of hours on my computer, maybe going over the files I'd been able to get set up and coming up with a few ideas for that article I was going to write for the journal. A little peace and quiet would do me well. Meemaw could deal with Hunter. Justin could see to Jeannie. I was going to take care of myself and mind my own business from there on in.

That's what I was thinking when Mama stopped at a traffic light and I looked over at The Squirrel and the people sitting in the front windows and saw Hunter sitting in a booth with "the blonde."

I didn't think what I was doing when I got out of the car and started back toward The Squirrel. In front of the big squirrel painted on the front window, I stopped, thinking I was going to compose myself, which proved not to be the case when I pulled the door open, brushed off Cecil's "Good evening," and walked directly to where Hunter and "the blonde" sat. I plunked down in their booth without a "by-your-leave." I smiled big at both of the startled people. Hunter fumbled around and then finally introduced me to Diana Richards, from Dallas, there for her brother-in-law's memorial.

I forgot what I was ready to launch into, stopped before my mouth got open.

"Brother-in-law?" I looked into the big blue eyes and stopped. "You're not related to Jeannie, are you?"

She shook her head and took a deep breath. "I'm Sally's sister. Sally was Eugene's first wife."

"Sally?" I acted as if I didn't know the name. "Sally? You mean Sally Wheatley?"

She nodded. "And you're Lindy Blanchard. Sally talked about you. Said you were the most fun in Riverville and that you were trying to do something for the pecan farmers. She was really impressed, from what she said."

My mouth must have been hanging open. Hunter reached over and closed it for me.

"I don't understand," I said and was sure I looked my confusion.

Meemaw came huffing in, saying she'd sent Mama on home and she hoped I had a bed upstairs in the apartment she could use for the night, since we were both stuck in town now. She pushed me to move over in the seat and sat down. I was thinking—while lost in a lot of confusion—that's where I get my pushiness from: Meemaw. She sure could fool people, with all her lady airs.

"You know who this is?" I turned to ask her.

She nodded. "We met once." She smiled over at Diana Richards then back at me. "Couldn't say anything about who she was. Hunter asked me not to."

Meemaw looked across the table at Hunter just as Cecil strolled up with four menus in his white little hands.

Hunter looked at the man and said something just came up and we were leaving, which was news to me. Cecil sniffed mightily and turned to me.

"I hope you're not making my restaurant into nothing more than a meeting place, Lindy. This is the second time—"

We were up and out of there and all piled into Hunter's scout car, heading for the Nut House and my apartment.

"Where we can talk," Hunter said as he pulled out into traffic. "Without you blowing a gasket."

Chapter Twenty-three

"You see, Lindy," Diana Richards began once I'd handed around glasses of sweet tea and a plate of Meemaw's Double Action Chocolate Chip and Pecan Cookies. "I never accepted Sally's death as an accident. Or maybe I should say, I thought somebody was trying to cover up something. I talked to Elizabeth about it, but she was too sad at that time to even think of such a thing—that's what she said. I hired a private detective. What he came up with was that they didn't know whose gun fired the bullet that hit Sally. It seems the game ranch, where they were shooting, only had one guide up in the hills with the whole group. They were shooting sika deer, and wandering around like they probably shouldn't have been. Everybody said the same thing, that the shot came out of nowhere, up in the hills. Nobody would say they were shooting at that time. I guess, because they couldn't think of anything else, the local police decided it had to be an accident. I'm still not so sure. And now, look what happened to Eugene."

I didn't know what to say, or think, and I was still mad at Hunter for not trusting me with this information and not ready to let it go.

"Why didn't you tell me who she was?" I turned on Hunter, a hint of suspicion still niggling at me—after all, Diana Richards sure was pretty.

"Couldn't. Until this morning she didn't want anybody to know she was in town."

"Sorry if I caused any trouble," Diana said, leaning back in her chair, drink in one hand, cookie in another. "I don't know what really happened to Sally, and to tell the truth, I was a little worried about even coming to the memorial today. If somebody saw me before . . . I mean, I'll bet anything Elizabeth isn't too happy with me. She knows I've still got questions about Sally's death and she sure doesn't want me here asking anything about Eugene's."

"I don't see why not," I said. "She wants this thing solved as bad as the rest of us."

"Elizabeth's kind of an odd . . . person," Diana went on. "But you know her. Wants everything neat and not messy, like what poor Eugene's memorial turned into. I'm just another mess to her right now."

"Too bad," Meemaw snorted.

"So." I was more interested in why she questioned Sally's death than in gossip about Elizabeth. "The police up there, in Ralston, near that game ranch, never got any real answer to who shot Sally. I didn't know any of that. Sally was a friend of mine. I just, well . . ."

Hunter lifted an eyebrow at me.

I turned back to Diana. "Who was there that day, shooting?"

"There were six or eight people in the group, is what I was told. Eugene and Sally. Elizabeth was there, too. She's an avid hunter. The rest were friends of both Eugene and Elizabeth."

"Do you have a list of names?"

She shook her head. "The game ranch wouldn't give it to the detective I hired. I guess we could ask Elizabeth. She's the only one who was there we can put a name to, and is still alive."

"I've been working on it, Lindy," Hunter said. "Miss Amelia's been checking, too. Even got a few names from Elizabeth."

I looked over at my meemaw. "How'd you do that?"

"Offered to send out notices of the memorial service to her friends in Dallas. Asked about Sally's friends. Brought up the hunting accident and came right out and asked her who was out there with them. She named two couples and said to be sure and invite them to the memorial. Said she figured anybody on that hunting trip would want to come see Eugene off." She hesitated. "Don't know if any of them were there tonight. In all that uproar, I didn't get a chance to check the memorial book."

"Couldn't you just go ask her, Hunter?" I asked.

"She's not a whole lot of help. Seems this battle over the money's made her skittish, like she doesn't want to give out anything to anybody. Had trouble just getting basic facts about people at the party out of her."

"Anybody named Curly on the hunt?"

Hunter shook his head. "If he was, then Elizabeth's been lying to me, that she didn't know him. Still, I've been looking into the man."

"You know he's been hanging around town?"

"Yeah, you told me."

"We saw him right after the memorial. He was standing across from the church, in the woods. I think Elizabeth saw him, too. Anyway, her limo stopped and then sped off."

"And he was near you yesterday." Meemaw thought a long time then looked over at Hunter.

"What I think your grandmother is getting at, Lindy, is maybe the man's after you now. I don't know why or what's going on in the man's head, but you see him yesterday and then today, outside the church. One thing I think we'd better do is make sure you've got somebody with you at all times until this is cleared up."

"Why me? I don't know him. Never saw him before in my life. I think you're both jumping at spooks. Coincidence. Maybe he was a friend of Eugene's and didn't want to come to the memorial for whatever reason."

"A friend?" Meemaw's eyebrows shot up. "He was a waiter at the party, Lindy. Not a friend."

"Well, yes, but—"

"Be careful. Don't go anywhere alone for a while," Hunter said. "And I was thinking of something else. What do you say to coming into the sheriff's office tomorrow morning. I'll get an artist in there. Maybe you can come up with a sketch that looks like him. I'll get a BOLO out to departments across Texas. Don't want to scare the guy. I just need to talk to him."

I agreed and mentioned Chantal. She'd seen him and could probably identify him better than I could. Hunter agreed to call her and get her into the department in the morning, along with me, to put together a composite picture of "Curly."

Hunter was going to drop Diana off at her hotel and then offered to take Meemaw back out to the ranch so she could sleep in her own bed. I was grateful all the way around, and especially grateful to Diana, now that I knew who she really was, and was happy to meet Sally's sister, and just plain glad to have my life settle back into what it used to be, with Hunter in it again. Well, almost. We still didn't get a chance to talk about how close we almost came to being enemies. And if we were going to get past all of that. And if we had a future. Three questions that kept me awake that night. I hoped they were keeping Hunter awake, too. In his own house. In his own bed—by himself. No, I forgot about his awful dog.

Chapter Twenty-four

After I met Hunter and Chantal at the sheriff's office the next morning and argued back and forth about what the man looked like, we came up with a pretty good drawing of him. Looked right to me. Chantal wasn't sure, changing her mind about the thick eyebrows, making them thinner at the last minute, then arguing with me about whether his hair was parted on the right side, the way I thought. She thought the left. Despite all of that, the woman artist came up with a good likeness and I was out of there, back to the ranch and checking in with Martin about the trees. There'd been a problem with one of the irrigation lines in the greenhouse, but he'd called the company and a man was on his way to fix it. I walked through my test grove, stopping to look at the three-year-old trees I was banking my reputation on—the three GraKing cultivars grafted with the Elliott I'd been able to fortify with a different genome. I would write my article based on these three trees, looking just a little droopy that morning, which made my heart leap up and down a little—or whatever happens in your chest when you get scared that you've inflated your importance as a scientist and are about to be proven wrong.

At my desk I started looking for the book on the Gra-King/Elliott experiments. I would base everything on what I did, how I did it, compare this set to other cultivars I've used, the timetable, watering schedule or lack of watering, even about that first scare—that they were dying. Then their resurrection, their growth rate—all preliminary to the first budding, and to an eventual crop of pecans. But that would be another paper. I hoped so hard that last paper would be the one about the complete success: drought resistant, scab resistant, a perfect crop every two years, and a time of prosperity for the pecan farmers. Not like the bad years my daddy and his daddy went through. When spring buds withered from lack of rain or when the nuts inside the shells turned black from fungus. Those were years when money was tight. When families lost their farms. When neighbors sold the groves for what they could get and moved away. All of that made a big impact on me. Going to see a friend, Lucy Kordes, for the last time. The tears running down her mother's face. Her daddy's grim smile and hard handshake before they climbed in their truck and drove away. And my own daddy, the year of a terrible drought, when it hadn't rained more than a half-inch all spring. I stood out in the groves with him and watched the sad, drooping trees with no blossoms.

I'd vowed then to do something about it if I could. I was little, didn't know what on earth I was talking about—until I got to Texas A&M and found that maybe there was something I could do. Found that men and women scientists were working on all kinds of projects to make farming easier. I felt, that first year, like I'd found a brave new world, right there in Texas. I wanted in. I changed my major to bioengineering and genome research and never looked back.

I usually kept my record book in the files. Sometimes it was out on my desk—if I was working on it. I checked both places. Nothing. Martin never touched my files, or even looked at my record books on the various experiments. Couldn't have been him, taking it out of the greenhouse. Me again. Maybe back in my apartment. I sometimes worked from there when I didn't get enough done during the day. One thing I half agreed with Mama about: That I had no business moving into town when my work was at the ranch. What Mama didn't understand was that though I came back home instead of taking a job in a lab somewhere, I still wanted at least the feeling of independence. I would be thirty in a few years. Something about living at home and working at home smacked of being an old maid and that wasn't something I wanted to have to think about.

Before I headed back into town to get the book, I went into the locked test grove to check on my latest successes. The little trees, barely more than a few feet tall, were just as I'd left them. Still doing well. I thought I could see new budding along the stems. I checked the water gauge. Martin had added a little more water. Another month and we'd reduce the amount again, see when and if they could withstand drought and still thrive.

I felt at peace for the first time in days, listening to the late morning wind in the trees beyond my wooden fence. I felt the dry heat on my face. Everything was as it always was and always would be. Not like that outer world where terrible things like murder and anger kept coming at me. Out there, people hated one another and worried about squirreling away as much money as they could, and even killed for money. Out there people turned on old friends and new relatives because they got funny ideas in their heads.

Fear and jealousy, most of it. Then I thought about Sally again. A funny woman. The best kind of new friend. Loved to hear about my work. She was thinking about using some of the Wheatley money to fund projects that would make the lives of pecan farmers better. She talked to Eugene and he was all for it, starting with scholarships for kids. I felt the hole in my life all over again. Grieved for the kind of friends we could have been. Maybe that was why her sister, Diana, felt someone shot her deliberately, wanted her dead. Just because she missed her so much.

That face in the sketch came back at me. Why was he hanging around town? Maybe a mental case, not stalking me at all. Not really dangerous. Be creepy, to know someone was out there taking a strange interest in me the way Meemaw and Hunter thought.

That's where I was in my head when my cell rang.

I checked the ID. Hunter.

Well, that was a good start, I told myself, and felt pretty happy at that moment. Maybe we'd go somewhere for dinner—not The Squirrel. Maybe we'd talk for hours—the way we used to. I made my voice bright when I answered.

"Lindy?" he asked as if he hadn't heard my voice since he was a little squirt, just a little bigger than I was.

"You know it's me, Hunter. What's going on?"

"We found him."

"Who? You mean the dark man?"

"Yup. Found him this morning. Got a call from George Watson, out at the KB Ranch."

"He was staying with George? I don't get it."

"No, Lindy. George found the man in a front ditch. Shot through the back. Very dead, Lindy. Guess you don't have to be afraid anymore."

I was speechless.

"Lindy? You there?" Hunter sounded as if he was in a

hurry, which wasn't going to allow time for me to grasp another death.

"You're the only one who really knows what he looked like. Outside of Chantal. Think you could meet me at the ME's office? Identify him for us?"

I agreed, even though I was in a kind of shock. Another murder. If Diana Richards was right, this was number three.

Chapter Twenty-five

There was nothing pleasant about looking at a dead man closer than I liked looking at dead men. At least the dark man's face was intact, which was better than what my imagination had been flashing at me.

I did turn a funny shade of gray, I guess. At least that's what Hunter said when he led me out of the morgue.

"You need to sit down?" he asked.

We went to The Squirrel to have a cup of Cecil's coffee, which tasted like swamp mud warmed up a few times—with a few grounds on the bottom thrown in for good measure—great for setting people back on their feet.

Cecil Darling, the little man of little sympathies, made the snide remark that at least I ordered something, after coming in and walking out the last few times. "As if my wonderful little restaurant weren't good enough for a Blanchard." Of course there was a sniff to go with that, but Hunter gave him a look that sent him running to annoy other customers.

"The sheriff gave the story to the newspaper this morning, along with that sketch you came up with. It's going on TV at noon. We're hoping to get some calls. Somebody in town has to know him. He had to stay somewhere close, since he was hanging around. I've got the feeling finding out who he was will push this thing along."

He stopped to look over the menu, since it was close to noon. "Might as well have dinner here as anywhere, I guess," Hunter said. He put a hand up to call Cecil, who was much more congenial now that he'd seen us both taking in his menu.

"What's kedgeree?" Hunter asked, pointing to one of the daily handwritten items.

"A fine fish dish, made with fish and cream and rice and all of those wonderful things." Cecil was ecstatic as he shaped the dish in the air above our heads.

We ordered it. A kind of apology for upsetting him. Cecil seemed to accept the apology, even breaking into a rare smile. When the plates came, filled with bits of fish and hard-boiled egg and rice and cream, it was a surprise. We both liked it and told Cecil, then called over to people we both knew to try the kedgeree. After the strange but good dish, we settled down with sweet tea and crumpets as Hunter checked his watch.

"Be on TV by now. Hope we hear something soon."

Full and happy to be back with the man who made me more comfortable than anybody in the world, except Meemaw, I figured it was time to start figuring things out. So much going on.

"You know that lets the dark man out as Eugene's killer," I said. "Or we've got two of them."

"Could be. Can't cut out anything, Lindy. But if this Curly turns out to be Eugene's murderer, then I'm taking another look at Billy for killing Curly."

"Why? I like Billy. Look what he did yesterday, at the

memorial. He stood up to that awful mother of theirs. Carried her out as if she were a stray cat. Seemed like a hero to me, not a murderer."

"Think about it. Billy really loves his sister, standing up to that mother of his the way he did. If he found out who killed Eugene—who made Jeannie so sad, and a widow—don't you think he'd go after the man? Sure wouldn't come to me." He took the measure of what I was thinking, looking closely at my face.

"Or if we go back to 'who benefits,'" he went on, "like your grandmother keeps saying, all I see is Jeannie and her family. Elizabeth's not losing anything with her brother dead. In fact, from what I hear, she will get everything and Jeannie gets nothing. Some kind of family trust."

"Okay. So, you're saying Billy killed Curly. And you're saying Billy killed Eugene, too, for the money."

He took a couple of nervous swallows. "I'm thinking. Maybe Curly knew about Billy. Saw something there at the party and was blackmailing him, or his mother, or Jeannie. That's why he was hangin' around town."

"But Jeannie might not get anything now. So what did they gain?"

He shrugged. "Maybe they didn't realize there wasn't a new will in her favor."

I came back at him. "I don't think Jeannie had any part in this. I just won't believe it."

He shrugged again. "Believe what you want to. I'm going where likelihood takes me."

Cecil came to clear our dishes and offer dessert, which we turned down. We waited for him to move on before talking.

"Did you get a bullet from Curly's body?"

"We did. They're comparing it to the bullet that killed Eugene right now. If they come from the same gun, we've got the same killer." He blew his lips out in exasperation. "Billy."

"But what about Sally? Could her death have any connection to Eugene's?" I asked.

He shook his head. "No idea."

"Seems like too much coincidence, the two of them shot like that."

When his phone rang, he slid from the booth to take it outside where others couldn't hear. It was almost a relief to have him gone a minute. My head was aching from trying to sort through things. All I could think of was Meemaw. She had a way of laying facts straight and making a single picture out of a mess of uneven sticks.

"Things are moving," he said, excited, when he came back into the restaurant and slid in across from me. "Got two calls. I'll tell you outside."

"You want to go share all of this with Meemaw? She has this way of—"

Hunter smiled and reached out to take my hand. "Don't have to tell me. She's been straightening things out for me since I was a kid trying to find where I was going to fit in life."

"And she told you to be a cop?" I know I looked incredulous.

He shook his head. "Nope. She told me to be a rancher. But I don't like cows. There was something else she told me: 'Don't listen to anybody. Be your own man.' That's what did it. That's one smart woman."

Next stop was the Nut House.

Chapter Twenty-six

One thing I didn't think about was who would be lounging around in the Nut House that time of day. There was Miss Ethelred and Freda Cromwell, big as life and twice as loud. And didn't Ethelred lean back on the heels of her run-down shoes and squeeze her eyes almost shut when Hunter and I walked in.

"So you got another murder on your hands, Deputy. Telling you, listen to Freda and me here and you'll have this thing solved. Now some stranger's dead. Who do you think, but gun runners are doing it? I've got something to show you here." She opened her black bag and pulled out a folded newspaper, thrusting it toward Hunter. "Take a look at that article. *Houston Chronicle*. Says they caught men in Galveston setting up a gun deal. Bet you didn't see it. So stands to reason that's what we've got going on in Riverville. Bet anything that man you found dead killed Eugene trying to get the guns out of there and now the other runners got him.

Probably kept the money he was supposed to give Eugene. So easy, if you just look at things right."

"You really think Eugene Wheatley was that kind of man? That he would even know men like that?" I couldn't keep quiet. Hunter was too polite and it drove me crazy.

"Maybe you should stay out of this, Lindy. Leave it to the professionals." Ethelred turned away from me, her broad back a wall I wanted to thump as hard as I could thump.

Freda, beside her, elbow high, nodded and grinned at me. Freda had the kind of eyes that light up like little penlights and stay on you until you think you're going to go blind.

Hunter shook his head and smiled. "Well, ladies, I sure do appreciate all your help, but the thing is, the courts want us to find proof before we go around arresting people."

"Look for those gun runners, I'm telling you." Ethelred turned to Hunter. "You'll find all the proof you want. Bet anything they've got messages they've been sending between them. Might be in some other language, but I figure you'll know somebody who can speak Colombian or whatever."

"Yes, ma'am." Hunter tipped his head. "I'll keep all of that in mind."

"Humph," Ethelred said and crossed her arms in front of her. "Do as you like, but you'll be sorry when people keep dying around here."

Meemaw came from the kitchen and rescued us, inviting us back for coffee and one of her just-out-of-the-oven pecan rolls, which sounded wonderful, but Hunter suggested we go up to my apartment to talk. Somehow the Nut House leaked gossip like a sieve.

Treenie Menendez came from the kitchen to take over for Meemaw with the customers. I saw her eye Ethelred and Freda and purse her lips. "You go on, Miss Amelia," Treenie said, almost gleefully. "I'll clean this place out pretty quick."

And I bet she would—pretty quick, moving Ethelred and

Freda to the rocking chairs on the front porch so she could sweep or mop or some excuse to get them out of there.

Meemaw brought the hot pecan rolls up with her. She knew the quickest way to Hunter's heart was through his love of pecan anything. I could see her watching the two of us in my tiny kitchen, eyes going back and forth until she knew it was real and then her face lit up—at least we were friends again. She set a huge pecan roll—dripping with glaze and tiny bit of pecans running over the cinnamon and sugar, and dough as light as a cloud—on a paper plate for each of us.

"So here's where we stand," Hunter started when he could talk again. I had to reach over to pick pecan bits out of his chin whiskers. There was no taking him seriously looking like a kid who got caught stealing from the kitchen.

"You heard that dark man was found dead this morning, over to the Watsons." He was talking to Meemaw. "Shot once. We got the bullet. I heard from ballistics a little time ago. The bullet's not from the same gun that killed Eugene."

"Didn't expect that," Meemaw said, a worried look moving over her face. "We don't usually have a whole lot of killers going around Riverville shooting people. Now we've got two."

"Could be the murderer just used a different gun on Eugene."

"Could be. But I kind of doubt it. Jobs like that, you'd want a gun you're familiar with."

"Then, like I was telling Lindy, I'm looking close at Billy Truly."

She dropped her head into her hands for a minute, thinking, then thumped her hands on the table, jiggling her cup. "How about Sally's death? Could Eugene's and Sally's deaths be connected?"

"That's what Lindy was asking. I'll get on that one, though Sally's death was ruled an accident at the inquest.

Be hard to prove different now. Too many miles and too many years between all of this."

He looked over at me. "Like I said before. I got two phone calls. We got a hit on the news program. Miss Lydia Hornbecker called the station, said she recognized the man we want information on. He was rooming at her boardinghouse. Said his name is Henry Wade. Wrote on her register he was from El Paso. Been with her a couple of weeks now."

"Lydia Hornbecker?" Meemaw sat back. "I've known Lydia since I first came to live in Riverville. Worked together a hundred times on bake sales for the church. Lydia makes the best apple pie you ever tasted. Almost beat me out in the pie contest at the fair a couple of times. Why, I'd love to go talk to Lydia. Had to take in borders since Sam died a few years ago. But she's got a flair for takin' care of people. I'd like to see her, if you're heading over there and you don't mind."

And so the three of us were sitting on Miss Hornbecker's veranda a half hour later, going over her register of boarders and listening to her description of Henry Wade as a nice man who never caused her the least bit of trouble. "Cleaned his room for himself so all I had to do was change his bed every couple of days and give him fresh towels. You know, Miss Amelia, I found these dryer sheets that puff towels up like brand-new. Be happy to write down the kind, if you want it."

Meemaw was, of course, interested, but a little more interested in Henry Wade.

"Did he say he knew anybody in Riverville?" Meemaw asked as Hunter made notes.

Miss Hornbecker thought awhile. "Henry wasn't a talkative man, ya know. Kept to himself mostly. I didn't ask him questions 'cause I thought that would be pryin'."

"Did you notice anything in his room that wasn't right, when you did go in there?"

She thought again then shook her head. "He kept his room neat as a pin. Nothing ever layin' around like some people. You wouldn't believe how sloppy some are. And not just the men. Why, I've had women stay here leavin' a trail of powder behind them. Lipstick smears on the towels. I asked one to leave after two days because the smell of her perfume went all through my house. You wouldn't believe how I was sneezin'. Took me days to clear it out."

"Everything in his room just the way he left it?"

She nodded. "Saw the picture on the TV and knew enough to leave that room locked until you got over here." She was talking to Hunter.

"You mind if we go up?" he asked.

"Sure. All three of you, if you want. What you're gonna find is what he brought here with him. One suitcase. A long leather case—think it has to be a shotgun. I asked him and he told me he'd been hunting before he got to Riverville. Oh, and some kind of case I took for one of those computer things. Never asked me about Internet or anything. None of that password stuff. But y'all go on up and take a look. Only thing is, Hunter, you take anything out of there, I need some kind of receipt. There might be relatives coming and I don't want to be accused of stealing."

With that agreement, we made our way up a narrow staircase leading from the back of the house. Our weight made the stairs creak. Hunter's boots landed with heavy thuds that brought other boarders to their doors as we passed. That meant explaining again what we were doing there. A couple of the women seemed struck dumb when they heard a murdered man had been living amongst them.

Curly's room was bare but serviceable and neat. The bed was covered with a homemade spread made of different-colored quilt squares. I was willing to bet some of them were from collections Miss Hornbecker inherited from long-dead relatives. Next to the bed was a nightstand with a swivel lamp on it. There was a mahogany dresser, a chair and a floor lamp, and a small desk with one of those green bank lights sitting on top. The room was as neat as Miss Hornbecker had said. Nothing out of place. Nothing lying around. Nothing personal anywhere to be seen. I figured the dresser drawers and closet, maybe the bathroom, were the only places we would find anything.

Hunter nodded to Miss Hornbecker and told her we'd be down with a list of things we were taking. He had to back her out of the room. I could see she was reluctant to leave us alone rummaging through things she might be responsible for, but she got a promise from Meemaw not to make a mess and was gone, stopping along the hall, we heard, to reassure the other boarders things were under control.

The closet yielded the most: a suitcase tied with straps, something like a duffel bag. There was a computer case with an Apple computer in it, along with pads of notes and drawings. And there was that gun case, holding a rifle. Hunter didn't pull it all the way from the case.

"AR15," Hunter said, holding gun and case in his hands. "The military uses them. SWAT teams. Uses full metal jacket cartridges—like the gun we found in Eugene's gun room. It's accurate at a pretty good distance. Could be the one we're looking for."

He set the gun against the wall. "Fingerprints first," he said. "Then we'll get it to ballistics."

He wrote the gun down on the list for Miss Hornbecker.

"I'm taking everything," he said. "The man's dead. Who knows what we'll find here? Maybe the names of people he worked for . . ."

"Are you buying into what Ethelred Tomroy and Freda Cromwell are saying?" Meemaw gave him a shocked look.

"'Course not, but I don't know who he is, where he's really from, or why he was hanging around town. Didn't have a driver's license on him when he died. No Social Security card. Nothing."

"Then let's go through everything here," Meemaw said.

"I'm afraid I shouldn't let you go through anything, Miss Amelia. I'll get in a whole heap of trouble with the sheriff if I do that. I'm asking you to just note what I'm taking out and wait to hear what we find. I promise I'll let you know."

"I'm standing here now." Meemaw fixed him with one long look. "One peek isn't going to mess up anything."

"It's not so much me stopping you, Miss Amelia. It's about the defense attorney when we get whoever killed him. He'll be throwing fits if he knows you two were even up here."

She nodded and I agreed. There was the future trial to think of.

"Then you'll let me know what's here as soon as you find out yourself?" Meemaw gave in and Hunter agreed, giving his word. "The sheriff knows what a help you've been to us in the past. He's not going to mind—long as we follow procedure when we have to.

"Tell you one thing," he went on. "I'll get deputies out talking to the waiters and such from the party. See if any of them know anything about this Henry Wade."

"Back at the Nut House you said you got two phone calls," I asked before leaving. "What was the other one?"

Hunter gave me a sheepish grin. "Forgot to tell you. Your mama called, said you weren't answering your phone. That Dr. Franklin was out to your ranch wanting to talk to you. He was going to wait awhile . . ." Hunter looked at his watch. "That was two hours ago. Guess he's gone now."

I could have been mad at him, but I wasn't. "Let him wait. I don't much like the man and don't have a clue why he keeps hanging around me. Seems he's taken to Elizabeth Wheatley. He's with her every time I see her now."

Hunter nodded, both abashed and satisfied at the same time. I guess jealousy isn't something any of us want to admit about ourselves.

Chapter Twenty-seven

Back on Miss Hornbecker's front porch, Hunter turned to Meemaw, looking a little guilty.

"Miss Amelia," he said, his head down. "I didn't mean to shut you out the way I did. Suppose you come with me back to the sheriff's office and we look at the man's things together. If you don't mind waiting while I go up and get the suitcase . . ."

He was carrying the computer and gun case.

"I've already got an idea what you're going to find, Hunter. You don't need me for that and I got pies to make for a banquet this evening. We know that gun was there for some reason. I'd say it'll match the bullet that killed Eugene. Maybe I'm wrong." She shrugged. "I kind of doubt it, though. I'm thinking the murders of Eugene and Sally are tied together. Can't get it out of my head. And thinking about it, it has to be somebody here in town Wade was hanging around to see. Maybe Elizabeth. She's the third in the family. Maybe he was supposed to kill her, too."

"Said 'accident' about Sally's death," Hunter reminded her.

"And I'd say right back: Take another look."

Hunter nodded.

"I think that's settled then." Meemaw was ready to get back to her work. "Seems this man's job wasn't finished or he'd have been long gone. We find out what he was doing here and who he was after, I think your case will be closed."

"And I'll bet you another thing," she added. "Billy Truly's not involved in any of this. I know people pretty well after all the years running the Nut House. More than likely, if you check with Huntsville, Billy was in there 'cause he got in the middle of something he shouldn't have. And I'll bet you something else—that mother of his had some part in it, too. I've seen women like her a million times. Tie their sons to 'em closer than a husband and then lead them around like puppy dogs, but they don't love 'em. Don't know how to love anybody."

Hunter said, "I hope you know you're blowin' holes in everything I've been thinking."

"I don't mean to interfere, it's just that if Sally was murdered instead of being accidentally shot, Jeannie and her family weren't even in the picture back then. Takes them right off the front burner, I'd say."

"Speaking of Jeannie, I want to get out and see her today," I said, realizing it was what I should be doing. "See how she's doing and see how the legal business is progressing and how she's getting along with the Chaunceys."

"Aren't you going to the farm to see Dr. Franklin? He's been waiting a couple of hours by now." Hunter's concern for Peter struck an insincere note.

I shrugged the suggestion off. "Let him wait. He doesn't know half what I know about propagation or much of anything else. I think he's pumping me for information. Something going on with that man."

Meemaw agreed. "Got the same feeling from him. You

go on out and see the Chaunceys and Jeannie. I'm going over to have a talk with Ben Fordyce, see if he found out anything about what Elizabeth's pulling on Jeannie. Think he'll give me the rough edges of it even if he can't tell me specifics. You know, money always seems to be at the heart of bad feelings in a family. Well, money, and not getting the love a person needs." She took a breath. "First back to the Nut House. Can't forget those pies. Jack Holmes with the pecan co-op'll be over in a couple of hours to pick them up. You two call me with whatever you find out. Maybe I'll see you at home later, Lindy."

"I'll be there. I lost a valuable record book I need for an article I'm writing. Got to check my apartment first."

"Not like you to lose things," Hunter said, then smiled. "Except your shoes—down by the river; and your math book in school; and your sunglasses and your purse and—"

"My virginity."

I knew that would shut him up all the way back to the Nut House, where he dropped me and Meemaw off.

Hurrying up the steps of the wide porch filled with rockers, me and Meemaw were laughing though she elbowed me hard when she saw Miss Ethelred and Freda rocking amid a circle of friends. They looked our way, calling out, asking what we thought was so funny.

What can you do but stop and make up a lie to keep all the watchers happy?

Meemaw was on her way over to see Ben Fordyce after the pies were made. I was still upstairs, hunting for the book, then changing into shorts and a halter. The day was hot, hot, hot, and I felt clammy, my hair sticking to the back of my neck. I brushed it up into a ponytail, ran a cold washrag over my face and arms, and was out to my truck and on the road to the Chaunceys' ranch.

On the way, I checked the phone calls I'd missed. Three from Mama so I called her and told her where I was going.

"You know that Dr. Franklin's been sitting out in the back, waiting. I'm too busy to deal with him right now. Got orders for the pecans coming in right and left. He wants to sit there, that's fine with me. Asked if he could go on out to your greenhouse. I said no, nobody goes out there without permission. Hope that was all right. I know he's a friend of yours, but to tell you the truth, Lindy, I don't much like the man. What people are saying is he's suckin' up to Elizabeth because of her money. Maybe she's not much of a warm person, still I don't like seeing her taken for a fool."

Leave it to Mama. Chip off the old block. Or maybe, I was thinking, the nut doesn't fall far from the tree. Something like that. If she wasn't so busy running Rancho en el Colorado, where my grandfather used to raise cattle and now the family is firmly into pecan farming, I swear she'd be as good a detective as Meemaw.

"Could you, please, go tell him I'm not coming home today. Got too much to do." I hesitated. "And Mama, would you call Martin and tell him to keep an eye out, in case Dr. Franklin decides to go to the greenhouse anyway? Tell him to send him away. Just say I don't allow anybody out there when I'm not around. Okay?"

"Take care of it right now. Will I see you later?"

"I don't know, Mama. Maybe for supper."

By this time I was through the gates of the Chauncey Ranch and heading out the dusty two-track toward their house.

I groaned when I saw the blue car parked in front. Not the Trulys. I thought they'd be banned from the place. Now me and Jeannie wouldn't get anything talked about, not with Wanda and Billy listening. I couldn't imagine Wanda not having a comment on everything I said.

Melody was out of her chair first, waving and yelling she

was going in to get me some "honest tea." That was her name for iced tea with just a little Garrison's Bourbon in it—enough to take away your cares, whether they be the heat, or rain, a fight with your sister, or putting up with the likes of Wanda Truly. I yelled back I sure would appreciate it and joined the others, hugging Miranda and Jeannie and nodding to the other two. We exchanged pleasantries like "How you feeling?" and "How are you doing?" and "How do you like this heat?" and "Wasn't it awful about that man found dead this morning?"

"What kind of a town you got here, Lindy?" Wanda Truly was quick to sneer. "Seems like y'all keep killin' one another off."

"Mama," Jeannie chided.

"Seems like it, doesn't it, Ms. Truly? But this one's a stranger. Nobody knows him."

"I seen him on the TV," Wanda went on. "He was at Jeannie's party. Did you know that?"

"You weren't there, Mama. How'd you see—"

"I saw him 'cause I was out in the kitchen." Wanda slapped her hands together. "Wasn't invited to my own daughter's wedding celebration so I got myself a place helping the cook serve up the buffet."

"Mama!"

"She did," Billy put in, rocking slow as molasses, eyes shut. "Wanted me to do it, too. I told her 'no.' It was your special day, Jeannie. Think you about had enough of us."

"So you were that extra helper I heard about?" I said as if I didn't already know.

Wanda nodded. "Came in my own clothes. No servant's uniform or anything like that. I have my pride even though my own children don't think I deserve much."

"That's not true . . ." Jeannie frowned. Her voice was weary.

"Seems to me it is. Not even invited. Your own mother."

"How much longer are we gonna have to hear about it, Mama?" Billy said.

"Well, I'd like to see . . ."

Jeannie turned to me and asked if I'd come out about anything special, just as Melody slammed the screen door behind her and put a sweating glass wrapped in a white paper napkin into my hand.

I took a swig because I needed something fast. Three minutes with Wanda Truly and I was about to lose it. What I did was nod at Jeannie and try pretending there was no human being sitting in Wanda's chair. If the chair kept on mumbling things, I could just pretend it was all an illusion.

"Well, I did come out to ask you some questions," I said to Jeannie. "I kept seeing that Curly around town. Hunter was getting the idea he might be after me for some reason."

I noticed Wanda was stuck forward, holding her rocker still with her feet. She was taking in every word I said.

I leaned toward Jeannie. "Maybe we could go someplace else. This is information Hunter probably doesn't want out yet."

I was talking to Jeannie, but that didn't stop Wanda.

"You get his real name?" she demanded. "All he'd tell us was 'Curly.' Said to call him that."

"Why don't the two of you go on inside?" Miranda got up slowly, with just a little tight menace to her ample body. "Come on, I'll clear a couple of chairs for the two of you to sit in the big front room and talk in private."

"Well, I don't see . . ." Wanda protested.

Miranda stood tall, thumbs settling into the waistband of her khakis. She looked down her nose at Wanda. "Don't think you see a lot of things, Wanda. Beginning with what a pain in the petooties you can be."

We escaped into the house ahead of Miranda, taking seats at their big table and pushing stuff out of our way.

"Here's what's going on," I started. "The man's name is Henry Wade. We found a gun case in the closet of one of Lydia Hornbeck's rooms. That's where he was boarding. They already got the ballistics back on the bullet that killed him. Wasn't the same gun as the one that killed Eugene. Now we're all thinking maybe Sally's death had something to do with this."

"Sally!"

"Did you and Eugene ever talk about it?"

"He told me what happened that day, directly after we met. Took him a long time to get over Sally. Well, I don't think he was really over her yet. That was awful for him and memories of it haunted him. I heard she was really a special girl."

I nodded. "I thought she was funny and kind. Did he ever mention that maybe her death wasn't an accident?"

She shook her head slowly. "After that one time, he didn't talk about it at all."

"Did they have any enemies that you know of?"

"You mean Eugene and Sally? Or just Eugene?"

"Either one."

She shook her head. "Eugene had a lot of friends. We weren't married that long—a couple of weeks. If he had enemies, he didn't tell me about them."

"What do you think about the relationship between Eugene and Elizabeth? Was it really close?"

She sighed. "I don't think Elizabeth liked me at all. That made it hard on us. Eugene just wanted to get back to Dallas, maybe close up things there and move pretty fast. Or he said if Elizabeth went away, we'd come back here. Just so we weren't too close to her. She's got a way of taking over things. Like that party. Eugene and I didn't want it much. We're not . . . weren't . . . that kind of showy people. Still, she's his sister and she thought there should be something."

"So it was her idea."

She nodded. "She did everything, saying she knew I wouldn't know how to handle a party that size and she had all this experience."

I waited just a minute. "And that yellow dress you wore."

"Yellow Rose of Texas. I thought it was nice."

"But you know the history behind the Yellow Rose of Texas."

"I do now. Maybe Elizabeth doesn't know it, though. She's the one got it for me."

I remembered when she said it was Elizabeth's idea. Her own sister-in-law making a fool out of her at her wedding celebration.

"I noticed that Elizabeth didn't have a date there with her. Doesn't she usually have some kind of escort?"

"I thought her escort was that Dr. Franklin. They seemed kind of friendly."

"She say anything about him? Did she introduce him as her date or what have you?"

"Just introduced him around, kind of holding on to his arm. Then I saw him talking to you and I heard . . . well, that you two were out to dinner . . . and I didn't know what to think."

"Me either. He's been the one taking her everywhere since Eugene died. Guess maybe they became friends. Happened to meet and he asked her about me, because we're in the same profession." I was trying to put things together.

"Still and all . . ." She seemed to drop into deep thought.

"He's not staying there with Elizabeth, is he?"

"Not that I know of. But then I've been gone from the house a few days and so much has been going on." She waited a minute. "Anything else?"

"What's all this legal stuff Elizabeth's been talking about? Did Ben find out anything?"

She nodded. "A family trust. I guess all the money's in it and the house and a couple of apartments in Dallas and a boat and all the cars and just about everything. Ben says I'll get some of it, as Eugene's wife, but Eugene didn't put me in directly as a trust holder so Elizabeth will get most. That's what Elizabeth claims, which is kind of strange. I remember Eugene saying he was going into Dallas to make sure I got taken care of if something happened to him. That was the morning of the party. Maybe he just forgot."

"Doesn't seem right."

"Ask Mama if she thinks it's right. She's been having fits. Threatening to find the best lawyer in the county, all of that stuff. I'm tired. I just want this over. I want to go someplace and start my life again. Eugene didn't owe me anything. Elizabeth's right about that. A few weeks of marriage. I was thinking if we ever had a baby, that would be the time to get me and the baby covered somehow. Guess I'm naïve, the way Mr. Fordyce says. It was never about the money, not with me. It is with Mama. Driving me crazy."

I believed she was innocent of everything happening around her. And I believed she was naïve—maybe too much for her own good.

I sat back, looking at Jeannie's open and sad face and wished I could go back outside, on that porch, pick up a big broom, and chase Wanda Truly out over the Chaunceys' hills until she could never find her way back.

Chapter Twenty-eight

The notebook wasn't anywhere. I told myself I could remember most of it—for the article—but really I knew I couldn't duplicate the watering: amounts, times, withdrawals, increases. That took solid facts behind it. Awful, that I was that careless. Not what a dedicated scientist should do—be so unprofessional as to lose data backing up experiments.

I walked through the greenhouse, checking the stainless steel tables, in case I'd laid the book down somewhere. Nothing there but my yellow pods of seedlings and pots of newly developed saplings.

No notebook. I had a deadline facing me. I had to have the article in to the journal at least six months ahead of the publication date. It had to be vetted by other scientists. There would be questions to answer and maybe even challenges. How could I defend my work without records to back up what I'd done? It wouldn't matter, in the long run, if the trees were what I hoped they'd turn out to be: drought resistant, scab resistant—all the things that killed off blossoms and nuts and even the trees themselves. It was my ego prodding me. I wanted credit for my work before someone else grabbed it. All along I'd told myself the effort was only for the good of the pecan farmers and here I was, needing to be known for the breakthrough. One thing I was finding out about me: I was no selfless Mother Teresa after all.

Since I was going to have supper with my family at the ranch house, I stopped over at the Sanchezes' place to talk to Martin, and visit with Juanita and Jessie.

First thing we did was hug all around and catch up on the news. Juanita was cooking supper. The frying peppers about did my eyes in. The house was thick with the aroma of spice. Juanita invited me to stay and I would have loved to, but I'd promised Mama I'd be there that night. It seemed everyone I knew had something they wanted to talk about.

Jessie was helping her mother, a colorful apron wrapped around her as she cooked tortillas on her mother's battered old pan, flipping them as they bubbled and browned. I'd helped out many times in this kitchen. The smells were comforting. Even if my eyes burned, it felt good being there.

Martin was sitting at the table going over the newspaper. He pointed to the dark man's sketch. "I know I've seen him around. Maybe in town. Or over at the Wheatleys' when Elizabeth asked me if I could pick up some serving pieces from a rental place in Columbus."

Martin shrugged. "I just know I've seen him before."

I turned to Jessie. "Did you see the sketch?"

She nodded.

"He isn't that man who asked about me at the library, is he?"

She shook her head slowly. "No, I told you, that one was

more like that man at The Squirrel. The one with Elizabeth at the memorial."

"Dr. Franklin?"

"I would say he fits the description."

I got right to the notebook, asking Martin to please keep an eye out for it.

"The last time I noticed that book, it was on your desk. Right before that Dr. Franklin came to visit. Maybe that's where you should look. Call him. Maybe he picked it up then stuck it somewhere without thinking."

Of course. That's who was alone in my greenhouse before I got there. That's the only person within miles who would be interested, maybe stuck it in his jacket by mistake . . .

Or not by mistake. I didn't trust anybody at this point.

Except my family, and the Sanchezes, and Hunter . . .

And Meemaw, and Justin, and Mama, and . . .

So many.

"HAVE I SEEN YOUR NOTEBOOK? WHY, WHAT A QUESTION, Lindy!"

I called him at a number I had on my cell, from his previous calls. I wasn't accusing him of anything, just asking.

"It's been gone since that day you were out here and I wondered if you picked it up by mistake."

"I'm not in the habit of pocketing items when I am a guest. In fact, I'm rather hurt to have you asking."

"I told you about that article I'm working on. Without my record book on these specimens, I won't have proof . . ."

"Dear, dear, dear. I see the problem. I wish I could help. Are you certain you've looked everywhere? I mean, we can be so absentminded when we're in the midst of one of these discoveries. Ah, the hope. Don't you find it appalling how single-minded we get?"

Since I found nothing appalling about doing the job I'd

set out to do and since I was hungry and wanted to get off the phone, I ended the conversation when he was about to go on about some self-puffery that would make him come out looking good.

All that was left to me was to decide when to call the journal editor and admit I had nothing to send.

Chapter Twenty-nine

Supper was set when I walked in. My family ringed the huge trestle table where a tureen of Meemaw's spicy, hot pecan soup sat steaming.

"Hunter called for you. Didn't want to bother you if you were working. Could you call him back after you eat?" Mama smiled her tired smile and lifted an eyebrow at me. "Looks like you two are friends again."

I took a seat between Justin and Bethany and held my bowl out to Meemaw to be filled. And a plate of tortillas to go with it. Nice, that I didn't miss anything by not eating with the Sanchezes.

I rolled my eyes at Mama. She sure did push about the marriage thing. As if hers had been so splendid, with my daddy being murdered in the grove and her having to take over running the farm—at least all the bookwork, the sales, the ordering, and mailing. Tough job. I always wondered what would have happened if she'd stayed in Dallas, with Meemaw and my grandfather, who was a state senator. What if Mama never met my daddy? Sure would've been an easier life for her. Trouble with that was Mama loved the groves as much as the rest of us, and wouldn't I have hated living in a city.

But then there wouldn't have been a "me." No Justin. No Bethany. I looked around at this family I loved so much and gave them all a silly smile, which made Justin frown, Bethany cluck her tongue, and Mama purse her lips, waiting for an answer about me and Hunter.

"Yes, Mama, me and Hunter are friends again."

"Can I start planning a wedding in the tent anytime soon?" Bethany stuck her nose in.

"You getting married?"

"I was only asking."

"Anything happens in that department, you'll be the first to know."

"Maybe you should start bringing that boy over to supper more often," Mama said. "Seems like we don't see him half enough."

The rest of the talk was about the dark man's murder and who on earth was killing people in Riverville. Meemaw led most of that conversation, leaving out a lot of information we'd learned earlier, and turning the conversation neatly from the murders in town around to what the county fair committee was coming up with this year, including an appearance by Randy Travis, which made me think about asking Hunter to go with me.

I didn't call Hunter until I got back to my apartment. I had questions for him, and things to tell him. Most of that I forgot when he launched into what he'd learned about the dead man.

"Sheriff Higsby thinks we're getting close to solving most of what's been happening."

"How's that?" I asked, hoping the sheriff was right.

"First of all—the fingerprints. Name is really Henry Wade. No lie about that. Forty-three years old. Got a record in Dallas: larceny from a building, malicious destruction of property, attempted manslaughter. He got off on that last one. Let's see here. There's an assault and battery charge—when he was in his twenties. Did time on that one.

"Born in El Paso. Seems he's got some family there. Somebody's going out to talk to them and break the news. We've got a whole batch of questions we want answered—like who his friends are, what he was doing here in Riverville, did he know anybody around here—things like that."

"What about the gun?"

"Let me finish, okay? Just heard from the lab about the rifle. The bullet's a match with the bullet that killed Eugene Wheatley."

"What? You mean this Henry Wade killed Eugene?"

"That's what it looks like. Checked with the Defense Department, seeing if he was in the service. Turns out he was a Marine. Honorable discharge. Special forces. Sharpshooter . . ."

"Oh, my God. Have you talked to Elizabeth yet?"

"Not yet."

"It's all so—"

"I know."

"You want to come on over and talk?"

"About the case?"

"About anything you want to talk about."

"How about your virginity?"

"I was only joking."

"Still, seems as good a topic as any if we're going to get back together."

"What do you mean 'if'?"

"Give me a half hour," he said and hung up.

Chapter Thirty

He brought the dog to my apartment. The animal eyed me and I eyed him. I think I won because he laid down on my kitchen floor and went right to sleep.

"What are we going to do with him? I don't have room for a dog here."

Hunter shrugged and spread his hands. "Nothing, I guess. Can't leave him home. He howls and the neighbors call the sheriff."

Hunter was hungry, as usual, and all I had were three eggs, a few slices of hard bread, lots of pecan butter, and a brick of cheese. The toast would only get harder in the toaster and the pecan butter would cover that. The cheese called for more toast. And a pitcher of sweet tea.

I made all of it while stepping back and forth across the dog, who awoke at the smell of food and sat next to Hunter's chair.

"What do you call him?" I asked, giving the long-haired animal the fish-eye.

"Flasher. He answers to it—when he answers at all."

"Where'd you get that name?"

"I used to have a dog named Flasher."

"You name that one, too?"

He shook his head. "No. My mama did. Don't know why."

"So now you've got a second Flasher. Seems right for a cop."

As we discussed the dog, his head swung back and forth—from Hunter to me and around again. I could have sworn he got what we were talking about, but then I decided he was clueless because I didn't want to think of a dog as smart as I was.

"You staying the night?" I asked, the way I'd ask any friend to sleep over.

"Thought so. If you don't mind."

"Mind? Why should I mind?"

He nodded at the dog. "He's kind of used to sleeping in bed with me."

"I've only got one bed."

"Maybe on the sofa then."

"You and him? On my sofa?"

Hunter laughed. "No. You and me on the sofa. Flasher can have the bed."

"You better be kidding." I gave him a narrow look.

Hunter ate the eggs and toast and butter and all the cheese, then gave some to Flasher on a paper towel. He drank two glasses of tea and thanked me for the great meal—which reminded me what an easy guy he was to be with.

"Got more," he said.

I took that for a question and shook my head—no more food.

"I've got more on the things we took out of Henry Wade's room."

"What'd you find?"

"That computer. Wiped clean like he was worried about somebody stealing it."

"So no help."

"Now, hold on a minute. Sheriff Higsby's already got it going to Columbus. A computer forensics specialist will look at it tomorrow morning. He'll get to the hard drive and pick up anything that's on there. If Henry wanted to really hide something, he should have destroyed the whole thing. Taken a hammer to it."

"What do you think there could be?"

He shrugged and moved to the sofa, taking his boots off, stretching his legs, and wriggling his toes. "What we're hoping is that we'll find a connection to Eugene. One of our men went through all Eugene's records: sales and purchases. No Henry Wade there. 'Course Henry could've used a phony name. Next we're talking to people in Eugene's office in Dallas. See if there's any record of a Henry Wade there. Maybe even in his secretary's logbook. A phone call or something." He paused to think a minute. "That gun of Wade's was an AR15, like I thought. Assault rifle. One in seven twist."

"But there wasn't that much open space in Eugene's gun room, was there? I mean, didn't the shooter have to be pretty close?"

"Not if he stood in the doorway and shot. That table where Eugene was sitting was across the room. One shot to the back. There was a lot of damage."

"Just like there was to Henry Wade's heart. One shot."

"Yeah, you're right," Hunter said. "That's really bothering me. What the heck's going on here? We got us a nest of snipers?"

"What kind of gun killed Wade? Same thing?"

He shook his head. "Far as we know, it was a Remington 700P, 7.62 caliber. Sniper rifle. Must have had a scope on it. Forensics man said he thought it was Remington's Tactical

Weapons System. Comes with a Bi-Pod and a Tactical Scope. Probably a five round."

"So what we've got is Henry Wade killed Eugene. Sounds like a hired assassin, you ask me. Then somebody else killed Henry Wade. What a mess!"

He nodded.

"We've still got one more death to figure out," I said.

"You mean Sally Wheatley?"

I nodded.

Hunter gave me a satisfied shake of his head. "You know something? I like working with you and Miss Amelia. Things kind of take a new shape. Start making some kind of sense when the three of us talk things out."

"Just the two of us, here now."

That was enough of a reminder for Hunter. He reached out for me and all talk of murder was over for the night. I never did get to my bed. Flasher slept there alone.

Hunter's phone rang too early the next morning. Of course, Flasher barked and had to be shushed.

I was unhappy at the sound of chimes when it was only 6 a.m. Maybe there could have been a long, happy day ahead for us. Maybe no more murder and money and madness for a while. I was thinking I'd get up and make coffee. No breakfast—since he ate all my eggs. And then we could go out to a bend in the Colorado where it was wide, where there was a rope hanging from a tree to swing on out over the water. A private place where a lot of teenagers swim in the buff. I could already feel the muddy water sliding off my skin. Cold, like the air never was. And quiet. In an inner tube, you could float for hours. 'Course now I had to worry about where I parked my car, getting my hair wet, hiding my clothes so no idiot stole them, and then getting back against the current—

"That was the sheriff. Gotta go." Hunter stood in the doorway, tying his tie.

"No coffee?"

"Nope. Deputy Brent's bringing back one of Henry Wade's brothers from Dallas. The man wants to help, but he said he hasn't seen his brother in months. Something was going on, though. Wade suddenly had a lot of money and was doing some bragging. I'm going into the department, meet them when they get there. Sheriff told me to bring Miss Amelia on over. Figures she can make something of what the brother says."

"You're asking her on your way out?" I had to laugh. "Won't she be surprised to see you in the store this early?"

He shrugged and snickered. "Guess so, but your grandmother's a pretty savvy woman. Wouldn't try to put anything past her."

"Maybe Ethelred will be down there, too. Wouldn't that be nice? Town could really use another scandal about now."

He rolled his eyes and turned to go. "Oh, and Deputy Harner talked to the waitstaff from the party. Asked about Henry Wade. Somebody said she'd seen him before around Riverville. Didn't know his name but recognized him that night. That means the guy's either been here before or was here way before the party. Hope all this leads us somewhere."

I got up from the couch feeling bent and broken and stiff. Flasher came trotting out of my bedroom, stopping to shake a time or two, and head toward the door.

"You taking him with you?" The question was a formality.

"Could you keep him?"

"Are you crazy?"

"Then could you take him over to my house and close him in the kitchen?"

I groaned. "Okay. But you owe me."

He kissed me before leaving. I held on to him, looking

up into his deep blue eyes and wanting more than anything to hang on for at least a week.

"I've been thinking, Hunter," I started while rubbing my head against his chin. "You have to get out to that game ranch. See if either bullet—from Henry Wade's gun, or the bullet that killed him—matches the gun that killed Sally. Meemaw really has a feeling Sally's death is part of all this. And I know better than to ignore one of her feelings."

He nodded, folding his arms around my back and pulling me close. "Me, too. I'll bring it up this morning. See about going to Ralston and going over Sally's case with that sheriff."

He turned to go.

"No shower?"

"Can't. Later."

"I'm taking one."

He stopped. "Maybe later."

"Sure you don't have time for coffee?"

"Nope. And don't try to entice me. I've got a lot of work to do."

He came back to where I stood, smiling wide. The smell of him, when he leaned down to kiss me, was of warm skin and a not too fresh shirt. "About that shower," he said. "Hope never to miss an offer like that again in my life."

He left and Flasher crawled up on the sofa, stretched out, and began to snore.

Chapter Thirty-one

I was thinking about his last remark as I showered, dressed, and made tea for myself: *"Hope never to miss an offer like that again in my life."*

I was back to being scared he would ask me to marry him. Funny how that works—one minute wanting something so bad and the next minute scared to death you might get it.

I sat at my kitchen table, in front of a small window looking down on Riverville. Flasher nosed the bowl of water I'd set on the floor for him and then sent it sailing across the room. I hollered then picked up the bowl, sopped up the floor, and told him he wasn't getting anything until I got him home, which turned him back in to the living room, where I saw him lift his leg on the end of my sofa. I was too astonished even to scream at him, and then too mad to do anything more than find a piece of rope and take him downstairs, through the store, which wasn't opened yet, and out to Carya Street, where he peed on every lamppost and every live oak like he had a bladder the size of the *Titanic*.

I sat on the store's porch for a minute. Flasher settled on the floor beside me with a deep grunt. All I wanted to do was sit and think about last night. About Hunter. About things he was saying—like maybe he was getting close to proposing and I didn't know if that's what I wanted at all now that I was in danger of getting it.

People walked slowly across Carya Street, mostly twos and threes, talking, hailing other people. Two women pushed baby carriages, one had a stroller, and another woman was pulling a two-year-old along by his hand, though he didn't want to go anywhere and was letting her know it.

All people in a long line of people. A man and woman fall in love and the next thing you know you've got a first baby and everybody's excited and then you have another and another and nobody really cares, just doing your duty for the human race.

But that musing left out a lot: the way I felt about Hunter, the way he felt about me, about biological happiness. No matter what my analytical mind was telling me, the rest of me was saying Yes, Yes, Yes. And a baby—from both of us. I'd held plenty of babies—my friends all had them now. I'd felt how warm they were in my arms and what they smelled like and what their eyes said when they looked up at you, and that toothless smile . . .

Ech. I wasn't ready for stuff like that. I pushed Flasher off my foot. I had enough babies to take care of: all my trees.

That reminded me I had other things to do today. A last search for my record book on the trees, and if I couldn't find it, I had a tough phone call to make to the editor of *Propagation*. There was no getting around it. I had nothing for him but photographs of the trees in different stages, and very few of those. Since the article was supposed to be about drought resistance, I would need background of the grafts, a genome study, and my watering schedule: from full-on watering to the slow reduction of water; the trees' responses—all of that, with dates and times.

I was still cursing myself for not keeping everything on my computer.

I put Flasher in my truck, rolled down a window, and ran back up to my apartment. Scrubbing the leg of my couch and the wooden floor under it took some time. I dug out a different pair of sandals from my closet, changed my shorts, and headed back down the stairs, locking my apartment behind me.

It was going to be a tough day, making that phone call to *Propagation*. I didn't like letting people down after I'd given my word I would deliver something really groundbreaking. But life is life, I told myself while waving back at Treenie, who stood behind the counter, waiting on people holding their bags of pecans and boxes of pecan candy and books of pecan recipes in their arms while talking a mile a minute and smiling and yelling "Mornin', Lindy" over at me.

"Hope ya had a good night," someone called out in a sarcastic voice.

Somebody else snickered and I remembered why all that small-town togetherness sometimes gave me a bad case of hives.

I hurried out the door, got in my truck, and started it. I had to get to the greenhouse—one more hunt for the notebook and then call Joshua Lightley at *Propagation*.

That's when I missed Flasher.

He was gone.

I turned the truck around and went back to the front of the Nut House. A few people were gathered on the porch. They swore they didn't see any dog in my truck.

People down the walk shook their heads. "Nope. Big black dog? Think I would've seen him."

I hunted in and around the stores for two blocks. I walked the streets behind the stores and then went back for my truck. This was awful. The first time I'd watched the animal for Hunter. Failed!

For the next hour I drove around town. Up one street. Down the next. No Flasher.

He was a wraith. Maybe not a real dog at all. Maybe he could disappear and reappear at will. I had to call Hunter and tell him. I didn't want to. I just kept driving until I was going in circles and hours had passed.

A two-failure day, I told myself. I had to let Hunter know what happened. This wasn't going to be an easy phone call either.

Hunter was busy so I had to wait. When he finally came on the phone, I wanted to burst out crying, letting him know how sad I was, what an awful person I was.

"I think I lost Flasher," I blurted out. "I've looked everywhere. He was in my truck, but when I came out, he was gone. I only ran up to my apartment for a couple—"

He laughed at me.

"My neighbor called. Flasher's sitting on my back porch. I'll go over there and put him inside. The dog's kind of nuts, Lindy. Got a real mind of his own."

I could have been mad—wasting my whole morning. I could have hollered at Hunter, saying I didn't want to watch the miserable creature in the first place.

All I said was, "I'm glad he's safe."

I think I meant it.

The greenhouse felt dank and empty. I didn't feel the usual welcome. I searched the files again, thinking I'd misfiled the notebook, but there was nothing out of place.

I had another tough call ahead in my day of tough phone calls.

And, of course, Joshua wasn't happy with me though he did add, "Might have to accept another article offered to me. Sorry about that, Lindy."

"An article about what?"

"Same thing you're working on. The man called just a day or so ago, offering me his work on the same grafts you're using. He's got all his timetables to back up his findings. Sorry. I was going to stick with you, naturally. But now—"

"Same work as I'm doing?"

"Sounded almost identical."

"What's the man's name?"

"Hmm." I could hear paper shuffling right through the phone. He put the phone down. Then was back briefly. "Give me a minute. Must've filed it for future contact."

When he was back, he read off, "Dr. Peter Franklin. Guess a lab in Italy's working on your same materials."

I was very quiet. I was thinking, and I was furious. My blood began to boil, but I couldn't let out a string of curses with Joshua Lightley listening.

"Are you there?" Joshua asked.

"Yup." Okay, did I tell him I knew Peter Franklin and suspected him of stealing my records? He'd think I was unprofessional. But what the . . .

"Said he was in the U.S. to visit other scientists, get an idea of what's being done in the field."

"He's visiting all right," I said. "At the moment he seems to be stuck here in Riverville, where I live."

"Stuck?"

"Well, something like that. There was a murder at a party we both attended. He stayed in town and came to my greenhouse. If I may speak frankly, Mr. Lightley, my notebook was stolen from my desk and I suspect Dr. Franklin was the one who took it. And now this. I am almost speechless."

He cleared his throat. "Well, eh, Miss Blanchard. I don't know what to say."

He sounded as if he thought there was something wrong with me. I wanted to groan. I should have kept my mouth shut.

"Do you know Peter Franklin?" I asked, hoping I wiped out my whining.

"Of course. Well credentialed. He was affiliated with Harvard, if I'm not mistaken. Many articles. Well thought of in his field. I thought he'd gone off the grid to do some work in less populated and, therefore, less disturbed areas. I could be mistaken. So many scientists working on so many projects. Hard to keep up with."

He hesitated while he thought of a way to get me off the line. Or so I thought. "I suppose I'd better look into this, if there is a problem," he said. "Wouldn't be the first time two scientists worked on the same thing at the same time."

"We weren't." I couldn't help myself. "Nothing like what I'm doing. At least not when we talked about my new trees."

"Well then, I don't quite know what to say . . ." He sounded dubious, not believing me. After all, who was I compared to this man with a long list of credits to his name?

"Why don't I look into it? I'll check him out though I'm sure it's the same man. Doctor . . . eh . . . Miss Blanchard. I'll be in touch."

I put the phone down and sat in complete misery. I was going to be a laughingstock when people heard how I accused Dr. Peter Franklin of stealing my work. It wouldn't be out in the open. Scientists didn't stoop to that level—often. But my name would be whispered in labs across the country, in fields, and in greenhouses. *"Accused Dr. Franklin of stealing from her. You ever hear of a Lindy Blanchard?"*

They'd hear of me now.

I sat still in my rolling chair, in my greenhouse, and

thought long murderous thoughts about Peter Franklin. Friend of Elizabeth's all right. Just as devious. Just as underhanded.

And then I thought other thoughts. Like how to get even.

Beginning with an easy phone call.

Chapter Thirty-two

"Lindy! How nice to hear from you." Peter affected joy at the sound of my voice. "I was just beginning to wonder why you were being so standoffish. I've been busy here, with Elizabeth. So many problems about the estate and Eugene's wife running off to stay with those old ladies out in the country. I mean, people here are making it very difficult for Elizabeth. She's thinking of leaving Riverville for good. Putting this house on the market. Poor thing. Of course, I have to stay and do what I can to help."

"Of course, Peter. I understand. We've all got to do what we've got to do."

"Did you call about anything in particular? Or just to say hello?"

"To say 'hello,' of course. And then I needed to talk to somebody who would understand—" I provided a little catch in my throat.

"Oh dear, is there something wrong?"

"Yes. Terrible. It's my trees."

He hesitated. I could almost hear him thinking. "What is it?" he said. "I hope nothing's wrong with your latest attempts at drought resistance."

"That's it. My poor little trees. I was so happy about them. Coming along just fine. I told you, didn't I? That day you were out to my greenhouse?"

"I think you mentioned something—"

"Well, they died. And I was just getting ready to write an article on them, too. Real breakthrough in drought resistance. It was for *Propagation.* Remember? I told you about it."

He mulled that over. "Hmmm. I seem to remember. How sad for you. Are you certain? Perhaps this is a kind of dormancy. You were cutting the water back severely. I think that's what you were saying."

"Yes. All going so well. Now they are stone-cold dead. We pulled them up today. Doesn't matter that I lost my record book. Won't be necessary. I'll have to begin again."

"Well. The way you spoke—" He was working up to high dudgeon. "I mean, I took it this experiment was further along that it must have been. I feel . . . I don't know . . . somewhat fooled."

"Really?" I said then had to infuse my voice with apology. "Sorry about that. I didn't mean to mislead you. But you, of all people, know what a scientist's life is like. So many disappointments. So many grants rescinded. Articles canceled."

I played him along, holding him for a good while, enjoying his outrage. Next he'd be calling Joshua Lightley to cancel his offer of an article. I hoped I'd get to learn what his excuse was. Too bad it might hurt him professionally.

I could only hope.

Jessie and I went to see *Saving Mr. Banks* at the Bijou that night, and loved it. Took both of us back to when we were kids and watched *Mary Poppins* over and over again. We used to walk with a duck-footed Mary Poppins walk and dance with a cane, like Bert. The movie brought it all back and we were pretty happy until we left the theater and ran into Ethelred Tomroy on her way out.

Not knowing much else to talk about as we stood there, all looking blankly at one another, I asked how her investigation was going. She stumbled back, fingers clawing at me as she tripped and almost fell, right there on the sidewalk.

I think my mouth was open. What the heck?

She looked hard around, at the people standing nearby. "Oh dear, don't mention that out loud," she begged in the smallest voice I ever heard Ethelred use.

"I'm sorry," I said, and meant it.

"Hunter came to see me. They're gettin' close to all those drug and gun lords. My heavens!" She wrung her hands. "This last murder, that man over to Lydia Hornbecker's boardinghouse—Hunter thinks he maybe came to town to shut me up. Can you imagine? Me—the target of some South American drug lord? I can't believe I let Freda talk me into hunting those men down."

She threw her hands to her chest, as if to quiet her beating heart. "I'm out of it. I told Hunter everything I suspected. It's his job. Far as I can see, it won't do to have civilians doing police work. Freda and me coulda gotten killed. Now, because of all this, Freda's stopped talking to me, though it's mostly her fault. I'm going over to the Nut House and tell Miss Amelia what's going on. She gets herself too tangled up in police business, you ask me. She's got to be more careful. A woman her age."

I agreed wholehearted and reminded her the Nut House was closed and said to go over there in the morning. I was just so sure, I went on telling her, that Meemaw would be only too happy to have Ethelred warning her how dangerous it was to interfere in police business.

"Well, I didn't think of it as interfering, as such. More helping out. Now I can see it's better if citizens trust in their police force and let them do their business. I know Miss Amelia might get mad at me, trying to tell her what to do, but she's got to listen. This is dangerous and I don't want anything happening to my old friend."

I had to smile at Miss Ethelred. For all her posing and posturing and putting other people down, Meemaw's old friend really did care about her.

What I did next shocked Miss Ethelred so that her buggy eyes almost popped out of her head. I leaned up and kissed her cheek.

Chapter Thirty-three

The next day Hunter and I were sharing a piece of Meemaw's pie we'd stolen out of the cooler. We were in the kitchen, laughing because I told him I'd seen Ethelred and she was shaking in her shoes after he'd warned her away from her investigation. When Meemaw came in, her stiff face warned us that something was up and it couldn't be just the stolen pie—though she didn't like people helping themselves to her valuable stock—*"Which I might need on the spur of the moment and here you are, Lindy Blanchard, eating up everything without as much as a 'by-your-leave.'"*

We found out soon enough why Meemaw was mad. And it didn't have to do with me, for once.

"Hear you warned Ethelred away from her investigation." She stood next to the table, looking down at our guilty faces. She was talking to Hunter, who knew enough to color up.

"Now maybe you'd like to go out there"—she extended a pointy finger back toward the swinging doors to the store—"and tell her I'm not going to be murdered in my bed because I help the sheriff out from time to time. Poor soul is worried sick I'm going to get myself killed. Think I'm the only one in town who really cares about that silly woman. She knows that and wants me kept alive."

She stopped and shook that finger at Hunter. "I know you did it just to keep her and Freda quiet, and get their noses out of things. Still, I don't think I can put up with one more minute—"

Hunter, often the object of Meemaw's wrath when we were little and dumb, stuttered out an apology then went right into praise for the pie, which quieted her down enough so she pulled out a chair, sat, and calmed herself.

"What else are you two up to this morning?" She looked from our faces to our pie dishes—clean as a whistle.

"Just came to see you." Hunter wiped filling from his chin. "Sheriff was wanting to know if you'd go along with me over to Ralston. We're kinda short on men right now."

"That game ranch where Sally died? That's the only reason you want me to leave my store and go trekkin' with you? You're 'short on men'?"

Hunter sure knew how to get Meemaw going.

I sat back to watch the fireworks.

"I didn't put that just right." Hunter slid down in his chair and frowned. "What I meant to say is, the sheriff really needs me to get over there and he's got the other deputies busy checking everywhere he can and . . ." His words trailed off, like he was talking to the floor and forgot what he was saying.

Meemaw waved a hand at him. "Sorry, didn't mean to take out after you, Hunter. That Ethelred's got me going."

She smiled over at him the way she used to do. One thing with Meemaw, she never could stay mad at people she loved.

"Okay, now . . . What for? Why do you want me to go with you to Ralston?"

"Sheriff Higsby talked to the sheriff up there. The man

said to come on out and go through the file he's got on Sally Wheatley's shooting. We can see if there's a match with the cartridge that killed Eugene or the one that killed Henry Wade. Two different guns. I'm taking both ballistics reports with me. Seems like, if somebody shot Sally on purpose, it's got to be one or the other of the guns we know about. Too much coincidence, that she was killed just like her husband. Can't tell me we've got that many killers around. The sheriff there in Ralston says he still thinks it was an accident, but the man's got an open mind. Wants to get it right."

"You don't need me to go talk to a sheriff," Meemaw said.

"Me and Sheriff Higsby thought it might be good to have a woman go along. Kind of look around and see things the way Sally would've seen 'em. You know, keep your eyes and ears open."

"As I told you, I've got a store to run, Hunter. Glad to help you out, but I don't see how I'd be necessary over to Ralston. Can't help you with guns. I don't own one. Never will. Can't help you with ballistics. Can't help you find the other people on that hunt along with Sally. Can't question the guide who took them out—you're better at that than I am. Can't question people in Ralston if they've seen the man around town. You know, take that sketch along. Maybe go into restaurants. Maybe the bank. Maybe a gas station. Places like that where outsiders go. Could try any hotels or motels in the area. But I don't have the stamina for all that searching. You need somebody younger for that footwork, son."

"Guess you gave me my playbook right there, Miss Amelia." Hunter grinned from ear to ear. "Now I'm sorrier than ever you can't go along."

I saw Meemaw thinking a minute. She had her grandmother face on. Her *"I'm going to fix something for Lindy, who never can seem to fix things right for herself"* face.

"I'll tell you what, take Lindy, here, along. She knows as much as I do about all of this. Let's see what she thinks. Why were the women there to begin with? I never took Sally for a hunter. What was it they were after that day?"

"Sika deer."

"There in the hills?"

"Yes, ma'am. Rich man's hobby. Those deer cost hunters anywhere from fifteen hundred up."

"Terrain's hilly?"

"Some rolling country. Lots of big rocks."

"How many acres? You know?"

"Not exactly. Maybe a couple thousand."

Meemaw shook her head. "Who'd mistake Sally for a deer? Wasn't she standing in a group of people?"

Hunter shrugged. "Wild shot. Some of those folks don't know a shotgun from a hockey stick."

"I'm glad you're going. Show that sketch of Henry Wade around at the wildlife ranch, too, while you're there. See if anybody saw him on the hunt."

"Showed it to Elizabeth," Hunter said. "Never saw him before. Didn't even remember him from the wedding party. Said it must've been the caterers she hired brought him along."

Meemaw shrugged. "Doesn't hurt to ask around Ralston. Maybe he was a hired hand out there at the game ranch."

"And maybe you should go after all, Meemaw," I protested. "You've got all the questions. I don't know what I'd even be looking for. And," I stopped to put in a slight complaint, "maybe I don't like being second choice."

"Hush," was all Meemaw said, giving me one of her narrow-eyed looks that told me she wasn't going to take any back talk.

I knew what she was doing. I think Hunter knew, too. I pretended to reconsider. We all sat there nodding, acting like we thought it was a great idea for me and Hunter to go off for a day or so together, catching a couple of murderers and righting a few wrongs along the way.

A couple of days. A couple of days alone to talk. I sure was willing to help out. I'd take a look around the game ranch. I'd tell Hunter what I thought and make my grandmother proud. I couldn't help but think *"chip off the old block"* and then tried to get the pictures out of my head: Meemaw, like me, with some wild man, riding toward danger in a truck. Staying in a cheap motel with her wild man . . .

"Okay." Meemaw thumped her hands on the table. "Now, I've got a couple more questions. If I'm treading where I shouldn't be going, you let me know."

Hunter nodded. "Yes, ma'am."

"Did you get fingerprints from Henry Wade's gun?"

"Yes, ma'am. All of 'em Wade's."

"What about that gun expert you brought in to go over Eugene's collection? He find anything missing?"

Hunter shook his head.

"Anybody help with who could've come to that back door to shoot Eugene?"

"Still asking. Trying to find out if somebody was supposed to take a tray out to 'im and if one was sent. Chantal didn't remember."

"Maybe there was no tray."

We all looked at each other.

"But didn't somebody mention Eugene saying there was a tray coming out to him?"

We let it pass.

"Any follow-up on that stuff Elizabeth was saying? I mean, about Eugene being sorry he'd married Jeannie?" Meemaw asked.

Hunter shook his head. "Just the opposite. Friends I talked to said he was happier than he's been since Sally died."

We were all thinking hard.

"Maybe the killer switched guns to make it look like Wade killed Eugene," Meemaw said after a while. "But with only Wade's fingerprints on the gun, his body found miles from the boardinghouse, and Lydia Hornbeck hovering around that house of hers, no stranger's going to get by her dragging a dead body, and no stranger's gonna wander in and out with a rifle in his hands. I'd say it's Henry Wade's gun all right."

"So we have Eugene's killer. Wade. Now here comes another killer."

"Looks like it," Meemaw said.

"And no clue as to a motive for this whole thing."

"You've got to dig as deep as you can into Wade's background, Hunter. You talk to the relatives who came for the body?"

"Yes, ma'am. Said he was a bragger. Came back to El Paso from time to time only to show off all the money he had on him. They didn't know much else—like where the money came from. Told them he was some kind of 'soldier of fortune' or something like that. I got the impression nobody liked him much. His brother and uncle came for him. Didn't see a lot of sadness. We tried to get a photograph of him. Nobody even had one."

"What I figured," Meemaw sighed. "Some people choose ugly paths."

She thought some more. "Soldier of fortune—fancy name for a hired gun. So who would be after the Wheatleys? And why? They're pretty prominent folks in Texas. Eugene always struck me as a nice man, despite the money. Elizabeth's too worried about her social standing to do anything that would make her look bad. Who'd want any of them dead, let alone all of them?"

Meemaw shook her head after a while. "'Fraid I'm not much help, Hunter. Got to be tied to whoever killed Henry Wade. Or not. Could be he was just an evil man and somebody else he did dirt to killed him. I suppose you've got to take another look at Billy. Hate to say it, but I've got to admit—maybe for his sister's sake he'd do away with Henry Wade. But I just know he had nothing to do with Eugene's death."

"That's what I was thinking, too. At least to rule him out."

"Tell you something." Meemaw looked from Hunter to me and back. "This thing is getting to the point where I can't tell up from down. I'd say, knowing human beings the way I do, if Henry Wade killed Eugene, there was nothing personal about it."

"Then why didn't Henry Wade get right out of town? Why hang around, waiting to get shot?" I asked.

"If he was a hired killer, I'd say he was either waiting to get paid or he had another job to do. Sharpshooter, eh. Looks like both killers were that—only a single shot each. Guess it's gonna take more time and shoe leather. That right, Hunter?" She smiled big at him.

"Right you are, Miss Amelia."

"So best you two get going over there to Ralston. Get that answer on the bullet. It's important to know if the same gun that killed Eugene killed Sally. Jeannie wasn't in the picture when Sally was killed so that lets her whole family out as to being involved. Can't see Billy—who was incarcerated when Sally was killed, or his mother—who wouldn't have the money to hire a hit man anyway—doing that. And unless one of 'em's a fortune-teller, how could they know Eugene would ever marry Jeannie?

"You two get going. See what you can find at the game ranch."

I ran upstairs and threw a few things into an overnight bag while Hunter went home to do the same. I stopped to look at myself in the bathroom mirror, running a brush through my hair and winding it into a ponytail that came out standing up like a fountain on top—the way little girls wear their hair. I checked my lipstick, wiped a smudge off my teeth, and looked into my eyes. "Maybe this whole thing is dishonest," I told myself. "You're not going along to investigate a murder and you know it."

Myself answered, "So what?"

And I was off.

We took my truck. There wasn't an extra patrol in town. We tussled over who was going to drive with the loser, me, muttering and promising dire consequences. Hunter said he'd drive until he got tired. A few hours. Be there before noon.

It was already feeling comfortable, the way we always were together. It was almost easy to forget why we were going to Ralston, forget there were murderers in Riverville, and pretend the world was back to being a nice place.

Chapter Thirty-four

First thing I said to Hunter as we drove out of town was, "You really wanted to take Meemaw instead of me?"

He looked over from the driver's seat. His exasperation was clear. "Bein' polite. Your grandmother's got a brain like a steel trap. Good thing you got other things going for you."

"Pig." I hit him with the folder I was looking through.

"This shouldn't take more than a day or two, at most," he said after a while.

"Have you got an expense account or are we staying at the Bide-A-Wee down in some wash?"

"Brought a tent," he said, then laughed, taking it back.

"I don't want bedbugs."

"Won't be no bedbugs where we're going. Sheriff invited us to stay with him."

"What kind of fun will that be?"

He gave me a hard look. "You along on a murder investigation or out for fun?"

"Of course, an investigation." I really was ashamed of myself.

"Kidding," he said. "Got us a reservation at a big hotel outside Austin. You see a bedbug there, I'll sue 'em."

It hit me then that there was no big dog riding shotgun. "What'd you do with Flasher? You didn't ask Finula to watch him, did you?"

"Heck no. Not with those late hours of hers. The new deputy took him. Said he likes dogs. I'm hoping they get attached and I'll be rid of 'im."

Hunter drove until we stopped near Round Rock at lunchtime. New Orleans food, and the best seafood in the county. After that he was sleepy and I drove up into the hills, where the road dropped and climbed and rain gauges in the washes showed nothing but dry ground.

Next thing we were in Ralston. I woke up Hunter to let him drive because I didn't know where I was going, though the town was small—a lot of the false-fronted stores hung with FOR SALE signs.

Hunter wiped his eyes as he sat up. "So soon? Good job, Lindy."

The wildlife ranch was about thirty miles farther north, but he wanted to stop in and talk to the sheriff before we headed out.

"Department should be right here on Main Street somewhere." He peered out the windshield, into the midday sun, looking down the wide street with only a few cars pulled into parking places. Some of the stores had wide-open doors—since it was in the low eighties. Not into summer heat yet.

"If I can't find it, I'll just stop and ask."

"Or call him," I suggested, always opting for the easiest way to do anything.

I pulled out the sketch from the folder Hunter handed me earlier. Those cold eyes. I knew I'd gotten them right. They gave me chills, just looking at them, even with the man dead. I really hoped we'd find something that would clear up everything, tie the murders together, end this once and for all. Nothing felt normal to me anymore, not my work, not my up and down relationship with Hunter, not even my relationships with my family. It was all skewed. I hadn't asked about Sally's sister before then. Was she still around? Was Hunter still her protector?

Well, not if he was with me. Hmmm . . .

"What happened to Sally's sister after the memorial? Just asking."

He looked over to smile at me. "Gone back home. But we're in touch, in case you were worried about it. She wants to know what we find out here. You know she's always said Sally's death wasn't an accident."

"I know. And I'm glad she's in the loop. Who knows? Maybe I'll get to know her better, since I liked Sally so much. Or not . . ." I added, being honest with myself.

"Nothing to worry about, Lindy. If that's your problem. She's engaged and busy and there's nothing going on between us."

"Who said I was worried?"

Probably remembering when I burst in on the two of them at The Squirrel, he rolled his eyes at me.

And that was enough of that subject.

Hunter pointed toward a low building with a hard-to-see sign out front. It was just off the main drag. Evidently the sheriff wasn't advertising for business.

Hunter and I were welcomed by Sheriff Winston Homer in true Texas style. He was a big man with a big hat and a big smile. The men shook hands. I got a hug that felt like being wrapped in cotton. We nodded to the other deputy sitting at a desk and then went back with Sheriff Homer to his office. He talked all the way, saying he'd like to show us around Ralston, if we had the time, and maybe have us over for supper. He was sizing us up—probably wondering what I was doing there with a sheriff's deputy. Too polite to ask, he just kept welcoming me to town and then ordered tacos from a local restaurant even though we told him we'd already eaten.

I figured it might take a little longer than I thought to get down to business in Ralston. Then I figured that wasn't all bad. People sometimes worked out a lot of problems just by talking and eating. Folks, after all, did need to get to know one another before jumping into murder.

When we headed out to the wildlife ranch with Sheriff Homer, we were full enough of tacos and beans to burst wide open. We had a copy of everything in Sally Wheatley's file. The sheriff had Hunter's ballistics reports sent out immediately to a lab near Austin for comparison with the bullet that killed her.

"Hear back in a couple of hours, unless something else bumps us down a notch or two. Our man knew you was coming. Should settle that much—if somebody's after those Wheatleys or not."

We went out in the sheriff's car, driving over ninety on some pretty curvy roads, and up and down some pretty serious hills. Thirty miles flew—literally, with live and craggy dead oaks speeding past my backseat window—beyond the metal grate—like crazy Halloween decorations. We pulled down into a valley, stopping in front of a low wooden ranch house sitting out in the sun, surrounded by bushes and dry earth. All around were the sides of steep wooded and rocky hills, and dry two tracks leading up at different angles, in different places.

The game ranch looked about like I'd expected it to look. Not real overdone, but nowhere nearing shabby. The people who came here to hunt had money. They expected things to be kind of easy on them. Hunting meant trekking up into the hills until a guide pointed to some grazing animal and then BANG! and the hunter was out fifteen hundred or more.

After Jim Wardell, the ranch manager, came out and shook hands all around, we headed back to where a row of fancy bunkhouses stood with a blackened stone fire pit in front, and then on beyond to another row of low buildings—not fancy at all.

"This is where the guides stay," Jim turned to say as he toed his well-used cowboy boots into the dusty earth. "Figured you'd want to talk to Earl James. He's the one took the Wheatley group out that day."

He led us through a low doorway into a large room with a long, handmade table standing at the middle. A kitchen opened off at one end; a long hallway at another. Jim Wardell went on down the hall, his boots making a hollow thump as he walked. He came back with a thin man in old jeans and old boots you couldn't tell, to save your life, what the original color had been. The man had to be in his fifties—or sixties—or seventies. Who knew? Face wrinkled like a bad prune. Eyes squinting as if he never came indoors. When we were introduced, Earl stuck out a hard-used hand to take ours, hitting me with a very respectful, "Ma'am.

"Hear you wanna talk about that day back when the woman got shot." Earl's voice was wispy—like he'd had that one cigarette too many. He turned to cough, then back to us.

He gave me and Hunter a one-eyed, sidewise look and took a seat at the table, where we all sat down.

Hunter agreed, that's what we were there for.

"Couple a years now. Don't know as I remember all that much about it."

I pulled the sketch of Henry Wade from the folder and slid it across the table.

"Who's this?" Earl squinted up at us.

"A man shot down in Riverville."

"What's he got to do with anything? Don't mind my asking."

"Found a gun in his room. Bullet matched the bullet that killed Eugene Wheatley, the man out here hunting with his wife when she was killed."

He nodded and took another look at the sketch.

"Can't say as I know him. He wasn't on the hunt with those people. Had Mr. Wheatley; his wife—the one what got killed; his sister; a couple of friends. That's all I remember. And this man here wasn't with 'em."

Hunter went on to ask him about the hunt: Anything unusual? People seem relaxed? No trouble going on? Took them out to a new place or one he usually took folks up to?

All the answers added up to nothing out of the way about that day.

"And then you heard a shot?" Hunter asked.

He shrugged. "Heard lots a shots that day. Some of those folks weren't experienced hunters. Tell you the truth, only one of those women knew one end of a gun from the other."

"Any other groups out at the same time? Could the bullet that killed Sally Wheatley have come from them?"

He shook his head. "Only group out that day. I always figured it was some poacher. What else? Mr. Wardell will tell you. Checked all the guns people were using. The men and one woman had their own they'd brung with 'em. Other women used some we had. No bullet matched the cartridge we found."

Hunter leaned forward, resting on his forearms. He was getting down to business. "I know for a fact that guides notice a lot of things about the people they take up into the hills. And I know that guides listen to what folks say between themselves. And I know that guides like some of 'em and don't like others. What I'm askin' now is, give me your thoughts on that group."

Earl lowered his head in thought. After a couple of long minutes, he turned aging blue eyes up toward Hunter. "Liked 'em all well enough. That Eugene Wheatley was a fine fellow. Don't think his wife liked hunting much, but she was being a good sport. That sister—well, you coulda led her off to a hangin' and I wouldn't've stopped you."

"Why?"

"Mouth on'er that ran like a rabbit. Kind of nasty to the wife. You know what I mean? The way some of those ladies look down their noses and make fun like they wasn't really makin' fun and nobody should take offense? Even I could see what she was up to and felt sorry for that poor wife."

"What happened after the shooting?"

"All hell broke loose, is what happened. The shot woman was down on the ground. The husband was kneeling next to her, yellin' out her name."

"What about the sister?"

He thought again. "Seemed upset, like everybody else. Won't fault her for that. Seemed to care."

"You remember the other folks on that hunt?"

He shrugged, took a pack of Camels out of his pocket and a book of matches. He lit a cigarette, pulled in a long breath, and let the smoke out in the air over our heads.

"Think there was two other men and their wives."

"Anything about them?"

He thought, pursed his lips, took another drag on his cigarette, and then shook his head.

"Just people. A lot of joking. I remember that. Women teasing the men about what bad shots they were. Don't think any of those women, except the sister, took as much as one shot right up to the time that Sally Wheatley got killed."

"What did the women look like?" I asked.

Again he thought awhile. "I remember them bein' in their thirties, I'd say. Older than Wheatley's wife. She was a young, pretty thing. Real nice. The others—well, they acted like most rich women. Like they got to show off. You know what I mean? Like they got to be seen and heard so no other woman sneaks up and steals their husband. Always thought, women like that, pretty sad, you ask me."

I had to smile at this gentle, perceptive cowboy.

That was all we got out of Earl. Jim Wardell, walking back up to his place with us, wasn't much more help except he had a record of everyone on that hunt—names and addresses. For his own benefit, he told us. In case of any trouble—like there was.

We looked over the names: Tom and Maud Fritchey; George and Winifred Tillis. Names I kind of recognized. Maybe they were at the costume party. I couldn't have told you which ones they were.

Hunter copied the names and contact info into his notebook.

"Have to talk to them," he said. "Don't know where any of this is going to lead."

We said good-bye to Jim Wardell just as a couple of Jeeps filled with men came up the dusty drive. I figured it was the next hunt coming in.

Back at the sheriff's office, Winston Homer called the forensics lab over near Austin but was told he wouldn't have the results before morning. Hunter made arrangements to check back in the morning and we were on our own.

Taking a page from Meemaw's book, I wanted to hit a few of the stores in Ralston, check out if anybody in town had ever seen Henry Wade around. I wanted to take the sketch into the bank—see if Henry Wade cashed any checks there. Maybe ask at the two barbecue places I'd seen on either end of town. I was thinking about where most people go. Maybe the local saloon. We'd have to check all those out. Maybe a market—there was a small one along the six blocks of what you could call their downtown. Since it was getting on into the afternoon, we figured this would be a good time to catch people out and about.

Nobody in the small bank recognized the man in the sketch. The bank manager wished us good luck with finding anybody who'd remember the man from a couple of years ago and suggested we go over to Good Ole Boys Barbecue. "Waitresses have long memories. Especially if the man was a good tipper. Or a bad tipper. They'd know. If I was you, I'd head right over there."

Knowing good advice when we heard it, Hunter and I walked down to the barbecue restaurant on the east end of town, where a huge plaster bull stood outside and inside were hung posters like WE DON'T CALL 911 with a picture of a pistol staring at you. The place had a low ceiling with everything imaginable, having to do with nothing in particular, hanging from it. There were shiny wooden tables with stools to sit on. Lots of flags draped the walls—U.S. and Texas, with the Lone Star flag winning out by about ten to one—if I counted right.

The girl who came over with menus had on blue shorts and a yellow blouse open at the neck, where she'd tied a red scarf. She was young and said her name was Margie and what could she get for us on this fine day.

I showed Margie the sketch of Henry Wade and she shook her head when she learned this was about an incident going back a few years. "I've only been working here six months."

She went back for an older waitress who'd been around longer.

This one was heavier. Wearing shorts just as short as Margie's. She had the kind of lined face that told you right off she'd seen some doings in her life.

"Carol," she said and folded her hands in front of her, order pad hanging over her fingers, "you asking questions about somebody?"

We told her why we were there. Hunter asked her to sit a minute, see if she could help us out. I showed her the picture of Wade. She took the sketch in her hands and stared hard at it awhile.

"Why are you asking about this man?" She narrowed her eyes and turned to me, giving me the once-over, then to Hunter. "Since you're a cop, must be serious. He missing or something?"

Hunter shook his head. "The man's dead. We know where he is. It's what he did in the past that concerns us."

"Why?" Carol was in no hurry to give out information.

"Because we already know he killed a man in Riverville. We're here to see if we can connect him to another killing."

"Who got killed in Riverville? And what's that got to do with us, here in Ralston?"

"The man and his wife were up here on a hunt when the wife was shot. The man was shot in Riverville."

She shrugged. "Happens. I mean, the one killed at the game ranch."

"Nobody's gun matched the bullet that killed her."

"So you're talking two murders?"

Hunter nodded.

You had to give it to Carol. She wasn't going to get herself tied up in anything that might come back to bite her.

She sighed. "If that's the case, and this man's dead . . ." She tapped the sketch with a long, red fingernail. "I'll tell ya. I remember that face. Mean looking. I didn't want to wait on him, but neither did the other girl who worked here then. Sat a long time after he finished eating, like he was waiting for somebody. Went out looking mad as a wet hen, checking his watch, and stuff like that. Then he was back the next evening. Again, I had to wait on the bastard even though he didn't bother to tip me the night before. I can tell you I wasn't too friendly and shook off some of his fries into the garbage before I brought them out. Same thing. Barbecue with onions and pickles, fries, Sam Adams. Ate. Sat there waiting again. And then this woman walks in and over to his table. She didn't sit down long. Waved me away when I tried to hand her a menu even though this is a restaurant and I'm not just standing around 'cause I got nothing better to do. Waved me away like I was nothing." She closed her eyes and blew out her lips. When her eyes opened again, I could see she was holding in a lot of anger, whether at Henry Wade and this woman or at all the people, throughout all her years as a waitress, who treated her as if she could just be waved away.

"What'd they do? The two of them," Hunter asked.

"He paid his bill and they left. No tip again. That's the last time I saw the man. Good riddance."

"What about the woman?"

She shook her head. "Never saw her again either."

"You remember what she looked like?"

Carol shook her head slowly. "You're askin' a couple of years ago. I only saw her the once. The only reason I remember was because she treated me like I was dirt."

"Can you give it a try? How old, would you say?"

"I don't know. Maybe thirties. Maybe forties. Had on jeans and a suede jacket over the jeans—if I remember right. Big, dark sunglasses. A lotta gold. Long earrings, necklaces. You know how they do. Still, I could be mixin' her up with lots of other women."

"How tall?"

"'Bout like me. Five feet six and a half, I'd say."

"That's pretty good." Hunter was admiring her memory though she claimed she could barely think back that far.

"Brown hair, I'd say. Nothing much else about her. Kind of deep voice. That's it."

"Color of eyes? Anything she said that you remember?"

She shook her head slowly. "I told ya, she had on sunglasses and didn't take 'em off the whole time she was in here."

That was all we got out of the Good Ole Boys Barbecue. It felt like plenty.

Back in my truck, Hunter turned to give a tight shake of his fist. “So he was here.”

“And with a woman. Maybe one of the friends on the trip—”

“And what do you want to bet it’s going to show the bullet that killed Sally came from Henry Wade’s gun.” Hunter was feeling pretty good about then. In true Hunter fashion, he wanted to go back out to the game ranch. He had more questions. That made me mad and I dug my heels in.

Chapter Thirty-five

I was tired and said it was too late to go back out there, the way Hunter wanted to do. He wanted to talk to Earl James about the woman who came into the barbecue place. See if he could identify her as one of the women on the Wheatley hunt. We had that suede jacket. Lots of gold jewelry. Low voice.

"He's out on that other hunt. Remember? We'll just be spinning our wheels," I complained, then went on complaining. "I'm tired. This morning I didn't even know I'd be spending the day here in Ralston. Let's go get supper and see this hotel you booked."

"You're hungry? After all those tacos on top of seafood?"

"That was hours ago."

"Geez, Lindy. I'll have to start driving you around in a tank pretty soon, you don't cut back on the calories."

"You think I'm fat?" I used the outrage all women used expressing "fat" anger.

He turned from behind the wheel to grin. He always knew the places to poke to get me mad. "Wouldn't call it fat. I'd call it nice and curvy."

"Then don't say things like that. Hurts my feelings."

"You and those feelings of yours. Heard about them since you was six years old."

I made a noise and nodded fast. "Still got 'em, Hunter. And you better watch yourself or I'll be telling folks about the time you—"

"Okay! Okay! Truce." Now he was the one bothered. "We'll head toward Austin and come back tomorrow morning early. The sheriff should know about the cartridge by then and we can take a run out to the game ranch. Have one more go at Earl James."

Austin was Austin and we were just on the outskirts anyway, so I didn't see too much and Hunter didn't want to go to the entertainment district to hear music.

The Hidalgo was a beautiful hotel. A lot better than I expected Hunter would have booked. Our room was spacious. A huge colorful mural hung on the wall behind the bed. This was luxury, but I'd bet anything Hunter had gotten a good price for the night. The thing about Hunter was that he wasn't a cheap, or even frugal, man. He was careful, was all. Liked to get his money's worth. I could have bet anything he'd asked around to a lot of his friends about a place to stay near Austin. He hadn't let me down.

We had supper in their dining room though neither of us was really hungry. I'd been lying earlier, to get my own way and save the ranch for morning. Trouble was we drank a couple of beers—both not used to drinking much—and almost fell asleep at the dining room table. Getting upstairs was a lot of fun, both yawning and making faces. I think I got into my pajamas. He never made it into anything beyond his shorts. Still, it was kind of a night to remember. If for nothing else, for how late we slept the next morning.

Chapter Thirty-six

Hunter was reaching for me the next morning then looking over my shoulder at the bedside clock. He let me go and gave a "Whoop."

"Ten thirty!" he yelled and almost bounced me off the bed. "Can't be. No way!"

He ran to the chair where he'd laid his pants, fumbled around in the pocket, and called Sheriff Homer.

"Been checking things out," he sputtered. "Be right out there. Oh. Good. Give me an hour."

I was headed for the shower. I'd spotted nice little bottles of shampoo and conditioner, a nice body lotion. This was going to be a great shower. Then maybe breakfast in the dining room. I was thinking a kolache—if they had them. Apple or cheese. And a big pot of tea . . .

Hunter read my mind. "No time, Lindy. Sorry. Got to get back to Ralston. The sheriff's calling for the results now. Promised we'd be right out."

Of course. What was I thinking? Sometimes, I swear, I get off track and just want nice times to keep going.

We were back to Ralston in forty minutes flat. When we walked in, it was like we were already old timers in town. The deputy behind a desk up front smiled wide and bade us "Mornin'."

"Sheriff said to tell you to go on in. He's out getting some kolache and coffee. Be right back."

So I had half my breakfast wish though by now I was back on track and just wanted to hear what the forensics people found.

"Got news." The sheriff bustled into his office and set rolls and coffee in front of both me and Hunter.

Hunter ignored everything else. "What'd he come up with?"

"A match. You got your gun that killed Sally Wheatley. No doubt about it. That cartridge that killed your Wade guy—no match. Different gun. Either you got a man with a lot of guns or you've got two killers."

Hunter leaned forward and whistled. "That's something. Thanks, Sheriff."

"Welcome," the big man said. "What more can I help you with?"

He made a motion with his hand as if pushing the coffee and kolaches at us. I was ready to celebrate and found an apple roll in the bag.

Hunter was thinking. I knew that meant trouble ahead. Maybe a trip to Dallas to find those guests on the Wheatley hunt or something else he'd come up with. What I wanted to do most was call Meemaw, tell her what we'd found, and see what she had to say.

"All I need now is a motive for killing both Wheatleys," Hunter said.

"From your killer's shot, he was a good marksman. Had to come from up on one of the hills, behind a boulder, I'd say."

"A Marine," Hunter told him. "Sharpshooter."

"And the shot that took out your Marine?"

"Straight through the heart. Looks like it could've been a hundred yards or more. No powder burns. Kill shot."

"Whew. And here I thought Riverville, Texas, was a quiet little town."

"Was, until we got these two."

"From the looks of things," the sheriff said, "you'd better find that other killer pretty fast. Sounds like a professional hit to me. Not something you want in Riverville or anyplace else. Still, you don't want him gettin' away."

The sheriff sipped at his hot coffee and set it down to take a big bite of his sweet roll. "To tell you the truth, I'm just as glad to hear the guy who murdered that Wheatley woman is dead. I can close the books on that one now. Don't like loose ends hanging around to devil me for years. Not like we get much in the way of killings here in Ralston. Once in a while. Mostly a husband. Sometimes a wife. But no hired killers."

Hunter turned to me. "Let's get back out to that game ranch. Ask Earl about that woman—see if he recognizes the description the waitress gave us."

I nodded. That was agreed on.

"Then maybe I'll have to go into Dallas. Talk to people at Eugene's office. Could be this is all connected to his oil business."

The sheriff nodded. I mumbled something. I wasn't going to Dallas or anywhere else after we got out of here. I had to get home to my own work.

We thanked the sheriff for his hospitality and help and left, though I did take one more roll—in case I didn't get to eat again that day.

Chapter Thirty-seven

It was the lazy part of the early afternoon when we drove through the hills back out toward the game ranch. Still not really hot, but the air was wet, like it picked up half the Gulf and moved it into Texas. I was tired again. Leaning against the seat, closing my eyes from time to time and yawning. I put in a call to Martin Sanchez and we discussed watering and feeding for a while. Any grafting or other biological pairings would be put off until I got back. The thing about Martin was that he was so good with the trees he knew them intuitively. Not trained in any of my work, but he knew what to do without being told. He could look at a tree—see a yellow leaf—and be on the job that minute. As a farm manager, Martin was the best in the business.

Hunter drove in and passed the ranch house, heading instead into the parking places out by the clients' houses. From there we walked back to where the guides stayed and walked in on three of them having their noonday meal. The three, including Earl James, looked up, surprised. Earl recognized us from the day before and raised a hand in greeting, pointing to the pot of stew on the table and then pointing to a stack of clean white bowls sitting off at the side.

"All had morning hunts," Earl said after halfway introducing us to the other two, who kept right on eating. "Kind of late eating."

"Ate already," Hunter said. "Could you come outside when you're done? Like to ask you just a few more questions."

"You find out if that killer from Riverville killed this lady here?" he asked as he took a paper napkin to wipe his chin.

Hunter nodded. "That was him."

"Wow!" Earl exclaimed as he got up. "Wonder what that was all about?"

The other two men nodded toward us as we headed back for the door, taking no interest in what we were talking about or why we were there.

Out in the lane, in front of all the housing, Hunter turned to Earl and asked him to show us where Sally had been shot.

He hesitated a minute, thinking hard while fumbling in his shirt pocket for a cigarette. That found and lighted, he looked off to the hills, eyes closed to slits, for a long minute.

He pointed to a track leading up, disappearing behind huge boulders.

"Have to climb a bit." He looked down at the sandals I was wearing and shook his head.

"Maybe better you stay here," he said.

I wasn't about to come this far with Hunter and miss the next thing he was after. I said I'd be fine and followed the two men out across the mowed grass to where the trail began and quickly led upward, between rocks, to bigger rocks.

We were at a flat, open area, when Earl James stopped and pointed to a place just ahead. "That's about it. Wouldn't go any farther," he said to me. "Rattlers in there. No boots. Shouldn't go."

I agreed, having forgotten about rattlesnakes. I stopped to

watch as Hunter and Earl moved on a couple of hundred yards and stopped to look around at the higher hills, probably gauging where a shooter would put himself to get the best shot at people crossing this wide, open place between boulders.

I looked up, too. Not that I was expecting to see anything. Couple of years ago, after all. Doubted anybody was lying in wait, hoping for a second shot.

There was no seeing without putting a hand up to shade my eyes. The sun was at its highest. My sunglasses were back in the truck. Still, I caught a flash of something pretty far up in the hills. Probably a bottle left up there. Even mica in the rocks could give off flashes when the sun hit it right. I stood there hoping to see the flash again and maybe tell Hunter about it, when the flash became something like fireworks, or at least a lot brighter. More like an explosion.

Before I could do any real thinking, something hit me and I was down on the ground, putting a hand to my left shoulder and coming away with a palm full of blood. I was damned mad at first and then the pain hit and all I could do was bend over and groan, then try to roll out of the way of another bullet.

I opened one eye and looked up into Hunter's face. Scared. Worried. Saying my name and telling me to stay still, right where I was. He was going after the shooter, he told me. Earl was on his way back to the house to call the sheriff and get an ambulance.

I lay there thinking, This is no fun, and then I kind of passed out and came back when the pain hit again and I was yelling that I wanted a doctor while watching the blood spread down my arm and around the fingers I'd clasped over the hole there.

Then I was crying and swearing at the same time and so grateful when men rushed up the path with a stretcher. They cut off my blouse—which was okay because I had a new bra on—and did some poking at the wound with something

I figured was to sterilize it, and then I was bound up and on the stretcher and taking a bumpy ride toward a hospital somewhere. I didn't care where. Just wanted to get there and be knocked out so the pain would stop, which happened right away after the EMT gave me a shot in my other arm.

I woke up in a very nice hospital with a very nice and reassuring doctor's face above mine.

"How are you feeling?" the face asked.

I said I felt like hell and wanted to know how I got shot in the shoulder.

He said he couldn't tell me that. The shot was a clean one, he said. "Right through your shoulder. Should be fine. Some bone fragments, but I got them all. Be out of commission for a while, is all."

I looked around then asked for Hunter when I saw he wasn't in the room.

"The deputy?" the doctor asked.

I nodded until I winced at the pain. Any movement seemed to set my arm on fire.

"He's on his way. Been calling the desk every couple of minutes to see how you are. Should be here soon."

I relaxed back against the pillow and had to pull my arm—in a sling now—over me.

I was shot, I kept telling myself. What for? Who did it? I wasn't a Wheatley. No value in me to anyone. And then I shut my eyes and fell asleep.

When I awoke the next time, Hunter was sitting in a chair beside my bed. He looked tired and worried. When I opened my eyes, he leaned forward and smiled down at me.

"You've got to learn how to duck, Lindy. You'll never make a cop, standing out there like you've got a target painted on you."

"I wasn't expecting to get shot. Who's that mad at me?"

He shrugged. "Couldn't find him. I climbed right up to where the shot came from. Got the cartridge, is all. Could have a fingerprint on it. The guy was long gone."

I took a minute to let the pain settle then asked him, "What the heck, Hunter. Why me?"

"We'll know soon. Unless they've got some maniac here in Ralston, too, it should be the same gun that killed Henry Wade."

"I'm not a Wheatley. I'm not some Marine sharpshooter who killed the Wheatleys. Why would anyone want to shoot me? You think they were after you? Makes more sense. Go after the cop who is working the case."

He shrugged. "Don't think it was me he was after. Clean shot, the doctor said. Could have been straight through your head—if that's what the shooter wanted to happen."

I moaned because I was thinking I had the right not to be brave through this one. All I could think of was how Meemaw would feel when she heard about me getting shot. And after she sent me up here with Hunter. There was going to be a lot of beating of breasts around here.

Reading my mind, as he could always do, Hunter said, "Your mama and grandma and sister and brother are all on their way. I'll tell ya, Miss Amelia's mad as hell. I wouldn't want to be that shooter when we catch him. Got a feeling she'll be taking out her own pistol—if she has one—and putting an end to him—whoever he is."

"When can I get out of here? Maybe we can beat my family to the punch and get on home."

I barely got the words out when Bethany burst into the room and rushed to my bed, hands to her cheeks, eyes filled with tears. She moaned as she fell to her knees beside me. I figured, if nothing else, I was going to get a lot of TLC from my family.

"How did this happen? Are you going to be okay? We're all sick about what happened . . ."

Behind Bethany came Meemaw, just about as distraught as Bethany, but in tighter control of herself.

"I should've known, Lindy. They're probably after me. I was supposed to come. That bullet in you should've been—"

"Cut it out, Meemaw." I used the sternest voice I could come up with before Mama was hugging me and Justin was standing behind her talking to Hunter, demanding to know when he was going to get the man who did this.

And that went on for a half an hour before everybody was kicked out.

The next morning I was released with orders to see my own doctor and not to move the arm any more than I had to. I was happy for the prescription for pain pills. What else could a wounded woman ask for in life except maybe not to be told on the way back to Riverville that the gun that shot her was the same gun that killed Henry Wade. I didn't like being anybody's target, least of all a sharpshooter who would always know where to find me.

And even worse, we never asked Earl about that mysterious lady.

Chapter Thirty-eight

The next few days were quiet. The pain was almost gone—great pain pills—unless I moved my arm too much. Which I tried not to do. I was in something like a happy fog, willing to let Hunter and the sheriff go after whoever shot me. I wasn't afraid, having convinced myself it was all a mistake. That shot came from a long way off. Took me for somebody else or it was a poacher after a big sika. If it was a person they wanted, it had to be Jeannie—though why they'd think she'd be out there was beyond me. But a lot of things were beyond me right then and that's the way I wanted it to stay.

I did make sure Meemaw called the girls to warn them to be on the lookout and Elizabeth, too. She and Jeannie were the only Wheatleys left, and this whole thing seemed aimed at the family. Miranda said she'd put a gun by every window and door and be ready for anybody who came looking for trouble. It was a lot of the Old West mentality, but awfully reassuring.

Meemaw wouldn't pass on phone calls or let anybody in who came to see me, except Jessie and Martin and Hunter. Jessie and Martin found me in my greenhouse, making notes on some of the seedlings in my yellow pods and feeling very happy to be back home and back to work and not thinking . . . much . . . about some dude taking a shot at me.

Jessie, ever colorful and ever worried about me and having a few hard curses to settle the shooter's hash, had something to say about the man who'd been to the library earlier, asking about the Blanchards and me in particular.

"They were back at The Squirrel the other morning," she said. "Elizabeth and that man she's been going around with. Took a picture of 'em with my cell phone when they weren't looking. Showed it to our summer intern. She said he was definitely the man who was asking about all you Blanchards. Funny, how he'd come in like that. If he came to town to meet you, why didn't he know about your work already?"

I shrugged. "Maybe just curious. Who knows? Kind of a snob, like Elizabeth. Maybe he wanted to see if I was worth his time or not."

Jessie shrugged. Martin got down to business: what he'd been doing with the trees in the test grove, water reduction according to my notes, stuff like that.

"You find my notebook yet?"

He shook his head. "Can't think of anything, but that man who was out there. That man from Switzerland or wherever it was. Nobody else was ever there without you. I'm always careful about that."

"Peter Franklin. Turns out you're right. He called the journal I was supposed write the article for and offered one of his own—same thing I'm doing. I don't know what's with that man, but I settled him. Told him the trees died. Notebook was useless now. He won't be writing any articles any more than I will."

Meemaw didn't tell me Peter'd been calling for me, leaving only the message that it was urgent and I should get back to him as soon as possible. Hunter told me that. I told her I'd been an invalid long enough—three days—and I wanted my cell phone back, which she gave me then watched as I scrolled through calls from just about everybody in town, as well as people I knew at Texas A&M. After she left to get back to the store, I hit the two calls from Peter Franklin and was pulled up short. That wasn't the phone number I had for him. It wasn't a phone number I had for anybody. Beginning with 011-254 and then nine more numbers.

Crazy. I called my cell phone carrier and asked about a number like that.

"Give me the whole number, ma'am, and I'll help you out."

When I did, the woman took a minute to look it up and come back to me.

"Ma'am. That's Mombasa, Kenya, Africa. You might not want to call from your cell phone. Your plan doesn't include that kind of service."

I was too astounded—*a phone call from Africa?*—to complain about my service plan as I usually did. How the heck did Peter Franklin get over there so fast? I just talked to him. What? A couple of days ago? I thanked the helpful lady and hung up.

I got up, showered, dressed, then went down to pull Meemaw away from a group of women complaining about rude teenagers in the park. They forgot their complaints and made a fuss over me for about ten minutes.

When I got Meemaw alone in the kitchen, after being scolded for walking around too much, I told her those phone calls she'd been dodging were from Africa. "Now that's funny. I mean, who gets wrong numbers from Africa?"

"Nobody, Meemaw. It takes some doing to call there at all."

"Well, got to be a wrong number. I saw Peter Franklin walking past with Elizabeth just this morning. Guess you better ignore it."

So I confessed all the trouble I'd been having with the good Dr. Franklin and watched as her face settled into steely-eyed anger. "Why, that thieving rattler. I never heard of such a thing. Here I thought scientists were so far above anything underhanded."

She sputtered until I put my hands up and told her that the editor at *Propagation* was looking into Dr. Franklin's bona fides for me.

"You think some other Dr. Franklin's trying to get ahold of you?"

I shrugged. Who knew what was going to happen now?

"Then you better call the man back. I'd do it right now, you ask me. Maybe there's two by the same name. Common enough: Peter Franklin."

We agreed and she followed me upstairs so I could use my landline instead of the cell. I let the phone ring a long time and then called back again since there'd been no message machine on the other end.

This time a man answered. It was a deep and slow "Hello." He said it again and then asked who was calling. The accent was American.

"Dr. Peter Franklin?"

"Yes, that's me."

"I'm Lindy Blanchard, calling you from Texas."

"Ah, yes, I called you twice. A woman there told me you'd been shot and couldn't come to the phone. I thought it was a bad joke—being Texas, and all."

"No joke, Doctor. I was out of commission for a couple of days. I just got your number."

"The editor of *Propagation* called me."

"I'm glad he found you. There might still be some mistake."

"I am the only Dr. Peter Franklin either of us could find listed anywhere. I'm the only one from Harvard. I don't know who this other man is. The editor is still trying to track him down. I never offered that journal an article on pecan propagation. That isn't what I'm working on. This has really perplexed me. Do you think I should come to Texas and meet this man? I mean, my reputation is at stake here."

"I don't know. I was the one preparing the article. It seems Dr. Franklin offered the magazine one on the same subject. And that was after he came to my greenhouse. When he left, a valuable notebook was missing."

"Terrible thing, a scientist being such a knave. Not me, you know now. I'm doing something like your work, but on species here in Africa, which are dying out. I've been away from civilization for about eight years. The work is too important to spend time bragging. But I didn't expect another scientist to usurp my name and reputation. That's against the law."

"Yes, it is."

"Would you have any idea how to stop him?"

"I think he's stopped already."

"If he isn't, and you think I should come to Texas . . . well, keep my number. Please. And I'll call *Propagation* back. I'm grateful to the man. Who knows what might have happened . . ."

I promised I'd call if it was necessary. The man hung up much happier than he'd been earlier.

Meemaw and I sat at my kitchen table looking at each other with our eyes wide. Finally Meemaw shook her head. "Lord, Lord, what's going on in Riverville? It's like a mini New York City, so much lawlessness."

"We've only got a few bad apples. Seems like this Dr. Peter Franklin, or whoever he is, is one of them."

"Well, I'd say you get on the phone with Hunter and tell him about all this."

She got up to go back to the Nut House but turned at the top of the stairway. "You know what, Lindy? I'm thinking this Peter Franklin might not be wanting you to let people know he's a fraud. Seems like he smells money here. He's always with Elizabeth. You knowing he's a fraud could have set him off, warning you to keep your mouth shut. Don't you think?"

"You mean the reason I was shot?"

She nodded. "Shot by somebody who had to be pretty darned good with a rifle, you ask me. If he'd wanted you dead, I'd say you'd be dead now. Somebody who wanted you out of commission for a while."

I was catching on. "Another possible murderer, you think?"

"No," she said. "Not another one."

"Should we call Elizabeth and warn her? He's fooling her, too."

"You know what, Lindy? Let's call the sheriff and Hunter. We gotta talk to them. I think there are some things we better do real fast now. Don't want word to get out to anybody or that man will be gone—Elizabeth's money or no money."

"I see what you mean. If he's an imposter, we've got to find out who he really is."

"And what he came to Riverville for."

"And if he has any connection to the Wheatleys."

Chapter Thirty-nine

Neither man was in the office. When Deputy Harner, taking the calls, heard it was an extreme emergency, he promised to dig them both up, though it would probably only be Hunter since Sheriff Higsby was in Dallas, and going to be there all day.

We were too nervous to sit around doing nothing until Hunter called. It was like dangling over a deep hole by a thin piece of string.

What the heck was going on? We knew Peter Franklin didn't kill Sally and Eugene Wheatley—Wade's gun proved he was the killer. But could Peter Franklin, or whoever he was, have killed Henry Wade? Why?

Only thing we figured we could do until we heard from Hunter was go check on the women out at the Chaunceys'.

The day was working up to be a hot one. Man on KULM said it could get over one hundred degrees by afternoon. Could've been worse, we both figured, and drove on out with the air-conditioning going full blast though Meemaw let me know she didn't like that cold air smacking her in the face and she was in charge, since she was driving.

We pulled up their long drive kicking a cloud of dust into the air behind us. The dust was the Chaunceys' early warning system. A bunch of them were sitting in the rockers on the tin-roofed porch when we pulled in front of the old house and parked.

Melody—ever the hostess—was the first to get up and wave us to take a chair.

"Gonna be a hot one," Miranda said from her rocker, fanning herself a mile a minute.

Jeannie and her brother, Billy, gave us a wave and Melody said she was going in for sweet tea and some of her special oatmeal cookies.

Miranda let out a splash of sound. "Those cookies ain't special, Melody. Out of a bag. You offering Miss Amelia Blanchard, of the famous Nut House, cookies straight out of a bag and telling her they're special?"

Melody put both hands on her hips and glared at Miranda.

"Just sayin'," Miranda shrugged. "You wanna be a fancy hostess, like you said, can't buy bag cookies."

Meemaw said how she looked forward to bag cookies once in a while. At least they weren't her own baking. With that, Melody gave Miranda a smug smile and went in for her refreshments.

We sat talking about the weather for a while—which was only the polite thing to do. You didn't jump into problems, no matter what was going on.

"Jeannie's just back from town," Miranda said after reaching around to straighten the rifle leaning against the house wall. "Went in with Billy."

"So . . . Billy." Meemaw turned to look hard at the silent man. "Didn't expect to find you here. Your mama around, too?"

Jeannie spoke up for him. "Billy's doing some mowing in the groves for the girls. It's so good to have him. Ever since he carried Mama out of Eugene's memorial service, he's been keeping a close eye on me."

Meemaw muttered she was glad to hear it.

"Mama's gone." Jeannie leaned out in her chair to tell us. "Billy took her to the station in town and put her on a train. She was carrying on up to the last minute, but he stood there until that train was gone. He told her not to come back."

She grinned at us, her face more relaxed and cheerful than I'd seen since the party. "We been talking a lot ever since."

Miranda thumped her hands on the table. "Nothing wrong with Billy. Any trouble this boy got into his whole life long was his mama's doing. Always after him to get even with somebody for her. Or to go settle some grievance. A woman like that can drive a man crazy. That's what got him in prison to start with. Now he's staying here. Him and Jeannie."

She nodded toward Jeannie. "And if you don't mind, I'm gonna tell Lindy and Miss Amelia what happened the last time that sister-in-law of yers came out here. Brought that blown-up doctor with her—"

Meemaw stepped right in. "That's kind of what we're here about. We found out that Dr. Franklin isn't who he says he is. Tried to steal an article Lindy was writing and publish it under his own name."

"Not the article, Meemaw," I corrected her. "He stole my notebook. I was basing the article on it and had to cancel with the journal. That's when I found out somebody by his name called and offered an article on the same thing. All hell's been breaking loose ever since. The real Dr. Peter Franklin is working in Africa. Been there a long time. Called all the way from Mombasa to tell me whoever this was, it wasn't him."

"What'd you know." Melody was back, handing around sweating glasses of sweet tea and a plate full of oatmeal cookies as perfectly round and sugared as a big machine could make them. "Thought something was off about the man."

Jeannie took her glass but set it on the floor beside her rocker. She shook her head at me. "Elizabeth brought him out here yesterday. If he's not who he says he is, what's he doing mixing in all of this?"

"The two of them. Walked right on in without a by yer leave," Melody put in. "Started on Jeannie. How she had to call Elizabeth's lawyer 'cause he couldn't get anything started on the family trust until she signed some papers. And that Peter Franklin—none of his business—going on about how poor Elizabeth's been crying her eyes out since Jeannie, here, left the house like she was fleeing General Sherman."

Miranda sat up straight and put her hand in the air. "It was real sad until Elizabeth started telling Jeannie to go pack her clothes. They were takin' her with 'em. And something about how kind Elizabeth was willing to be and how sorry she was Jeannie's expectations couldn't be higher, but then she was going on about the family trust and Eugene never put Jeannie in and never changed the beneficiary of the trust, which, according to Elizabeth, is only her."

"Eugene warned me about his sister. Said I had to watch her," Jeannie said. "That's why he wanted to move to Dallas or anywhere Elizabeth wasn't. Then he was thinking Riverville, if she wasn't going to stay in the house."

It got quiet, only clinking glasses, and rockers on creaking floorboards.

Finally Jeannie said, "Funny, though, how he told me the afternoon of the party he was running into Dallas to put me into the family trust and change the beneficiaries to include me. He wanted it all amended since there's no . . . what did he call it? Something like 'dower rights,' in Texas law."

"Yup." Meemaw nodded. "Know it well enough myself, after my husband died. He saw to my rights, too, so the government wouldn't get all his money. Good for Eugene. He was a good husband."

"Thing is," Jeannie went on, "with the party and all, we never got to talk about it. Then, Gene was . . . gone."

Jeannie rocked gently.

"That Elizabeth wouldn't leave Jeannie alone," Billy put in. "I chased the both of them right out of here."

Melody was back and serving more sweet tea from an icy pitcher.

"Met your brother out here, Lindy," Billy said after a while, then glanced over at Jeannie.

"Justin?" I asked.

Billy nodded. "Offered to help any way he can. Said he sure hoped Jeannie was planning to settle here in Riverville."

Meemaw was chuckling. I was mad. That was the thing about Justin. Closed mouth so bad you wouldn't know he even had one, except to other people.

"He came out with Hunter to tell us about you getting shot," Miranda said. "I tried calling, but yer meemaw here wouldn't let nobody talk to you. Probably the smartest thing, with everybody in the area up in arms about it."

"Hunter told us about the man who killed Eugene," Jeannie said. "Never heard of him and I guess Hunter can't figure out why he did it. Then he said Sally, too. This is like . . . I don't know . . . a vendetta against all the Wheatleys."

"Except Elizabeth," Miranda said, slapping her hands down on her knees. "Seems like she's the only one not getting shot at."

"And me," Jeannie said, frowning.

"And you. Yes. And I plan on keeping it that way," Miranda said with an "amen" coming from Melody.

"And you know somebody murdered the man that shot your husband." Meemaw turned to Jeannie, who made a face and bit hard at her lower lip.

"That's what we came out to warn you about. This second killer. We're getting an idea—"

"Can you say what it is yer worried about?" Melody asked, her elderly face unhappy.

Meemaw shook her head. "Got to talk to Hunter first. Be a couple of hours. We'll call you. Just don't let anybody come around."

Miranda sat up and slapped a hand on a holster at her hip. "Got my rifle, too."

"Bet you can handle a gun, eh, Billy?" She sat forward, looking at Billy.

"Can't. No guns. A condition of my release—"

"Well, I'll just give Jeannie one to carry, and in case you see somebody who shouldn't be around here, Jeannie could hand you the gun—case I'm in the bathroom or somewhere. Protection. That all right, you think?"

"Whatever I have to do, Miss Miranda."

With that agreed to, Meemaw and I thanked Melody for her gracious hospitality—which brought a grunt from Miranda—and we were off the porch and into the truck, waving at the brave people lined up rocking and sipping.

We headed back to town. I called the sheriff's office on the way. Deputy Harner said Hunter was still out on a loose cow on the highway call and he'd tell him as soon as he got ahold of him.

Chapter Forty

The thing I was thinking, on the way back to town, was how Hunter picked up Flasher out on the highway. And look where that got him. Stuck with that ignorant, lumpish dog. Now he was out after a loose cow. So what next? A cow staked out in his yard? No matter how he asked, a cow was one animal that wasn't coming to my apartment.

My cell rang as soon as I was back in signal range. It was Joshua Lightley from *Propagation.*

"Did you hear from Dr. Franklin?" he asked quickly.

I said I had.

"He's the real deal. Not that other one."

"I kind of figured that out."

"So you've got a phony on your hands. You said he'd been in your greenhouse."

"Yes, sir. Any idea who he really is?"

"Not a clue, Lindy."

"Well, he's still here and there's sure a lot been happening around him. Nothing good."

"Can't figure out why he'd want to do that to you."

"Me either. Not like I knew him or anything. Like he'd want to get even for something I did."

"Well, I called to give you the number he gave me. Make sure we're talking about the same man."

I took the number, saying it out loud as I wrote it down.

"That's him all right."

Joshua wished me luck and told me to send him anything I had, soon as I could get it all back together. That was the one thing in the day that made me feel good about myself.

What Meemaw and I agreed on was getting over to Elizabeth's. She may be a miserable snob and a pain in the butt to deal with, but the woman had to be warned about Peter Franklin, and fast. He could be out there. We had no plan if he was. Maybe one of us could get Elizabeth aside and tell her what was going on.

"I guess we'll just play it by ear," I said.

"Terrible thing. I feel sorry for Elizabeth. Caught up with this man. You know he could be a killer, Lindy."

"I'm starting to see it, Meemaw. Wish Hunter would get back."

"I gotta think. Just gotta think." Meemaw was the most discombobulated I'd ever seen her. Her usually neat hair was standing up at the back, like little white weeds. And she was driving too fast. "That other man, that Henry Wade, shot Sally Wheatley and Eugene both. Then he gets shot."

She thought awhile longer, narrowing her eyes and staring straight out the windshield as we drove up shady Carya Street and back out to the highway, going in the other direction, toward the Wheatley mansion.

"The Wheatleys are at the heart of this." She was mumbling to herself. "Only two left: Elizabeth and Jeannie. Makes you think."

I shrugged. "Guess so."

"No, I mean motive."

"Guess so," I said again, not in tune with her.

"Eugene's dead. Sally, his first wife, is dead. If the motive had anything to do with money and maybe inheriting, why, I'd expect Jeannie to be the one killed, not Eugene." She looked over at me. "You think this could have anything to do with the oil company he ran?"

"I don't know how. From what I've always heard, Eugene wasn't exactly a hands-on executive. Had men who'd run everything since his father passed. He left them alone to do it."

Meemaw was thinking hard. "Well, if you take a look at the top reasons people kill one another, it's either over love or hate; or money or lack of money. Let me see: revenge. Those awful domestic things—arguing and a gun in the vicinity. Now what category would these murders come under?"

"Seems like a couple of them, if you ask me. Since the Wheatleys are rich, money's got to be part of it. I don't see revenge here. Maybe love or hate? But who hated whom? Domestic . . . no. If Elizabeth was shot, well, I'd say, yes, domestic all right. Couldn't keep her mouth shut around Eugene's wives. That "superior" business of hers. If she'd only tried to get along . . . well . . . Jeannie wouldn't have felt she had to leave the mansion the way she did. Elizabeth would have at least one female friend."

I pulled in the tree-lined driveway leading to the Wheatleys' mansion and parked along the curve.

No parking attendant this time. No lines of limos and fancy pickups. And no white rental that Peter Franklin was driving.

Just a quiet June morning in Texas. The trees were moving in the woods around the house. I guessed their property ran on and on for a couple of miles. Nice place. Was a house a good enough reason to kill? I wondered.

Meemaw pushed the bell.

Martha, the housekeeper, in her little ruffled apron, opened the door.

"Miss Elizabeth's not home right now." She smiled a wide smile and greeted Meemaw especially. "Why, I was just going into town for one of those pecan pies of yours, Miss Amelia."

"Got plenty of 'em waiting."

"That's a good thing. My granddaughter's birthday party's tonight."

Impatient with the usual slow pace we lived at, I broke in. "Do you know were Elizabeth's gone to?"

Martha shook her dark head, her hair bundled up in the back into some kind of bun. "Left before I got here. Never knew her to leave so early. Probably off with that Dr. Franklin. He's here most of the time now. She usually has a list ready or calls to tell me the million and a half things she wants me to do. Nothing so far. Tried calling her. She doesn't answer."

"Think I'll try." I stepped out into the drive and dialed the number I had for Elizabeth.

No answer. I tried again, and again there was still no answer. Not even a recording telling me to leave a message. The phone had to be turned off. If she was with whoever Dr. Peter Franklin really was, I was starting to get afraid for her.

Back at the door Martha was saying, "Thought that man'd be moving in the way he treats this place like it's his. And the staff, too. Treats us all like dirt. Don't say a word to Miss Elizabeth or I'll lose my job, but there's not a single one of us that like the man. She's had a lot others better than that one."

Martha crossed her arms and leaned against the doorway. "Tell you another thing, everybody here's talking about how she's carrying on about Miss Jeannie. Just going on and on, like the poor soul's trying to steal from her. And with her own brother not cold in his grave yet."

She shook her head and sighed.

"Would you have her call one of us as soon as she gets back?" Meemaw asked. "Tell her it's real important."

She looked around at me. "You got anything to add, Lindy?"

I shook my head. "Or tell her to call the sheriff. Maybe that'll get to her. I got the feeling, ever since the party, she doesn't like me much."

"You mean that ghost thing you were wearing?" Martha laughed. "Yup, got yerself talked about a whole lot that night. And got Elizabeth going on and on."

We left, but neither one of us was happy.

"Think we should go back to town and sit there at the sheriff's office until somebody gets back," Meemaw said. "I feel like something's about to blow up and we're just chasing our tails. You know, I'm afraid Elizabeth could've gotten herself into deep trouble."

I felt the same way—expecting an explosion at any minute, and worrying about a woman I never expected to worry about. I called Deputy Harner at the sheriff's again and told him about Elizabeth Wheatley and that we were headed back to Riverville.

Chapter Forty-one

I wanted to hug Hunter when I saw him on the steps of the sheriff's office.

"Harner called just as I got back in my car. Cow, name was Sara, was too smart for that bunch of cowboys out there. Took a while to catch her."

I guess he could see Meemaw and I were both upset as we told him what we'd learned about Peter Franklin—that he was an imposter, maybe not a scientist at all. And now Elizabeth was missing.

"Harner gave me the details. Put an APB out on that rental Franklin drove. Got a BOLO statewide on him. Sheriff Higsby's checking with the Wheatley offices in Dallas. Nobody there knows a single reason anybody would want to kill Eugene. Nobody has a bad word to say about him. Nothing in his past. Always been a straight-up hard worker. Not at all like some of those oilmen. You know, big spenders and big egos and don't give a crap for the people who work for them."

"There's got to be something about the Wheatleys," I said. "Two killers after them. Some kind of vendetta. Somebody's paying these men to kill. Probably paying big. Why? How would they get at the Wheatley money? Can't be that. So, revenge?"

Hunter shrugged. "Gotta find that second rifle."

Meemaw held a finger in the air. "Know where we should go? The Columbus Inn. Where Peter Franklin was staying. George and Clarissa Pickens own it. Clarissa's behind the front desk most days. If not, it will be George. Not like some big city hotels. The Columbus is known for their down home hospitality. And I bet you anything, between the two of them, Clarissa and George know as much about their guests as Lydia Hornbecker does about hers. Those kids sank every dime they had into that hotel. You can bet your bottom dollar they keep an eye on what's going on."

Hunter smiled at Meemaw. "You know, Miss Amelia, there are times I get the feeling I'm following that Sherlock Holmes around. All I have to do is wait and you'll come up with something."

"Logical, Hunter. Just logical."

The Columbus Inn, over on Allred Avenue, was one of the prettiest in Riverville. It sat on a nice piece of property with the Colombia River running along down a grassy slope. I'd say it was all Texas, from the ochre adobe walls to the Texas flags flying across the front of the building. I'd been in school with Clarissa Tomplin. That was her maiden name. Me and Clarissa'd been kind of friends but never got that close. I think me being so interested in the pecan trees, maybe a little preachy about them, kept some people away. Maybe a lot of people, come to think of it.

It was good to see her standing behind the front desk when the three of us walked in.

Me and Meemaw got greeted with hugs. There was a lot of "How y'all doin'?" and "What a sight fer sore eyes." And then me and Meemaw were oohing and ahhing and patting her pregnant belly while Hunter waited impatiently behind us.

He knew better than to rush a couple of Southern women who hadn't seen each other in a while. There was catching up to do and family to hear about, like we didn't run into each other at the bank every once in a while. Something, I think, about meeting in unexpected places. There were requirements for greetings. We were kind of in Clarissa's home, here at the Columbus Inn, and that had a strict code of conduct to go along with it.

Refreshments went with the strict code. And us throwing up our hands and refusing daintily.

And then Meemaw got down to business. "You know Hunter Austen, don't you, Clarissa?"

She smiled big and nodded at Austen. "Sure, knew you from school. See you're with the sheriff. Should be proud of yerself, helping the good people of Riverville to stay safe in their beds. I always said, the sheriff and his men are our first defense against evil that can move into town and we don't even know it. Pastor Rogan was sayin' just the other day how we got to always keep in mind the men here at home who stand and serve. Why, George and I were talking about having some kind of appreciation day here at the Columbus. You know, have all the men who protect us come in and give them a big supper and ask the town to come over, maybe have a patriotic concert out in the back and . . ."

Hunter was nodding along until we were all afraid she was never going to get to the end of her oration. Now I remembered why me and Clarissa never got to be friends. It wasn't me and my pecans after all. It was her talking. There was no good way to turn her off.

Hunter stopped nodding and put up his hand, cutting the speech straight through so it came to a stop.

"I'm kind of here on business, Miz Pickens. It's about one of your guests."

It was almost funny, how her face froze and her eyes got wary. "Ya don't say? Which one, if you don't mind my askin'? You know I'm not at liberty to talk about my guests behind their backs. George always says maybe they're stayin' with us for personal reasons, like a husband or wife after 'em, and it's none of our business to give out information, so if yer goin' to ask things I can't tell you, well, you'll just have to forgive me, Hunter. I'm gonna stick a key in it and lock it up tight."

That last went along with the motions of sticking an imaginary key between her lips, locking it up, and throwing the key away.

"I understand," Hunter pushed on. "But we've got a very serious situation going on here in Riverville and one of your guests just might be involved in it."

Her mouth made a perfect "O." Her lashes fluttered. "Not the murders!" She was whispering now. "I wouldn't like to think we took somebody in who would get involved in things like that. Why, me and George were reading in the paper just this morning how there was another murder somewhere up near Austin that was connected to our very own murder here in Riverville and George was saying—"

Hunter had his hand in the air again, which magically brought a scaling down of the sound and then quiet. I wished I'd learned that back in school, I was thinking. Me and Clarissa might have been friends after all.

"His name is Dr. Peter Franklin."

The lashes fluttered again. The red mouth made a circle. "Why, don't tell me that. Not the doctor. He's an important man. He was tellin' George himself about all the things he's done for farmers and how he's working over some place in Italy and how he was here in Riverville to see . . ." She thought awhile. "My goodness! I think it was you, Lindy. Said the two of you are close friends and—"

I raised my hand and made the magic happen.

"We think he knows something about the tragic events that happened here." Hunter knew to jump in fast. "In fact, he might at this moment be a fugitive from justice."

"You don't say." Clarissa lowered her head and snapped off the three words, then stopped talking.

"I need to get up into his room. See if he's hidden any weapons in there—"

"No, no. We couldn't allow a thing like that."

"Even if the man turns out to be a killer?"

"That case maybe George would look the other way, so to speak. But—"

"Could I get into his room?" Hunter pressed on fast.

Clarissa shook her head. "Not without a search warrant. I know my law. I let you in there and they could sue us because we're not supposed to do a thing like that."

"I'll get a warrant to cover you, it's just that the man may be holding a woman hostage and we've got to find him."

She shook her head harder. "No, sir. Can't do that. We run an up-and-up place here at the Columbus Inn. You better go get yourself—"

George Pickens, a round man in his late thirties, stepped out of the inner office to interrupt his wife.

"Heard what you was sayin.'" George put his hand on his wife's shoulder. "I'll take you up, Hunter. Everybody in town knows what's been going on with the Wheatleys. I wouldn't stand in the way for nothing."

George got a key from behind the desk and led the way to the elevator.

The Columbus was known for pretty rooms. A lot of lace curtains and homemade bedspreads on four-posters. Pretty blue wallpaper. Texas history was caught in framed pictures around the walls.

The place was neat. You'd think nobody was staying there except for a suitcase on the wooden stand at the foot of the made-up bed.

I leaned over to whisper in Meemaw's ear, "Killers sure are neat."

Meemaw shushed me. "Watch your mouth."

George stood in the doorway. "Gotta watch," he said. "I know y'all, but I don't want to get caught in the middle of anything."

"Understand," Hunter told him as he opened the closet door. He pushed aside summer jackets on the pole, feeling the pockets of each of them. And then through a row of shirts—mostly white and blue. He checked the shoes lined in correct order along the floor.

Meemaw was in the bathroom, going through a shaving kit and looking at pill bottles.

She called out, "Nothing here."

I pulled out dresser drawer after dresser drawer. I was going to avoid the neatly folded boxer shorts, but something told me not to be prudish. This wasn't about me touching his shorts—a thing a lady would never do—it was about discovering who he really was and what he was doing here in Riverville.

I struck gold in those boxers. Inside the last neatly folded pair I found an iPad.

I held it up in my hand. "Gotta be something on here. He hid it in his shorts."

Hunter wasn't listening. He pulled a gun case from the back of the closet, set it on the floor beside him, and looked from one to the other of us as he unzipped the long zipper.

"Remington 700P. Sniper. The kind I've been looking for. I'll bet anything it's the gun that shot you in Ralston."

Which did nothing to make me feel any better about Peter Franklin.

George, scowling, was taking all of this in.

"You think the man's in physical danger?" he asked. "Heard I can't stop you taking things if you think the man's in physical danger. That right?"

"Worst kind of danger there is." Hunter nodded.

George backed into the hall without another word and left, giving us free run of the room.

Hunter smiled. "Good citizen, that George. Let's take what we think is necessary. I'm going to call in and get people here with a search warrant and get the techs to go over the room. We need fingerprints. One found on that empty cartridge from the Henry Wade shooting. Bet anything—"

"Hope we haven't compromised the evidence." Meemaw looked worried and backed toward the door.

"From here on in, let me be the bad guy." Hunter was looking down at the locked suitcase. I watched as he slipped a knife out of his pocket and opened the case.

"Think we got him," he said, pulling out a box of cartridges and holding it up in his hands.

He looked over at me. "Looks like the same make of cartridges. I'll be taking these." He tucked the box under his arm and pawed through whatever was left in the suitcase. From a side pocket he pulled papers out and fingered through them.

"Credit cards in different names, a driver's license," he said, not looking up. "There's some bigger sheets, looks like copies of e-mails." He hesitated over another side pocket and then held something above his head. "An address book."

I couldn't help myself, I went to stand beside him, asking to see the driver's license, which he held up for me to read.

The face was certainly Dr. Peter Franklin. The name was Peter Voorhees. The address was in Anaheim, California.

I stood there, trying to figure out what was going on, who this guy was, and why he'd wanted to come meet me when I wasn't the real target of any of this. Or was I? But then *why?*

Hunter called Deputy Harner, asking him to run a check on a Peter Voorhees from Anaheim, California. He added the license number. “Real fast, Greg,” Hunter was saying. “I’d say this was really life and death.”

He asked if there’d been anything on the APB yet. He seemed to get a negative.

With that done, he got put through to Sheriff Higsby, in Dallas, and they talked about what to do next.

I stood there praying that, whoever this guy was, he didn’t come back while we were standing in his room. Meemaw was clearing her throat and rolling her eyes at me, evidently thinking the same thing.

Hunter put his hand over the phone, still talking to Sheriff Higsby, but wanting to tell me something.

“Call the station on your phone,” he said. “Tell Harner to get ahold of Judge London about the warrant. Got to cover our—”

Which I did. Deputy Greg Harner would only talk to Hunter so he waited until Hunter and the sheriff had put together their plan and Hunter was free to talk.

All we got on our end was “Un-huh. Un-huh.”

He hung up and turned to us.

“Greg got feedback immediately. Peter Voorhees is wanted in California. First-degree murder. They’re warning us to go slow and careful. The guy’s dangerous. Got out of prison a year ago. That was for larceny and impersonation. Guess it was a doctor then, too. Don’t know what kind of doctor that one was.”

“Billy got out three months ago. Could there be a connection between them?” I asked.

Hunter shook his head. “This Voorhees was in Folsom, making license plates, I guess.”

“And the sheriff?” Meemaw asked in a hurry, almost out of breath. “What’s he want us to do?”

“He says there is no ‘us.’ He wants you two women to go home and let me take care of it from here on in. He’s calling in backup.”

"You call him right back and tell him these 'two women' aren't pulling out now. Whatever we've got to do, we'll do it together. We've come too far—"

Meemaw was mad. "Could be Elizabeth's already dead. Then we've got to get out to the Chaunceys'. Jeannie's next."

Hunter looked from Meemaw to me. I could see by his face that he knew he didn't have a choice.

"We better get going," he said, gathering the box of cartridges and the papers he wanted to take along. He tucked the rifle case under his arm. "You have to drive, Miss Amelia. Can't get up that drive of the Chaunceys' without a cloud of dust warning them somebody's coming. Don't want this Voorhees guy to see us in a police vehicle, if that's where he's at."

We stopped at his car long enough for him to get his own rifle from the rack behind the driver's seat. He called Harner back and told him to get somebody over there to pick up his squad car and said where we were headed.

Chapter Forty-two

"Here!" Hunter shouted at me when we were half a mile in on the Chaunceys' road. "Let me out. I don't want 'em knowing I'm anywhere around."

I slowed, so as not to be seen stopping.

"We'll call if his car's up there," Meemaw promised as Hunter slid out of the backseat, through the half-opened door and to the ground, kind of rolling down into an arroyo. I started moving just a little faster, giving him more dust for cover.

Meemaw reached over and put her hand on mine. "I hope we're not too late. God only knows how many people he could have killed by now."

I looked back at her, my throat tightening. "We've got his gun."

"You think killers only have one?"

"What else can we do?"

She shook her head. "We could wait until the sheriff gets enough deputies together to come out and surround the place, but by that time he'll be gone, if he's here. By then he will have killed everybody he came to town to kill, plus a few more—like us, I'd say."

I didn't have anything to add, just drove slowly until I could see the house, standing on its rise backed by the pecan groves. There was a car in front. Franklin's white rental. Meemaw saw it at the same time and ducked down to call Hunter.

"You think he brought Elizabeth with him?" I asked Meemaw.

"Kind of feel that's the way it's going to go now. Two birds with one stone. The last of the Wheatleys." When she turned back to me, there were tears in her eyes. "Oh, my child, I wish I could go in there alone."

I had no voice. My throat was tight. I could only croak out, "I've got the same wish, Meemaw. Wish I hadn't gotten you into any of this."

We got out of the car, but before we could get on the porch, the door opened and Melody stepped out. As I started up the steps, I not only tried to read Melody's face, but was also looking around for Hunter. He'd been running the last I saw him. I'd driven slowly. He should be somewhere close by.

"Land's sakes, come on in, you two. We was just sayin' we thought somebody was coming up the road."

I tried to read the elderly, wrinkled face and got nowhere. She didn't seem to be looking directly at us, kind of off to the side, saying things to be saying things.

"See you got company, Melody." Meemaw walked close beside me.

"Sure do. Just serving everybody a cold drink and cookies. Come on in. Come on in." Melody turned to wave us into the house, and as she did, she rolled her eyes at me. Some kind of signal, but I had no clue what it meant.

Melody held the door open. "Elizabeth Wheatley's here. And that friend of hers, Peter Franklin. You know, that scientist. Guess *you* know him, don't you, Lindy?"

I nodded, not ready to trust my voice.

Before I went inside, I looked around at the empty land in front of me, hoping to see Hunter. It seemed nobody was out there for miles and miles.

Melody went on talking at a great rate as I walked in and got a load of who was gathered around the twins' table. Billy Truly sat at the far side and I was happy to see him though his face was grim. Jeannie sat close beside her brother. At one end of the table, chairs pulled together, sat Peter Franklin, one hand wrapped in a bloody towel, with Elizabeth, eyes wide and scared, next to him. At the other end of the table, Miranda kind of lounged, her arm stretched out across the wooden tabletop, fingers beating a quick melody. Her other hand was hidden beneath the tabletop.

"Come on in, Blanchards. Take a look at what we got here." Miranda didn't sit up at first, just kind of half lay there as if somebody just woke her.

Meemaw and I stood inside, taking stock of what was in front of us.

"Happen that Hunter come out with you?" Miranda demanded.

I shook my head, not ready to give him away since I didn't know what was going on.

"I'll get the both of you something to drink," Melody said and headed around to the kitchen. "Not often we get this many visitors, I'll tell you."

I started to stop her, thinking maybe refreshments weren't in order at this kind of party.

"Let her go." Miranda lifted the hand on the table. "Better she stays out there."

Miranda leaned back in her chair, drawing her other hand out from under the table, holding the biggest, blackest, oldest pistol I'd ever seen in my life.

Meemaw gasped. "What the devil's going on, Miranda?"

"Bet you know some of it."

“I don’t think I know anything right now,” Meemaw answered and pulled a chair out from the table to sit.

“Well, I’ll tell you. That pair over there—” She waved the gun at Elizabeth and Peter, who kept their eyes fixed on the barrel.

“Hope one of you people notices I’m bleeding over here,” Peter moaned and held up the bloody hand.

Miranda fixed him with a look and went right on. “They came to get Jeannie, sayin’ she had to sign some important papers quick. All Jeannie said was she didn’t think she’d be goin’ anywhere. What Jeannie was tellin’ them, nice as can be, was that Eugene’s lawyer called Ben and Ben called here. Eugene did have that family trust business taken care of before he was killed. Was in Dallas the very day of the party. Not with their family lawyer. Had one of his own. She was tellin’ them she was happy everything was settled and Elizabeth didn’t have to worry anymore, the court would take care of it.”

She waved at Peter Franklin, or Voorhees, or whoever he was. “That one went straight out to his car and got a gun. Tried to bring it into my house. Can you imagine? Shot it right out of his hand. Think it’s somewhere out in the weeds. Hunter can find it when he gets here.”

She sighed. “We all been sitting quiet ever since. I called the sheriff’s office over and over, tried to get ahold of Hunter. Couldn’t get anybody so I told that deputy what answered, that I was holding a gun on these two and I think he’s tearing out here all by himself.”

All I could do was put my hands to my mouth. Meemaw looked like she’d had the wind knocked out of her.

“Ever since then Elizabeth, there, has been talking about how she doesn’t even know Dr. Franklin and he forced her to come out here with ’im. Thinks he’s going to kill her, she said. Like I didn’t see the two of them whispering on the way out of that car.”

Billy cleared his throat and jumped in. "'Course, that man—his name isn't Dr. Peter Franklin after all—says she's a liar and he's a private detective come here to prove she had her brother's wife and then her brother killed, all to keep their fortune in the family. Man, they both got big stories to tell."

Meemaw almost laughed, but not quite. "Bet they do."

I got up and headed back to the door.

On the porch I looked for Hunter, then called out his name.

I saw the gun coming around the corner before I caught a glimpse of him.

"You nuts? Yelling my name out like that?" He was in a half crouch, which looked uncomfortable for a man Hunter's size.

"Come on in. It's all over. Miranda's got her gun on 'em."

"What the hell!" He came running up on the porch. "You don't say. Miranda? Well, who would've figured . . ."

"Anybody who knows Miranda." I led the way back into the house.

Hunter, after taking in the two cowering at one end of the table, patted Miranda on the back. "He have a gun on him?" he asked her.

She nodded. "Blew it outta his hand. Should be in the dirt in front somewhere. That's why he's bleeding."

Voorhees held up the bad hand and was whining about brutality and needing to get to a hospital. Then he put his good hand up to his head and said he felt dizzy.

Hunter went back outside, and then in, carrying a rifle with the stock damaged.

"Guess this is yours," he said to Voorhees. "Got the one from your apartment. Looks like the gun that killed Henry Wade, and the gun you took a shot at Lindy with."

Hunter glared. "What in hell's your real name, fella? Voorhees. That it? Got out of prison what? Three months ago? Guess where you're going back to. For the rest of your life."

He turned to Elizabeth, who sat with her head down now. "And you, Miss Wheatley. What the heck's going on?"

"She's the one got me mixed up in it," Peter snarled before she could speak, his face dark and furious. "Set up the whole thing. First it was with my friend, Henry. Got him to do her dirty work—kill her brother's first wife to keep her from going into the will. Offered to pay Henry fifty thousand for the job. We were Marines together. Marksmen. Henry called me, said he fell into a money pit and got me to come out. He was blackmailing Elizabeth, here. Thought she'd never stand up to two of us. But what do you know? Out of a clear blue sky she called me. Wanted him gone. Offered me a hundred thousand to take care of it. Had to get rid of Henry. So don't believe her now, that she had nothing to do with it. Got e-mails back in my room. Gives you the whole story. This woman's mean as they come."

At the insult Elizabeth got her haughty look back fast, sneering, "Do you really think these people will believe an ex-con like you? They know who I am. They know the truth when I speak it."

"That's what I was figuring," Meemaw said. "I thought you had to be at the center of things, Elizabeth. Who else had to worry about losing the family money to one of Eugene's wives? Who else was on the scene of both killings? First Sally, but that wasn't enough. You had to have Eugene killed, too. Tell you the truth, Elizabeth, I didn't want to believe it of you, but here it is." Meemaw swept a hand out and around the people seated at the table.

"Yeah, Miz Wheatley," Hunter said. "Sure believe every word you say. You told your brother you were sending out a tray of food for him, didn't you? There at the party. I think Lindy mentioned it. Nice sisterly thing to do. You had Henry Wade brought on to be a waiter so he could get in the gun room and shoot Eugene. Your brother, expecting the food, got up to open the door and went back to sit where he was working. Eugene took a blast straight through the body. He didn't know what was coming. I guess you figured you couldn't just keep killing any wife he took so you might as well stop him."

Hunter stretched, seeming to enjoy his place in the sun.

"Just heard back from our computer man while I was out there waiting to come in the house. Found e-mails to you from Henry Wade on the hard drive of Wade's computer. He must've copied everything then thought he'd erased it all—I'll bet you ordered him to do that, get rid of evidence. The whole plan was all still there. People sure are dumb about computers."

I could hear sirens in the distance. I had to know. "Why shoot me?" I turned to Peter. "You almost killed me."

He got a cruel smile on his face, though he still held the bleeding hand up so everybody could see. "If I wanted to kill you, you'd be dead. It was Elizabeth." He tilted his head toward her. "First she had me do this scientist stuff for cover. Made me the kind of man who could hang around her. Then, when she heard you were going to be published, she thought it would be fun to mess that up for you. I don't think Elizabeth, here, likes you too much."

"Feeling's mutual." I glared at the flushed woman, who glared back at me.

"All her idea." He moved his head again. "I went along with it. Stealing your book. She thinks she's so smart. Was going to write the article to show you up. After she looked it over, she told me to toss it. Elizabeth thought it was good enough just to mess with you, for sticking your nose in her business."

The sirens got closer.

Meemaw stared straight at Elizabeth Wheatley. "Looks like the place you're going won't be half as big as that house you wanted to hold on to so bad."

"Shame on you, Miss Amelia. Turning on someone of your own class, like this," Elizabeth spit back.

"Why, bless yer heart, Elizabeth. If I know anything about me and my life, it's that I don't belong to a class of people who kill off their own kin." Meemaw sat back, looking pleased with herself.

That was the moment when deputies poured into the house with their guns drawn and all hell broke loose until everybody knew what was going on and Elizabeth Wheatley was off to jail. Peter Voorhees kept yelling "brutality" and waving his bloody hand as they took him to Riverville Memorial Hospital while I hugged my bandaged shoulder and thought how winning was a good thing even though it could hurt like hell.

EPILOGUE

Everybody was at the Barking Coyote that momentous night, celebrating Melody and Miranda's catching two murderers and delivering Riverville from a crime wave. Jeannie didn't come because she didn't think it was seemly, being in mourning for her husband and, in a way, for her sister-in-law who, by the way, was the woman in the suede jacket and gold jewelry who met Peter Voorhees in Ralston. So, of course, my smitten brother stayed behind at the Wheatley place with her.

"Don't want her left alone," Justin had muttered in his usual, untalkative way. Mama said something about never seeing her grown son so attentive to anything but the trees. I knew she was catching on to what was happening to Justin. We'd all seen it a dozen times, happening to other men. Poor fellows. Love sure did strange things to some of them. Like they weren't even who they used to be.

Meemaw worried out loud only once about how Jeannie was going to be very rich, and after all, she was a fresh widow. Justin could be waiting a long time for things to change on that front.

The rest of us came to the saloon to have a good time and celebrate the twins and locking up a couple of lowlifes. I included Elizabeth in that category because she was the worst of the worst. Without Elizabeth nobody would be dead. Sally and Eugene would be alive and happy. Jeannie would be single. And if Elizabeth hadn't hired two hit men like Henry Wade and Peter Voorhees, they would never have come to town. Meemaw said it was something like a vortex—one of those whirlwinds that once it got going couldn't be stopped until people were dying and blackmailing one another and who knew what all else.

"Dark hearts," she muttered more than once in the days since the twins caught the killers.

I was sitting at a table with Hunter, who was out of uniform. He was off duty and celebrating. "Gonna have one hell of a time tonight!"

Flasher was tied to Hunter's chair when we first got there. He gnawed through that rope in ten minutes. The dog just wandered after that, sniffing crotches, and then watching the dancers. Morton Shrift ignored him, like he did a lot of his customers.

Hunter had to bring Flasher with him because the dog chewed up too many pillows back at home. None of his neighbors wanted to watch him and everybody else was at the saloon to celebrate and weren't up to watching a hard-headed animal, or at least they planned on soon not being up to doing much of anything.

I thought having one hell of a time was a great idea, but all Hunter had done so far was sit sipping his 512 Pecan Porter beer. When I mentioned dancing, like everybody else was doing, he only shrugged one shoulder and made a face. Three times and I was getting mad.

Everybody else was on the dance floor, line dancing, slow dancing, leaning on one another and pretending to dance. The twins were the hit of the night and didn't miss a beat, whether dancing alone, together, or with a group of people.

Every couple of minutes Hunter looked over at me and tried to say something, but Waylon Jennings was singing out "Luckenbach, Texas" at the top of his lungs and people were drunk enough to sing along.

Not Meemaw, of course. She limited herself to one shot of Garrison's. But I'd say Mama was having herself a good time, line dancing with Ben Fordyce and other men who waited their turn.

Bethany was passing out cards for our event "pavilion," as she called it now, faster than a poker player with ten aces up her sleeve.

I put my beer down on the wet, stained table. I was kind of mad at the silent Hunter, and ready to go on home, where I might as well read a book as be here where the music was so loud I couldn't think and where everybody was having a good time but me. I had to pee bad and didn't want to have to go to the Coyotes' ladies', where I knew the room would be swimming in lipstick-smeared Kleenex all over the floor; and the counter and toilet seats would be wet.

What I was working myself up to was a fine snit so I could stomp out and go home.

"Lindy." The way Hunter said it made me look at him full-on instead of glaring from the sides of my eyes.

"Lindy," he said again.

"Luckenbach, Texas" finished and the DJ was talking about how Morton Shrift was giving out a free beer to everybody to celebrate what the sheriff and the citizens did to stop the murders in Riverville. There was a lot of hooting and hollering so I had to bend over the table to hear Hunter.

He was thinking. Maybe he'd decided to dance after all.

I was expecting "You wanna dance this next one?". Instead he leaned back, tipped the cowboy hat he wore over his eyes, and put one booted foot up on an empty chair.

"You gonna dance or not?" I demanded, as loud as I could, not caring who heard me.

He nodded. One of those nods to shut people up.

I got up just as the DJ put on another song. Hunter leaned over and grabbed my hand, pulling me back down near him.

"Don't go," he said. "I . . . I . . . Give me a minute here."

The song was loud. People were singing along. Billy Currington's "Like My Dog," bringing on the usual laughter and hollering.

Hunter took off his black hat and set it in the little space we had left on our table. He scooted his chair around closer. With the set look on his face, I started getting worried.

He leaned in, his lips almost touching my ear. "I been thinking . . ." he said and even that was hard to hear so I cupped my ear and bent in closer.

"I been thinking . . ." he started again.

Billy Currington was going on about his dog not minding a lot of things a wife would mind, like calling her sister a bitch.

I smiled at Hunter. Be good to hear what he'd been thinking about.

"You know, Lindy. We've known each other a long, long time."

"Since swimming naked in the Colorado." I had to yell to make him hear me. "You got so embarrassed because I saw your—"

He cut me short. "Yeah. Like I said, a long time now."

An old cowboy, stumbling up to dance, kicked the back of my chair and bent down to apologize while swaying above me. Hunter half got up and told him to keep moving.

Currington was hard to hear over the laughter and even harder because I was trying to hear Hunter. But I thought

Currington was saying something about the wife not listening any better than his dog does.

"So I've been thinking . . ."

I rolled my eyes at him. Come on, get on with it, fella!

Another long pull on his Porter, a stretch of his neck muscles, and he was back close to my ear, where I could smell the beer and his shaving lotion and maybe some good soap under that and I was thinking I wasn't mad at Hunter at all. In fact, I felt the opposite. I felt his arm against me at the back of my chair. I turned to look into those round eyes and thought how those eyes could melt my heart.

I watched the dancing and listened to the laughing and here I was with this guy who made me happy, no matter what. Talk about "lucky dogs." Not bad, Lindy, I told myself and reached out to touch Hunter's cheek, a little gritty with dark blond whiskers, and run my finger over his mouth.

"You know, Lindy. This is real hard on me."

I caught only the end of that and made him repeat it as Billy Currington wrapped up his song begging somebody to love him like his dog does.

And people were clapping and stomping.

And Hunter was yelling in my face. "Want you to marry me, Lindy."

Which everybody heard despite the noise. The whole place went up in a roar and they all came running over to where we sat, including Flasher, who leaped and danced and licked Hunter's face and then mine.

Morton Shrift was laughing, asking who was going to wear the noose in the family now and then offering another free beer for the whole saloon.

My hand was in Hunter's as everybody smacked him on the back and bent to give me a hug, especially Meemaw and Mama.

Hunter's face was redder than I ever saw a man's face get red.

He kept trying to look over at me, still waiting for an answer.

I only had a minute and was thinking fast about the stuff I wanted to do, the places I needed to go, and the time to myself I had to have.

I thought about all of that then leaned down, over Flasher, who was drooling on us, and yelled out, "Yes, I sure will marry you, Hunter Austen."

I stood, turned to my loving family, to my good neighbors, to friends like nobody else ever had, and nodded. "I'm gonna love this good man," I shouted real loud and lifted my beer over my head.

I can't sing, but I belted out my own line:

"I'm gonna love him like his dog does!"

Recipes from Miss Amelia's Nut House Kitchen

With all those guns going off in Riverville, Miss Amelia thought it would be a good idea to divert everybody's attention from the real things by having a special day with a little firepower of her own. That was a big day at the Nut House. PISTOL PACKING PECAN DAY, the banner over the door read. The hotter the day got, the hotter the food and the happier the people of Riverville. Again, Miss Amelia thinks a little Garrison's Bourbon never hurt one single soul in this world, so she's put it in the recipes. If you're a teetotaler, leave it out but you won't get to heaven any sooner than the rest of us.

TWENTY-ONE GUN SALUTE PECAN SOUP

Plenty of firepower in a bowl.

4 tbsps. butter
1 tsp. vegetable oil
1 large garlic clove, crushed
2 cups shelled and chopped pecans
1¼-inch-thick slice of round country bread
4 large tomatoes, quartered

4 chipotle chilies in adobo
7 cups milk
1 tsp. salt
½ tsp. freshly ground black pepper
6 pecan halves, for garnish
Dash of Garrison's Bourbon—for old time's sake

Melt butter in oil over medium heat in a big pot. Add garlic, pecans, and bread.

Cook about 5 minutes, stirring occasionally and turning garlic and bread once, until garlic is fragrant and bread is golden.

Transfer half the pecan mixture, half the tomatoes, half the chilies and 1½ cups milk to a blender. Puree until smooth.

Repeat with remaining pecan mixture, tomatoes, chilies and 1½ cups milk.

Pour mixture back into pot, along with remaining milk, salt and pepper, and bourbon.

Bring to a boil, then simmer about 3 minutes.

Serve hot, garnishing each bowl with a pecan half.

HUNTER'S SCATTERSHOT PECAN BREAD

Hunter swears by this sweet bread his mother used to make. One condition of their wedding is that Lindy learns to make it. If not, he'll make it himself. Which Lindy thinks is a better idea.

2 cups all-purpose flour
2 tsps. baking powder
2 tsps. baking soda
½ tsp. salt
1 cup sugar

1 cup sour cream
½ cup butter, softened
2 eggs
1 tbsp. Garrison's Bourbon
1 tsp. vanilla
1 cup chopped pecans

GLAZE

⅓ cup firmly packed brown sugar
⅓ cup butter
¼ cup chopped pecans

Heat oven to 350 degrees.

Combine flour, baking powder, baking soda, and salt in a bowl. Set aside.

Combine all remaining ingredients, except pecans, in a large bowl.

Beat at medium speed, scraping often, until well mixed.

Reduce speed to low, beat gradually.

Add in flour mixture until moistened.

Stir in 1 cup of pecans.

Spoon batter into greased 9x5 inch loaf pan.

Bake for 60–65 minutes or until a toothpick inserted in center comes out clean. Cool 10 minutes. Remove from pans.

Combine brown sugar and ⅓ cup butter in 1-quart saucepan. Cook over medium heat until mixture comes to a boil (3–4 minutes). Spoon glaze over warm loaf.

Sprinkle with ¼ cup of chopped pecans.

MORTON SHRIFT'S BARKING BETTY'S PRALINE PECAN BARK

A lot easier than pie and a great treat for the boys at the bar.

1 lb. milk chocolate candy coarsely chopped
½ cup toasted and chopped cashews
½ cup chopped pecans, toasted
½ tsp. cayenne pepper (you can use cinnamon if you want to)

In a microwave, melt candy; stir until smooth.

Stir in nuts and cayenne.

Spread onto a waxed paper-lined baking sheet.

Refrigerate for 20 minutes or until set.

Break into small pieces. Store in an airtight container in the refrigerator.

Yield: about 1½ pounds.

MISS EMILY'S OWN: BROWNING'S SMOKIN' BROWNIES

Miss Emily likes these brownies 'cause she likes food with an extra kick.

2 sticks unsalted butter, plus more for greasing
2 cups sugar
4 large eggs
2 tsps. Garrison's Bourbon
⅔ cup good-quality unsweetened cocoa powder

1 cup all-purpose flour
1 tsp. ground cinnamon
¼ tsp. cayenne pepper
½ tsp. salt
½ tsp. baking powder

Preheat the oven to 350 degrees. Line a 9x13 inch baking pan with parchment paper, leaving an overhang on two sides. Press the paper into the corners of the pan and lightly grease the paper with butter.

Melt the 2 sticks of butter in a nonstick saucepan over medium-low heat; do not boil.

Remove from the heat and let cool slightly.

Add the sugar, eggs, and vanilla to the saucepan and stir with a wooden spoon until combined. Add the cocoa, flour, cinnamon, chili powder, salt, and baking powder. Mix until smooth. Spread the batter in the prepared pan and bake until a toothpick inserted in the middle comes out fudgy, 20 to 25 minutes. Cool in the pan on a rack, then use the parchment paper to lift out the brownies before slicing.

Time: 35 minutes.

MISS ETHELRED'S HALF-COCKED CHICKEN WITH BOURBON MAPLE CREAM GRAVY AND A BUNCH OF PECANS

Miss Amelia swears Ethelred stole this recipe from her but you'll never get Ethelred to admit it. If you write her and say you hate the recipe, she will either tell you there's something wrong with your head, or she'll blame it all on Miss Amelia—depending on her mood at the moment. Serves 4

4 boneless, skinless chicken breasts
1 cup buttermilk
Vegetable oil—as needed in pan
¾ cup pecan halves
1 cup all-purpose flour
2 tsps. salt

Combine chicken and buttermilk in a large zip-lock bag and stick it in the refrigerator for 4–6 hours.

Place pecans in a food processor and process until finely chopped. Put in a pie plate and combine with flour and 2 tsp. salt.

Remove chicken from buttermilk and discard buttermilk. Dredge chicken in pecan-flour mix and turn to coat both sides well.

Heat oil in heavy pan. Fry chicken 6–7 minutes per side or until cooked through.

Place on wire rack to drain. Keep warm.

BOURBON MAPLE CREAM GRAVY

3 bacon slices
¼ cup chopped shallots
2½ tbsps. all-purpose flour
⅓ cup maple syrup
¼ cup whole grain Creole mustard
⅓ cup Garrison's Bourbon
½ tsp. Dijon mustard
½ tsp. salt
¼ tsp. black pepper
⅛ tsp. cayenne pepper
1½ cups heavy cream

Cook bacon until crispy. Place on towels to drain. Crumble.

Add shallots to bacon drippings and sauté over medium heat for 2 minutes.

Stir in flour and cook, stirring, for 2 minutes.

Whisk in maple syrup, all mustards, bourbon, salt, and peppers.

Cook, stirring, for 3 minutes. Gradually whisk in cream.

Bring to a simmer over medium heat. Cook, stirring frequently, for 5–8 minutes or until thickened. If it gets too thick, thin with a little milk.

Top chicken with gravy and sprinkle with bacon crumbles and any pecans you've got left.

CECIL'S FIRE IN THE HOLE CAKES

Of course, Cecil wasn't to be outdone. He brought these over to the Nut House himself. Miss Emily graciously accepted his cakes—with a sniff.

Makes 4 6-ounce cakes.

1 stick (4 oz.) unsalted butter plus more for buttering ramekins
6 oz. bittersweet chocolate, chopped
2 whole eggs plus one tsp. Garrison's Bourbon—for a taste of Texas
2 large egg yolks
¼ cup light brown sugar, packed
1 tsp. vanilla
Pinch of salt
3 tbsps. all-purpose flour
Chopped pecans

Preheat oven to 450 degrees.

Butter and lightly flour four 6-oz. ramekins. Tap out excess flour. Set ramekins on a baking sheet.

In a double boiler, over simmering water, melt butter with the chocolate.

In a medium bowl, beat the eggs, egg yolks, bourbon, brown sugar, and salt at high speed until thick and pale.

Add melted chocolate mixture and flour to egg mixture and fold together.

Spoon batter evenly into ramekins and bake for 10 minutes until cakes are set and puffed over the edges of ramekins.

Let the cakes set a minute or two. Hold hot ramekins with dishtowel over a dessert plate. If they don't come right out run a knife around the edges.

Serve with sweet whipped cream or vanilla ice cream.

Don't forget the chopped pecans on top.

MELODY AND MIRANDA'S DOUBLE-BARRELED BOURBON AND PECAN CAKE

The girls call this "A cake to make the gruffest cowboy howl at the moon."

Makes 10 servings.

3½ cups all-purpose flour
1 tbsp. baking powder
1 tsp. ground nutmeg
1¾ cups Garrison's Bourbon
¾ cup milk
1 tsp. vanilla extract

1½ cups butter
1 lb. dark brown sugar
6 eggs
2 lbs. chopped pecans
7 oz. pecan halves

Preheat oven to 350 degrees. Lightly grease an angel food cake pan.

Sift flour, baking powder, and nutmeg together in bowl.

In a small bowl, mix ¾ cup bourbon milk and vanilla together.

In a large bowl, with mixer at medium speed, beat butter until smooth and creamy.

Beat in brown sugar until mix is fluffed up.

Add eggs to the mix, beating one in at a time.

Beat flour mix and milk/bourbon mix into the large bowl, small amounts at a time.

With wooden spoon, stir chopped pecans into batter. Transfer batter to angel food cake pan.

Cover pan with foil and bake 1 hour 40 minutes.

Remove foil and bake another 20 minutes.

Let cake cool before removing from pan. Pierce the cake with a fork and pour 1 cup bourbon over the cake.

Decorate with pecan halves and serve.